To Mary with lo[illegible]
love from your
'old' friend, Charmian

Charmian M Coates
18th May 2006

The author, Charmian Coates, who lives in Blackpool, was born in Ilford, Essex, in 1937. At the outbreak of war her family moved to Oxford.

Aged nine she was taken to her mother's home in India and then spent two-and-a-half years there. The convent school she attended in Bangalore is the one to which she feels she owes the most for making her what she now is.

Charmian is married with four children, one now sadly deceased, five grandchildren and one great-grandchild. In 1972 she left Oxford, to run, alongside her husband, Alan, a small private hotel in Blackpool. This venture lasted four years.

Mark, the cerebral-palsied boy in this book, is based on her own late son, Neil, to whom she has dedicated it.

The author has also had three family sagas published by a Writers' Co-operative

LOVE WRITES
IN MANY COLOURS

Charmian Coates

Love Writes In Many Colours

Vanguard Press

VANGUARD PAPERBACK

A CIP catalogue record for this title is available from the British Library

ISBN 1 84386 229 8

Vanguard Press is an imprint of
Pegasus Elliot MacKenzie Publishers Ltd.
www.pegasuspublishers.com

First Published in 2005

Vanguard Press
Sheraton House Castle Park
Cambridge England

Printed & Bound in Great Britain

Dedication

Dedicated to the memory
of my dear son Neil Leonard Coates,
(The Raffle King)
who despite being so badly handicapped
was always organizing raffles for charity

9th January 1965 – 8th October 2002

Acknowledgments

With grateful thanks
to a very special
'Sandgrownun';
sadly, no longer
with us,
who gave me so much
help and encouragement
with this book
and all my writing
in general.

CHAPTER 1

"I'm sorry, Mrs Bellinger," said the policewoman, her manner sympathetic, "can we come in?"

Brenda agreed. Dazed, she let them help her into a chair, then hold a teacup to her lips; their words must surely refer to someone else going round and round in her head. "Your husband has had an accident - a fatal one, I'm afraid. Is there anyone we can call?"

There was no one, apart from her neighbour. Her father had died at Dunkirk, her mother was in Australia, and on John's side both his parents were dead. His only sister, a GI bride, lived in America.

The next few weeks were a blur. The funeral. Coming to terms with John's loss. She'd respected his wishes. Then, wished she hadn't. At least with a grave she could have visited him. The bed was so empty. The only way she could sleep at night was to add whisky to her cocoa. For a while, too, it looked as though they might lose the terraced house that John had modernised, with its pocket handkerchief-sized front garden. She certainly wouldn't have been able to meet the mortgage with her widows' pension and orphans' allowance. A painter-and-decorator, John had worked for a small building firm since leaving school in 1951. She'd not known how matters stood as regards finance. His former boss was able to put her mind at rest. The insurance he had on his employees would enable the amount owing on the James Street house to be paid off. Their home was safe.

Brenda leant over the pram and tucked the covers over one-and-a-half-year-old, Mark. He smiled up at her, brown eyes shining.

"Say, Ma...Mum..." she encouraged.

But the sound he made in reply was unintelligible.

Turning from the pram, her lips trembled; she only hoped she'd never have to endure another year like 1967. She glanced in the hall mirror; a fair complexioned young woman of medium height and build, and with a thick golden pigtail, looked back at her. She supposed she was still quite attractive, but there was no way she'd ever find another John. Anyway, who'd want a woman with three children, especially one who would always need so much looking after?

She missed John so much – from his passionate lovemaking – to him bringing her a cup of tea in bed on a Sunday morning. Sadly she recalled their strolls together on mild summer evenings with Mark in his pram, and Miranda and Melanie running on ahead, across Donnington Bridge and along the towpath to Iffley Lock, then home to a supper of John's home-grown runner beans and chipped potatoes. She even missed the laborious job of continually patching his white overalls.

Brenda called, "Come on, we're off to the shops." It was October and still warm so she'd not need to chivvy them into their coats.

Seven-year-old Melanie appeared, trailing five-year-old Miranda. Melanie's hair was brown like John's, while Miranda was fair like her own.

Melanie pulled a face. "Do we have to? I want to stay and play."

I want to stay too," repeated Miranda.

"Well you can't! I'm not leaving you two on your own again."

"Well, can we have a lucky-bag?" asked Melanie.

Brenda thought of her slim purse. There'd not be much left after she'd got the groceries. The snippet of news on the radio came to mind (at the Bank of England the pound had been devalued) her money wouldn't be going so far. Pay out at the Post Office was some days off. "Maybe, come on."

With Melanie and Miranda clutching the handlebars on either side of Mark's pram, they made their way to the shopping centre on the Cowley Road. Brenda's heart leapt as she spotted, halfway up a ladder, a broad-shouldered, brown-haired, white-clad figure, paintbrush in hand. She burst out, "John!"

The painter turned.

She swallowed, why did she keep imagining that she saw John everywhere?

A wolf whistle pierced the air. "Sorry dear, I'm Cyril," he called down cheerily, "but I'll be John for you if you like."

She averted her head and hurried on.

Reaching the Cowley Road she waited for a gap in the flow of traffic, cars, lorries, buses, even bicycles, before crossing over. The noise was deafening and the air reeked of petrol fumes.

In the supermarket entrance, she bent, tickling Mark beneath his chin. "Now, be a good boy 'till we get back."

He chuckled and grabbed at the woolly pompom that hung from the pram's hood.

Melanie appeared with a trolley. "I've got one, Mum," she said, proudly.

"Good girl."

They made their way around the aisles, Brenda deciding which items she needed most; jerking Miranda away from the wobbling pyramids of cat food and the bright packets of washing powder, which all swore that they, and only they, washed whitest. She pulled out her hanky, nostrils tickling, "Atishoo!!"

She paused by a display of sweets – an Aladdin's Cave of colour. She'd better get their lucky-bags or she'd never hear the end of it. She turned. Where had the girls got to? They were talking to a young black woman. Tall and willowy, with a complexion like milk chocolate, she wore a red miniskirt and a green blouse. Gold hoops hung from her ears and a yellow beret was perched on top of corkscrew black curls. She laughed, a pleasant tinkling laugh, as she answered the children's questions.

She was behind them at the checkout.

The assistant rang up the amount. How on earth am I going to get all this lot to the pram? Brenda thought, reluctantly handing over her last pound note.

The black woman hesitated. Her eyes made contact with the children's. She seemed to make up her mind. "Here, let me help you," she offered, her voice soft and musical, taking a bulging string bag.

"Thank you."

They reached the pram. Brenda pushed a cardboard box of groceries into the pram basket, and then attempted to hang the other bags from the handlebars. "It's no good, I've too much!"

Her woman laughed. "I'm not in a hurry. If you like, I'll carry this one for you."

"That's very good of you. Thanks. You sure it's not too much trouble? - I live in James Street."

"No trouble, it'll be a pleasure to accompany you and your little girls."

They made their way homewards. The woman walking beside her; the girls tucking into their sweets as they skipped ahead.

They reached Brenda's door. She made up her mind. "Why don't you come in for a cup of tea?"

The resulting smile revealed strong white teeth. "I'd be pleased to."

Minutes later they were sitting over tea and biscuits, Melanie and Miranda having disappeared with their orange squash and ginger nuts into the back room. "They've got all their toys in there," Brenda explained.

The woman nodded, the huge earrings jangling.

Mark lay chuckling on a rug. Brenda bent and placed a toy in the brown-haired, brown-eyed, boy's hand. She swept back her fair pigtail. "He's got cerebral palsy."

"I...I'm sorry."

"When Mark was a year he had to go into the Churchill Hospital for a lumber puncture. He'd been born normally at home, but developed pneumonia at three weeks and was rushed into hospital and into an oxygen tent. I thought all my troubles were over when they let me bring him home at three months. Though, he was never well. At ten-months-old he was x-rayed. I buttonholed the doctor and asked, "Surely Mark should be pulling himself up in the pram by now?" He'd bluntly replied, "Perhaps he is going to be retarded."

"How awful for you."

"It was." Both Brenda's little girls were strong and healthy. She'd just not expected her third child to be any different. "The lumber puncture showed that his brain was impaired, possibly due to lack of oxygen. I kept asking, 'But he will walk, won't he?' The consultant had shaken his head and said, "We can't say. You'll just have to wait and see."

The woman swallowed a mouthful of tea, her face revealing a sympathy that she was puzzled how to express. "He seems quite active the way he's kicking; his eyes are intelligent; surely he'll walk one day?"

Brenda had no answer. After a pause she said, "Have you been in Oxford long?"

"Not long. This is my first term at college. I'm reading English Lit' at Lady Margaret Hall."

"Gosh, you must be clever."

"Not really, but a degree helps. I want to be more than just a journalist. When I was a junior reporter, I had a small success, an article about racial discrimination in the Times. This made me even more determined. My name's Opal by the way, Opal Walker."

"Opal, that's a pretty name. It just suits you. I'm Brenda, Brenda Bellinger. He's Mark and those rascals in the back room are Melanie and Miranda."

"Melanie and Miranda - Miranda and Melanie - I like it."

"So you're hoping to make it as a writer? I tried writing some stories when I was a teenager, and more recently poems – at least, I think they're poems."

"Really! What are they about?"

Brenda bit her lip. "They're about John, my husband - he's dead - accident - six months ago."

"My goodness, you have had your share of troubles!"

"He fell from a boathouse roof in the course of his work." She would never forget the sight of the police at her door; hearing those words that seemed to come from the end of a long tunnel. She still woke at night shaking, after reliving those moments in her sleep.

"I understand."

They continued talking. Opal at twenty-four was three years younger than herself. She was also of mixed blood, her father being a white South African and her mother a black. They had come to England when she was a year old. "My parents could have never married in South Africa. In fact their relationship had to be kept a close secret. When it got out, they had to leave the country quickly."

"Why?"

"Apartheid," said Opal, "a black person can't even travel on the same bus as a white or use the same restaurant. Dad would have landed in prison if we'd stayed in Cape Town. My parents settled eventually in Birmingham, my father's a charge hand in a car factory. But it wasn't easy leaving all their friends and family behind, or being an immigrant. They've suffered terribly."

"I know what you mean. My mum's in Australia. When she married Brian, that's my step-dad, nine years ago, they emigrated there. I've really missed her, especially of late, and she writes that she feels helpless being so far away and unable to give me any support. I could do with her too, especially with my eldest. Melanie's such a monkey at times; leading Miranda into all sorts of mischief. Yesterday I slipped out for a loaf - I was only gone minutes. When I returned I found them cavorting on the shed roof. How on earth I got them down in one piece, I'll never know… Oh, do let me top up your cup?"

"Thank you."

Laughter and the scraping of furniture came from the other room.

"What on earth are they up to now? - excuse me a minute." Brenda dashed out. "I might have known it. If I've told you once,

I've told you a dozen times."

She returned, the children with her. "They were only playing trains with my dining room chairs."

"Melanie and Miranda, I'm ashamed of you," laughed Opal. She turned and behind her hand said, "Many a time I was in trouble for doing just that."

Brenda frowned fleetingly. She pointed to the plate and its remaining biscuits. "Here have another ginger nut each, then sit and be quiet - look at some picture books - how about those your Auntie Ivy sent you from America last Christmas? You've hardly bothered with them."

They did as they were told. Miranda sucked her thumb, her fair head bent over a book, while Melanie nibbled the end of one stubby plait.

"I do that when I'm concentrating on something," confided Brenda.

They chattered on. Half-past-three chimed. Followed by four. A ray of sunshine winking earlier on the mirror above the mantelpiece had past onto the wall.

The teapot was refilled. "And so," she said, pouring out yet another cup, "with John dying, me and the kids are on our own."

The gold earrings jangled sympathetically.

Opal nodded at the wedding photograph on the mantelpiece. "Is that you and your husband?"

"Yes."

"He was very good looking."

"I was so happy that day. Luckily I didn't know then what I know now."

"Perhaps it's a good thing we can't see the future."

"Eight years, that's all we had together. We'd made so many plans. We weren't going to stay in this house. John was going to buy a plot of land and build us a detached bungalow....still I don't suppose I'm the only one to lose a husband. My mum was in the same boat in the war. But of course she had an army pension."

"It can't be easy managing."

"It's not. Even though I make all the children's clothes, money goes nowhere." She indicated a Singer sewing machine on a treadle. "My late mother-in-laws."

"Isn't there some way you can earn extra money?" asked Opal.

"Not without going out to work. I used to type labels for Pergamon Press, at the bottom of Headington Hill. I was a shorthand typist at Morris' before I married. John bought me a portable typewriter, and I paid him back for it with what I earned. It was hard trying to type with Miranda sat on my lap, and as it was only a pound for a hundred labels, it wasn't worth it."

"I shouldn't think it was!"

"There's one way......I've been thinking of taking a lodger. It'd have to be another woman of course."

Opal's eyes gleamed. Brenda saw her glance around the room, taking in the red cottage suite protected by linen chair backs; the Axminster carpet square edged by well glossed linoleum; the pristine nets and floral curtains at the window and the vase of golden chrysanthemums on top of the polished sideboard. "You're thinking of letting a room?"

Was Opal interested? She was just the sort of person Brenda was looking for. "Why? Do you know someone who needs one?"

"Yes, myself. The digs I'm in at St Clements aren't up to much. I know it's near to town, but my landlady, well, to put it mildly, she's not as tidy as she could be."

"If it's that bad, why haven't you left?"

"Why?" Opal touched her face. "It's because of the colour of my skin. It's not always easy getting a room. Even in this country. I literally gave my feet blisters before anyone would take me in."

"I never realised."

"People don't."

Brenda rose. "Well the room's yours if you want it. You'd best come up and see it before you make up your mind. It's not very large, but at least it's clean – and tidy."

"Sounds grand to me. How much do you want for it?"

"I'm not sure. Let's see… say, seven pounds a week all in?"

Opal laughed as she followed her up the stairs. "I'm paying a tenner at Mrs Sharples and her meals… well, let's say that I weighed nine stone when I went there and now I weigh eight."

"You'd better leave before you fade away completely." Brenda pushed open a door, revealing a single bed covered by a white counterpane, rag-rug beside it, and a heavy mahogany wardrobe. "This is it. Will it do?"

Footsteps pounded up the stairs. "Is the lady going to live with us, Mummy?" asked Melanie.

"Is she, Mummy?" repeated Miranda, her blue eyes shining.

"If you'll have me," replied Opal, bending down to them. She fingered a lock of Miranda's hair, "it's like spun gold."

“You come from a hot country, don’t you? There’s a picture of a lady like you in one of my books - she’s wearing a grass skirt.”

“Melanie!”

Opal laughed. “It’s all right. “She turned to the child. “My parents come from South Africa, where the sun always shines, but I don’t think my mother’s ever worn a grass skirt.”

“Well, if you come to live with us, will you tell us stories?”

Brenda frowned. “Now Melanie, don’t pester Miss Walker.”

“Not Miss Walker, Opal. Of course I’ll tell you both stories, it’ll be my pleasure. I’ll tell you the ones my mother told me. The ones her mother told her; stories of her African village.”

CHAPTER 2

Opal entered the house, her ears blasted by the children's TV and a kettle's high-pitched wailing. Four months had passed. It was now February and in the front garden, snowdrops were showing and pale green shoots of crocuses were forcing themselves through the earth.

She'd settled in with Brenda and her children. She admired her, reflecting on all Brenda had to do - looking after the home and garden, plus two mischievous girls and a handicapped boy.

Melanie and Miranda, ran to Opal. "It's Opal, Mummy."

Opal hugged them. "I've something in my briefcase for you."

"Sweets?"

"You'll have to wait and see."

In the kitchen Brenda was dishing up the meal.

Opal popped her head round the door. "Hi there." Her eyes brightened. "My favourite. Sausages and mash."

"That's right. The kid's love it and it doesn't cost the earth."

"Can I help?"

"You could carry in these dinners for me."

Opal took them and set them around the dining table.

They took their places. Mark sitting in his special chair and being fed.

Melanie spilt tomato sauce.

Miranda dropped her fork.

Mark upended his dish.

Silence ensued, broken only by the clatter of cutlery.

Opal pushed back her plate. "That was delicious."

"Thank you. Prunes and custard?" asked Brenda

"Lovely," Opal replied.

Brenda removed the plates and left the room.

Opal wiped Mark's chin. "What a mucky face," she laughed, her earrings jangling; just pulling back in time as he made a grab for one. She sat back down and looked around her at the now familiar scene - the three children (two dark-haired and one fair) spoons at the ready; the table covered by an easy-to-clean plastic cloth; a sideboard with a lace runner. Her eyes came to rest on the solid fuel boiler, which fed the radiators around the house. The boiler itself was cast iron with a hinged lid, and of mottled brown and green enamel, resembling a squat toad. She fancied she could hear it croaking.

"That horrid boiler's burney!" said Miranda, pointing.

Opal turned to her. "What do you mean, sweetheart?"

"She got burnt by it," explained Melanie. "Stupid! - she poured water on the boiler."

"Was Miranda badly burnt?" asked Opal.

"She cried," said Melanie.

"It hurt!" said Miranda.

Their desserts were placed before them...

"Tinker, tailor, soldier, sailor," chanted Melanie, counting out her prune stones on the side of her dish. "I'm going to marry a sailor."

"Well, I'm going to marry a tinker," piped up Miranda.

"A tinker'd just suit you, seeing as you're one. Look at the custard in your hair. You make more mess than our Mark and he's got an excuse," said Brenda.

"Don't worry," said Opal, taking hold of Miranda, "I'll clean her up."

She wriggled and tried to pull away. "Can we have those sweets?"

"If your mother says so."

"Can we, Mummy?"

"I suppose so." Brenda pushed another spoonful into Mark's mouth and eyed Opal. "I don't know what I'd do without you."

"It's nothing. You'd manage."

After a leisurely cup of tea and talk about their day, the two women washed up. "I've got a lot of reading to get through tonight," said Opal.

Brenda flicked the dish mop over a plate. "Why don't you unwind and watch some television for a change? All work and no play, you know."

"Are you going to watch TV?" asked Opal.

"No, there's not much on," said Brenda.

"What about Steptoe and Son?"

"It's not bad, but I've got myself a library book and according to the blurb it's fantastic. As soon as I've got the children to bed I'm going to settle down with my quarter of liquorice allsorts for a quiet read - beggar my waistline!"

"Good for you!" Opal hung the tea towel over the cooker to

dry. At the door she turned. “Call me when it’s time for their bedtime story.”

“But you told them one last night. Aren’t we taking advantage of you?”

“Of course not. I’ve been looking forward to spending time with them all day.”

“They certainly love your stories of Toombi and the lion cub,” said Brenda.

“When I was little those old folk tales were my favourites too. I never got bored with them. I’d worry my mum night after night to tell them to me. Someday I may write them all down and send a parcel of them off to a publisher.” From the passage Opal called back,” Enjoy your read.”

It had been a lucky day for her when she’d met Brenda Bellinger. It was home from home for her at this terraced house in James Street. Mrs Sharples’ (her previous landlady) kitchen floor had been permanently littered with matchsticks, her dishes that were only washed when she’d no clean ones left, not to mention the grubby bed linen. Opal frowned. How had she stood it there for so long? She was doing well at college. Her tutors were pleased with her work. She was hoping that the degree course would help her to become a journalist.

She’d always wanted to write. Her dolls had been the first to hear her fairy stories. At Grammar School class work had had to come first. At eighteen, she’d become a star junior reporter on the ‘Birmingham Post’. This had stiffened her resolve. Her family had been very supportive; her mother delighted that a daughter of hers should be going to the University of Oxford. “In South Africa,” she’d said, “a black girl would have no chance for higher education.” Opal recalled her mother’s tale of how when she was small, her own mother, Opal’s grandmother, after a six-mile walk from her village, had had to wait in the hot sun for several hours to get a reference from the white vicar so that her daughter could go to school. His ‘boy’, told to say that the ‘Reverend’ was busy, had taken pity on her - bringing her some water in a tin can. But when a white man had driven up, he had been ushered inside immediately.

Opal was glad that only a minority in England were racially prejudiced. Settling herself at her table, she reflected on the white student she’d spoken to that afternoon in Blackwells. She had dropped a book and he’d picked it up, shrugging aside her thanks. In Birmingham there’d been several boyfriends. Some black, some not, but never anyone permanent. She'd been drawn to the thin, but personable young man with the fair crew-cut, sensing his response to her. Hadn't his eyes held hers as long as she'd allowed? Surely they'd 'clicked'. Hopefully, she would bump into him again. Opal picked up the text book smiling to herself and began to study.

* * *

She stretched. Her eyes ached, and her fingers were stiff. She eyed the clock. It was almost ten, and time for a bedtime drink. She smiled, relieved. She'd done enough for one night. As she came downstairs, she wondered how Brenda was enjoying her book. To her surprise, the television was on.

"Wasn't your novel any good?"

"Good! It was pathetic. Reckon I could write a better one myself."

"Why don't you then?"

"Do what?"

"Have a go at writing."

"I'm no writer."

"You don't know until you try."

"I'm not clever enough. I left school at fifteen – I never even won a scholarship. Though mind you, my best subject was English or rather, English composition. But a year's commercial course at technical college scarcely fits me for writing."

Opal tapped her lip. "Well, you can but try. A short story? Why don't you try that first? You told me you had a go at writing fiction once."

Brenda laughed. "I'd hardly call it that. Besides, I was only thirteen. They were in an exercise book and no more than a couple of pages long. I wouldn't know where to start, or I don't think I would."

"Start at the beginning and just write a brief outline of your idea and then flesh it out."

"I wouldn't know how."

"I'd help you with it."

"I suppose the other girls at school did rave about my stories when I read them out in the playground. But they were all about S E X, so I suppose they would. You know what thirteen-year-olds are like."

"Don't I!"

"I've just remembered. I attempted a play once for Children's

Hour on the wireless. It was a competition. Mine was all about a light-fingered Santa who tries to steal jewellery at a Christmas party and some children who foil his plans. It never got anywhere. Probably there were hundreds of entries. I think I might still have it somewhere."

"If you find it, let me look at it. Meanwhile what you need is some encouragement, and I'll supply that," said Opal.

"Would you really?"

"It would be a pleasure."

"I suppose it might be rather fun, and if I could get published, the money would come in useful. What do you think they pay for a short story?"

"Ask me another!"

"Even a couple of pounds would be welcome."

"There you are then, give it a whirl. But as well as fun, you know, expect hard labour!"

Brenda chewed the end of her pigtail. "I'll think about it. But first of all, I'll make us that cup of cocoa. And you can fill me in, if you will Opal, on the art of writing."

* * *

Some evenings later when Opal came down she was surprised to hear Brenda tapping away on her typewriter.

"You're not?" Opal hadn't really expected her to get started on a piece of writing, despite her enthusiasm. A lot of people have enthusiasm, but never actually do anything about it. It appeared she had misjudged her. Though Brenda could lose interest once she realised how much work was involved in producing anything publishable.

Brenda grinned. "I've taken your advice. I thought, do or die' - so here I am - though as you can see I'm not getting very far." She pointed to the rubbish bin that was half-filled with screwed up paper.

"Never mind, you've begun, and that's all that matters. Is it a story you're writing?"

"Trying to."

"Can I see it?"

"Not yet. I'd rather finish it first."

"Of course."

"I've been studying the womens' mags as you suggested."

"Good for you. You certainly don't let moss grow under your feet! Shout if you need help."

Brenda groaned. "No moss, just waste paper."

Opal made the cocoa.

"What's it about then?" she asked as they cradled their cups.

"It's a love story."

"From experience?"

"It happened to me and John when we first met."

"Mmmm."

"I thought I'd try 'The Peoples' Friend'."

"Perhaps." Dark eyes looked eagerly over to the table. "I can't wait to read it."

Brenda put a clean sheet of typing paper into the machine and flicking her pigtail behind her, laughed. "I hope you're patient. I keep changing the plot, so don't be surprised if it's a fair while before it's finished. Besides, my typing's rusty. I've made so many mistakes that my rubber's shrunk to almost nothing."

CHAPTER 3

Brenda's short story, 'Abigail's Secret Admirer', was finished.

It had taken her the best part of three weeks. She was on tenterhooks while Opal read it. The children were in bed and the house was quiet. At last she'd managed to pluck up enough courage to put her story to the test. Time slowed - the rain splattered the windowpane like gunshot pellets. What would Opal think of it? What, if after all, she should say that it was rubbish and only fit for the bin? When all was said and done, what did she know about writing?

A smile crept over Opal's face. Dark eyes met blue. "Not bad," she said, "the plot wants tightening, and there are one or two grammatical errors and some spelling mistakes, but nothing that can't be ironed out."

Brenda breathed again. "You really think so? You're not just being kind?"

"No. Certainly not. I'll tell you when it's good and I'll tell you when it's bad. This story has got potential. We'll work on it tomorrow night, and then you can type out a fair copy to send away."

"It's ever so good of you to go to so much trouble."

Opal's earrings jangled. "No trouble. When you're famous, I'll be able to say that I discovered you."

"I'd be really thrilled just to get into print."

"Yes, but perhaps I've been a little too encouraging. It'll take time. This is your first attempt. Don't expect too much too soon. I don't want you to be disappointed."

* * *

It was 9am and the girls had left for St Mary's and St John's Infants' in Essex Street, which was only a short distance away. Melanie had recently talked Brenda into allowing her and Miranda to go on their own. It was safe enough. After all, the girls were sensible as regards traffic - especially as all the neighbouring kids were going too. With having Mark to see to, not having to take them to school was a big help to Brenda.

She picked up the brown envelope from the breakfast table, slipping it into her shopping bag and said, “I best get this weighed at the Post Office. I’ve no idea what stamps to put on it.”

“I’ll keep my fingers crossed for you,” said Opal.

“Do you think they’ll like it?”

Opal hesitated. “It’s good, but even so, it’s not easy to get published. Don’t raise your hopes too high as a lot of famous authors got rejection after rejection when they first started. The main thing to do is keep writing. Take my advice. Start another story straight away.”

“I will, if I can. I’ll get down to it tonight.”

“That’s the ticket. Look, I must go; see you.” Opal swept up her briefcase.

Brenda lifted Mark from his chair and followed her into the passage. She tucked the squirming child into his pram. “How long do you think it’ll be before I hear anything? I’ll be on tenterhooks until I do.”

“Three or four weeks, maybe more,” said Opal, slipping into her scarlet coat. “You’ll just have to be patient.” She popped on her yellow beret. “Anyway, I’ll see you tonight. I’ve got a tutorial at ten-fifteen. I daren’t be late. The tutor’s a stickler for punctuality.”

The front door closed.

Brenda smiled at herself in the hall mirror. She’d a good feeling about her story.

* * *

A month passed. Every morning she hovered in the passage, listening for the postman’s step and his cheery whistle, followed by the rattle of the letterbox, but so far she’d been disappointed. The only deliveries being bills and an airmail letter that caused a pang, from John’s sister in Texas. She checked her watch with the kitchen clock. It was eight a.m. She tipped out cornflakes for Mark and the girls; settling down to feed him, with her mind only half on what she was doing. When Mark twisted his neck impatiently, she almost pushed the cereal spoon into his ear. What if the story was rejected? She knew she couldn’t really expect to get an acceptance first time; that she would need to grow a thick skin about rejections. All the same, she’d begun another. A love story based on an item she’d heard on the radio. It was going well. Mark was smearing cornflakes and milk all over himself. "Stop that, naughty boy," she scolded, dabbing at him.

He chuckled, muttering unintelligibly.

The letterbox rattled. She dashed out. There were two letters but no large brown envelope. But was that good or bad? She turned them over. One had a Birmingham postmark - it was Opal's. The other was a letter from the school.

The following morning, Brenda again dashed to the letterbox. She willed herself to see a small white envelope with the magazine's logo on it. On the mat was the brown envelope – her story. With shaking fingers, she tore it open and read the compliment slip: 'Sorry, not quite suitable for our magazine.'

She'd been so sure! Her throat tightened. So that's, that, then! Holding the manuscript she had typed so carefully in both hands, she ripped it into little pieces, letting them fall to the floor.

She heard Opal behind her. "What on earth are you doing?"

"It's no good! I can't write! I was daft to think I could!"

"Of course you can. You could have sent that away somewhere else. Just because one magazine doesn't like a story, it doesn't mean another won't. You can't give in so easily."

"It's too late now." She looked dully at the floor. "I'd best get a dustpan and brush and sweep up this mess."

* * *

Of course, Brenda let Opal talk her round – the writing bug had bitten her – and when that happens there's no way that one can stop. It is as inevitable as day following night. Finding out the rough draft of her story, she worked on it further, until satisfied, then sent it off to another magazine. The waiting and hoping began again – and the disappointment in reading the rejection slips. But she sent the story out again.

Eventually her persistence paid off. On the mat was a small white envelope with the 'Red Letter' logo.

She gasped. They'd not have written unless... excitement raced through her.

Opal appeared. "Anything for me?"

"It's here. I've a letter... from them... the magazine...the last one I sent my story to. Will you open it?... read what it says to me? Oh, there's one for you too."

"That'll be from my mother." Opal put it into her briefcase.

She smiled. “Here, give me your letter. You’re shaking like a leaf.”

She took it, ripped at the flap, and removed a folded sheet of paper.

“What does it say?”

“Give me a minute!” She read. “Brenda!! - you’ve done it!! - you’ve done it!! - and after only five times too.”

“Seven times you mean!”

“Now are you glad that I talked you into trying again?”

“You don’t mean?”

“You clever, clever girl! They’re only going to publish your story in their August issue.”

“No, I don’t believe it. It can’t be true?”

“It is.” She extracted a cheque, whistling. “Ten pounds! That’s a tidy sum. Here!”

Brenda took it. She kissed it extravagantly. “I’m rich,” she exclaimed.

Opal beamed. “Well, not quite that, but it’s certainly not to be sneezed at.”

“It’s all down to you. I know that,” Brenda told Opal.

“You put the work in, Brenda,” she replied.

Melanie and Miranda appeared.

“What’s happened, Mum?” asked Melanie.

Miranda tugged Brenda’s sleeve. “Mummy, Mummy...”

Opal turned to them. “You should be very proud of your Mum; she’s going to be published.”

“What like the lady who wrote about Noddy and Big Ears, Mummy?” asked Melanie.

Brenda never replied. “The first real money I’ve earned since I left Morris’,” she reflected. Eyeing the cheque, she added, “I’ll be able to get the kids new shoes. They could do with them.”

“Good for you.”

Brenda cuddled the girls to her.

Melanie’s eyes gleamed. “Can I have patent leather shoes?”

“You’ll have to wait and see.”

From the other room came a loud wailing.

“Mark!” she exclaimed, turning on her heel. “Poor darling, I’d forgotten all about him. He probably wonders what all the fuss is about.”

* * *

Every evening the click-clatter of typewriter keys resounded throughout the house. As Brenda became absorbed in her own magical world she began to realise that the writing bug that Opal had warned her about, had well and truly struck her. She could hardly wait to get the children off to bed so that she could get down to her writing. A week after getting the cheque for 'Abigail's Secret Admirer', her second short story had been despatched, followed by a third and then a fourth. Every morning for the last week she had waited on tenterhooks for the postman, feeling intense disappointment when nothing came back from the magazines.

"You've got to have patience," said Opal, smiling at Brenda's woebegone expression, "perhaps you'll hear tomorrow."

Hardly had she spoken when Brenda exclaimed, "The postman!" She rushed out, her eyes fixing on a white envelope. Excitement bubbled. Was this it? Would this letter contain her second acceptance? With fumbling fingers she picked it up and turned it over. Her spirits plummeted, the letter was for Opal.

It was to be a further week before her ordeal ended, but not in the way she'd hoped. On the mat, crumpled and rain-splattered were the brown envelopes that she had sent off so hopefully to three popular womens magazines, each containing a rejection slip.

* * *

"I don't think I'll bother to write anything else," Brenda said, as she and Opal washed up that evening, "I'll stick my typewriter back on top of the wardrobe, let it gather dust."

"You're not going to lose heart again?"

She swallowed. "I suppose not."

"Writers get dozens of stories rejected before they get even one acceptance, and you've actually had one published!"

"I'd have thought that, at least, 'Midsummer Madness' would have made the grade."

Opal dried the cup she was holding. "I would have thought so too, but maybe they'd just published one similar. Try it somewhere else. The others too, I reckon they're all good."

"You're not just saying that?"

"You should know me better by now. I mean what I say. No. Get them off somewhere else, and get more written. You mustn't give up. I reckon you'll make it. A lot of people take writing courses but don't get success immediately. Do they give up? No, they don't! They keep plugging away. Those poems I sent off, well, they've come back, but it hasn't stopped me writing. I'm working on a villanelle."

"I've got 'Her Prince Charming' almost finished."

Opal stacked the cups and plates in the cupboard. "There you are then; it'd be silly not to complete it. If you're feeling down, why not find that copy of 'The Red Letter' with your story in it?"

"I was riding high the day I first saw myself actually in print," reflected Brenda.

"Prop up the relevant page where you can see it. It'll give you confidence to carry on. Well, I must get off to my room. I've got a lot of college work to get through tonight. Call me for the girls' bedtime story."

* * *

Brenda re-addressed the rejects and posted them; 'Her Prince Charming' amongst them. Refusing to think of those she'd sent away, she concentrated on her latest effort.

The stories began returning. She tried not to dwell on the rejection slips, but it wasn't easy. Her 'Midsummer Madness' had been praised by one magazine's editor, but the woman still hadn't wanted it. She supposed it was like Opal said, a lot of people had to be satisfied with the pleasure they got from the actual writing. But she'd had one success, why not another?

The following morning an envelope plopped onto the mat. She picked it up gingerly. The logo danced before her eyes. With trembling fingers she read the letter. Elated, she danced a jig. She couldn't believe it. She'd done it again. The letter was from 'The Working Girls' Weekly', saying that they would like to publish 'Her Prince Charming' in their November issue. Opal had been right after all!

She felt in the envelope. Where was their cheque?

She tipped the envelope upside down and shook it. Nothing!

Puzzled, she re-read the letter. Then she noticed the small print. 'We must reluctantly request a five-pound donation to help with the printing costs.'

She crumpled it. "You'll be lucky," she exclaimed in disgust. Getting published meant a lot to her. But there was no way she was going to pay for the privilege.

CHAPTER 4

Brenda lifted the edge of the curtain and looked out into the street, just as a motorbike screeched round the corner and shuddered to a standstill. Opal jumped off the back. She was wearing a pink miniskirt and a jacket to rival 'the coat of many colours'. Her black corkscrew curls, threaded through with a scarlet ribbon, bobbed merrily. With her was a slight, fair-haired young man.

The front door opened. "We're here, Bren; is the kettle on?"

Melanie and Miranda were already in the passage. They had pestered to see Opal's boyfriend. Brenda had let them stay up later than usual, on the condition that they behaved themselves and went straight to bed afterwards.

Opal had asked her if she could bring Bob Brown, a fellow student to the house. She had confided that she'd first met Bob in Blackwells. How she had haunted the book shop ever since in the hope that their paths would cross. And how, a fortnight ago, they did. He had walked her back to college, and asked her for a date. That evening she was on the pillion of his bike, hands wrapped around him, on their way to the White Horse Hills. Brenda herself had seen that Iron Age horse that was carved out of the hillside, on a Sunday School outing as a child; and again when courting John. He had taken her there in a jalopy that he'd made roadworthy. It had been an Easter Monday. She'd been wearing, a blue and white spotted dress over a stiff net waist slip which had a dropped waist and a full skirt and was known as the A-line. She would never forget the wonder of that day, or the sunshine that warmed their pale winter complexions, as they picnicked on a grassy bank. Later John bought two shilling cornets, but then dropped the ice cream out of his. She'd offered to share hers - they ended up licking at the same ice cream. She smiled and smoothed an imaginary wrinkle from her skirt as she hurried into the passage.

As they hung up their coats, Opal and Bob replied to the excited girls' questions.

Brenda pulled them back. "Stop being nuisances!"

Melanie stamped her foot. "We're not! Are we Opal?"

"No, of course not, are they Bob?"

"Not at all. Now, which is Melanie and which is Miranda? Don't tell me," he pointed, and with a wink to Opal said, "You're Melanie, you're Miranda."

Melanie tossed her dark brown pigtails. "No, no, you've got it wrong! I'm Melanie, she's Miranda."

"Sorry, ladies."

Miranda giggled. "We're not ladies."

Brenda, comparing Opal's face to Bob's, was startled by the contrast. Unexpectedly, she saw them as others would and realised the difficulties that they might have to contend with. "I'm pleased to meet you," she said. "Come and sit down." She turned to Melanie and Miranda. "Now, say goodnight, and off to bed with you."

Both girls pulled faces. "It's not fair. I'm two years older than Miranda," grumbled Melanie.

"Let them stay a little longer," pleaded Opal, "they'll be good, won't you girls? I promised them a cake each. After all, they did help me make them."

Brenda frowned. "I certainly could tell they'd cleaned out the mixing bowl. All right then, but once you've finished eating, away you go."

Melanie looked smug. "Of course we will, Mummy."

"Me too, Mummy," piped up Miranda.

They went into the front room, where a tea tray, covered by a pink cloth, was set out with delicate rosebud decorated white china.

Brenda poured, handing Bob a cup. "Sugar?"

"Please, two spoonfuls, I'm afraid."

"Cake? Opal baked them. Do help yourself."

His eyes met Opal's. "They look delicious." He bit into one. "And taste even better than they look."

"Toady!"

Brenda smiled to herself at Opal's obvious pleasure. She remembered the first baking she'd done for John. He had come-to-tea to meet her mother; she'd made a fruit cake. It seemed funny now, but she'd been so apprehensive that she might have left out some vital ingredient. It would have been a major disaster if he hadn't liked it. Fortunately he had.

Miranda and Melanie were licking their lips in anticipation. She handed them both a tea plate with an iced fancy on it. "Now sit down and don't drop any crumbs."

Melanie sniffed. "Of course I shan't make a mess, Mummy."

"Nor me," said Miranda, "I'm not a baby."

"Well, how do you like Oxford, Bob? I suppose it's very different to Tunbridge Wells?"

He swallowed the remains of his second cake. "Yes. Vastly different, Brenda. It's a spa like Bath for a start. And that's not its only claim to fame. It's the birthplace of Charles II. Henrietta Maria, his mum; the wife of the King Charles who had his head chopped off, was forced to have him in a field."

"In a field! I don't believe it!"

"That's what the Tunbridge Wells Guide Book says. Evidently the royal party had to camp out as accommodation was scarce at the time."

"If I believed that, I'd believe anything!" Brenda wiped tears from her eyes. "What subjects are you studying, Bob? Tall tales, I should think!"

"He's taking History and English at Trinity College," said Opal.

"I feel quite ignorant compared to the both of you," said Brenda.

Opal laughed, her earrings jangling. "She isn't you know, she's a budding author. She's just had her second short story accepted."

"They only paid peanuts!" Brenda's second success had been a children's story read out at St Aldates Library. She had seen the writing competition advertised at the library, and had decided to write-up one of the tales she'd told Melanie and Miranda when ironing. A story of a squirrel, a nut thieving goblin, and the two elves who teach him a lesson. She'd entered this story in the competition. To her delight it had won first prize. She'd attended the 'Tiny-tots' Friday afternoon half-hour, taking Mark with her. The group of pre-school youngsters had cheered and clapped at the end of her story, read out by a librarian. But when Brenda's prize had been presented, she'd felt rather let down. All she had received from the Head Librarian were six Amami shampoo sachets. On every bath night since then, as she had washed and rubbed her hair dry, she had thought of the librarian and wished him as far away as Timbuktu. She had hoped for a tenner at the very least, and in her head had already spent it on the kids.

She realised Opal was smiling at her. "Sorry," she said, "I've been wool-gathering. No, I'm not that good; I don't suppose I'll ever make enough to buy myself a mansion."

Opal laughed. "You never know. Talking of mansions, Bob

showed me a photograph of his home. It's as huge as a castle."

Bob cleared his throat. "It's not as big as all that!"

Brenda changed the subject. "My late husband used to renovate old cars, that is, when he wasn't down by the river, fishing. Have you any hobbies, Bob?"

"Well, numismatics, coin collecting, you know, I've a thick cartwheel-penny, George III 1797. It weighs as much as three modern ones. I found it under a loose skirting-board at school. Then I've an 1840 Victorian half-farthing, which used to hang from my great uncle's watch-chain, and a George III silver half-crown. I recently discovered that in a junk shop. "

"It's a wonder he gets any study time in," said Opal. "He's always in the Ashmolean Museum, looking at their Saxon and Roman coin collections. That's when he's not overhauling his bike."

"It's a 500 cc maroon Triumph Speed Twin with telescopic forks," enthused Bob.

"And his pride and joy."

"I'm afraid I don't know one motorbike from another."

"Me neither," said Opal.

Brenda picked up the teapot, "A refill?"

"I'll have another cake," put in Melanie, licking her fingers.

"Me too," chirped Miranda.

"That's what you think. It's off to bed for the both of you, and don't forget to clean your teeth!" Rolling up a newspaper, Brenda playfully chased them from the room.

* * *

It was several weeks since Opal had taken Bob to meet Brenda. Whenever they had any spare time, they spent it together. They would walk hand in hand through Christ Church Meadows that were alive with colour; the white and pink blossoms of the trees putting Opal in mind of bridal bouquets. Or along the towpath that overlooked the Cherwell, watching the punts and their passengers skimming past like leaves in flood water. On one occasion, she took out a punt from Lady Margaret Hall's boathouse. Bob, half-heartedly offering to do the poling, had lost the punt pole in the mud. Late in letting go, he'd ended up in the water with the pole. He had to squelch back to his digs to change into dry clothing.

Another time, he'd talked her into going to Speedway.

They had ridden up past the Pressed Steel Works at Cowley - Opal perched on the bike's pillion and clinging to Bob's jacket. They'd joined the other motorbike enthusiasts that were avidly watching the races. Up went the tapes to a roar from the onlookers; away whizzed the four bikes around the red, shale track, ridden by two of the home team; the Oxford Cheetahs; in their red and blue helmets and two of the away team, the Swindon Robins, in yellow and black.

She'd never forget the dust or the smell of the burning Castrol R combined with the reek from the nearby sewer works. As far as Opal was concerned the only enjoyable part of the evening had been the pop music blasted out over the Tannoy.

"You weren't too keen," he said later.

She had to admit that she wasn't.

"It wasn't as exciting to me as it usually is." He pulled her to him. "I seem to find other things more exciting now."

"And what might they be?"

He dropped a kiss on her hair. "A certain Miss Opal Walker."

Strolling around town, they called in for a drink at the Eastgate Hotel, which rubbed shoulders with the grey stoned colleges, hundreds of years old, in the High Street.

Opal took a sip of her port and lemon, inwardly cringing at the disapproving looks from a couple sitting nearby. The woman, greying and overweight, wore a floral dress that was too tight; her gaunt husband wore a pinstriped suit. She knew all too well what they were thinking - it being written all over their faces: how can that white man lower himself by taking out a black girl?

"You're quiet," said Bob, reaching for her hand. "Is something up?"

"No," she replied hurriedly. She hoped that the cow of a woman would choke on her gin and orange, and her husband would choke on his pint! She was as good as them. Better!

"I thought..."

She pointed at the low-beamed ceiling, the brass warming pans and ancient muskets upon the lathe and plaster walls. "How old worldly everything is. I can almost imagine cavaliers tossing back their porter as they play dice."

Putting down his glass, he agreed that it was.

"I suppose the floor would have been covered in rushes, not to mention creepy-crawlies in those days."

"Maybe, but ye ladies swished in silks and satins," he said

comically, and quoted:

"When as in silks my Julia goes,
Then, then, methinks, how sweetly flows
That liquefaction of her clothes."

He smiled, "That's Herrick - fits I think."

"I suppose it does, but what about the second verse?"

"Next, when I cast mine eyes and see
That brave vibration each way free;
O how that glittering taketh me."

She smiled smugly, "Robert Herrick. 1591 - 1674. And it's called 'Upon Julia's Clothes'. You're not the only poetry buff, you know."

He laughed and lightly kissed her cheek.

She studied Bob's features. She was falling in love, a love stronger than any she'd ever felt before. But how did he really feel about her? His kisses were all she could desire. But was he serious? Opal remembered their earlier conversation. She'd said that she hoped one day to meet his mother.

He'd changed the subject.

Opal knew that Bob's late father had been a consultant surgeon - that the family were well off - that he'd been educated at a private school, but little more. Why did he clam up when she asked him such questions. Could it be that he was ashamed of her? She denied the thought, it being too painful. But another, equally upsetting immediately took its place. Could he already have a girl back home?

CHAPTER 5

"If I can write a short story, why can't I write a novel?" For some time Brenda had been feeling that she would like the challenge of writing a longer piece of work. She visualised the best sellers on the shelves of the book shops and all the money that their authors coined in. She could do with some of that for the kids – more words, more money!

Opal smiled wryly. "Why not indeed."

With the dish mop, Brenda rubbed vigorously at a blob of hardened spaghetti cheese. "Surely it's only the case of writing the equivalent of around a hundred short stories, with some research thrown in?"

"It's a lot more than that. You need to have a very good idea for a start. And as for research, well, it depends what period of time you're writing about. A contemporary novel is one thing, but anything else could be a great deal of research."

"I know that. I've been reading up about writing a novel."

"And what did you learn?"

"Well, first I have to write something called a synopsis of my idea, plus a chapter plan, and also the brief biographies of the main characters, even down to what they eat for breakfast and any little habits that they might have – like your jangling earrings."

"Funny!" Opal laid down the dried plate. "You have been doing your homework."

"Yes, I have."

"But, Bren, a novel is such a grind. You'll really have to be dedicated."

"I will be. Look, I want to give it a try. I'm going to start as soon as I've got the children to bed tonight."

"Striking while the irons hot!"

"Something like that. It's a pity they won't take Mark until he's five at the Mabel Pritchard Training Centre. I could have perhaps sneaked some time to write during the day."

"Is that the place you told me about at Littlemore? The place where Mark'll be able to get physiotherapy?"

"Yes. There's a girl in the next street who goes there. She's in the Special Care unit, that's where Mark will be. They take her there each morning in an ambulance."

"That must be helpful to her mother."

"Must be. She's got six other children!"

Opal put the plates into the cupboard. "Well, it goes without saying that I'll give you all the help I can."

"Thanks."

"But even when you've finished your novel, there's no guarantee that you'll be able to get it published. A lot of good writers have first novels gathering dust - and second - and third. I've heard of some people writing a dozen and still not get published. I don't like to pour cold water on your enthusiasm, but you've got to be prepared. Yours will have to be really outstanding to get anywhere."

"I still want to try."

"Fair enough. What's your idea about then? Is it going to be contemporary or historical?"

"I always loved history at school; the reign of King Charles II fascinated me - Nell Gwyn - the plague and the Great Fire of London."

"Is that the period you've in mind?"

"I think so."

"And is it going to be a romance?"

A dreamy expression passed over Brenda's face, her dish-mop disappearing into the sudsy water. "Of course, passion and derring-do in a bygone age. That's the stuff that women love. At least most of them, I reckon."

"A kind of Restoration, 'Gone with the Wind'?"

"Yes. Why not? I've always enjoyed books in that vein."

"It's best to tackle the sort of story you enjoy yourself." Opal hung the tea towel on the cooker. "I shall expect to see your synopsis later on tonight."

"What do you think I am? - a miracle worker!"

"I'm joking, of course. Though it's never taken you very long to come up with the goods in the past, despite all you have to do."

"Mummy, Mummy," shrieked Miranda from the dining room, "Melanie's taken my doll's tea set, and she won't let me have it back."

Brenda winced. "Like keeping the peace with those two."

* * *

It was two Saturday afternoons later. Both Miranda and Melanie had left for a classmate's birthday party, and Opal was out with Bob.

Brenda was happy for her; pleased that her relationship seemed to be developing, even if, in consequence, she didn't get as much of her company. Before Bob had come on the scene, apart from the one night a week when Opal dined at College, her evenings were spent with Brenda. But these days, as soon as their meal was cleared away, Opal would be off upstairs, readying herself for her date.

She didn't mind. Since becoming involved in writing, she didn't feel lonely anymore. The writing itself, seeming to answer an emotional need in her – her daydreams of a tall, dark and handsome young man entering her life, being less insistent in her imagination.

Having suspended Mark in his Baby-bouncer from the lintel of the kitchen door, she carried in her typewriter to do some work on the first chapter of her, as yet, untitled novel, keeping an eye on him at the same time. She had, after a great deal of thought, decided that the story would be set in 1666, the period of the Great Fire of London.

Mark jumped around on one leg, grinning and squealing excitedly.

"You like that, don't you, darling?" she said, threading a sheet of paper into her machine.

Mark made a gurgling sound that might have been, "Yes."

Was he, in his own way trying to answer her? He certainly loved going in the bouncer, although it didn't seem to do him much good; not so far as getting him to sit up and walk was concerned. She remembered how excited she had been the day she had seen the Baby-bouncer in a shop window on the Cowley Road. She had rushed home with it, imagining in her ignorance that it would do the trick and make his muscles stronger. John had suspended the bouncer in the very spot in which it was now – she, waiting and praying. Mark had enjoyed going in it, hopping around on one leg with a huge grin on his face, but it hadn't done what she'd hoped it would. Neither had rubbing in the olive oil, recommended by her neighbour, Mrs Briggs. Brenda sighed. What on earth would become of her boy in the future if he remained as helpless as he was now? He'd have to go into a home, should something happen to her. She turned back to her typewriter, determined not to worry about it. It did no good facing the future in advance. She'd think positively. Perhaps her writing would take off, and she'd make enough money to provide everything Mark might need. With an effort, she emptied her mind of her personal problems; concentrating on those of her fictional hero and heroine who were trapped in a burning house.

* * *

The front door opened. "Bren!"

She laid down her iron.

Opal entered the room. "What a journey!"

Mark chuckled. She went over to where he lay on the hearth rug and gave him a kiss and a cuddle; he, chuckling louder than ever. "And where's the other two?"

Brenda smoothed the iron over a cotton bed sheet, an odour of starch and steam filling the air. "They're fine. Melanie's driving me mad as usual. Won't I be glad when the school holidays are over. I've given them a shilling each and sent them off to Temple Cowley Swimming Baths to use up some of their surplus energy. I know Long Bridges is nearer and free, but I'm not too happy about the river; those hard pebbles on the bottom are murder on the feet. I can remember!"

Opal flopped onto a chair. "Good idea. Today's a roaster - must be 80 degrees at least." She flapped a tea towel in front of her face, "it's certainly baking in here!"

"Don't I know it. But I wouldn't have thought that you'd feel the heat."

"Why shouldn't I? I've spent most of my life in England."

"I didn't mean..."

"I know that, Bren. It was cool on the pillion of Bob's bike though, too cool!"

It being late June, and the college break, Opal had taken Bob home to meet her people.

"I think you're brave. I wouldn't fancy travelling all the way to Birmingham on the back of a motorbike."

"Nor I, but it was cheaper."

"Well, how did your parents take to Bob?"

"Really well. My mum spoiled him rotten, quite over-indulged him with her cakes and pies. Of course he lapped it all up."

"Like all men! What about your dad?"

Opal laughed, her earrings jangling. "He took Bob to our local, and Bob let him beat him at darts, or so he claims, but knowing my dad, he could probably have beaten Bob with one eye shut."

Brenda placed some ironing to air on clotheshorses. "Now that Bob's met your parents, when's he taking you to Tunbridge Wells?"

"That's the question. I just don't seem to be able to pin him down. He says that his mother's not very well, and can't have visitors. Changes the subject."

"So you don't believe him?" It sounded fishy to her. She'd not believe Bob if she were Opal.

Opal frowned. "I don't know what to think, I really don't. I wonder sometimes whether he has a girl back home, and is stringing us both along."

"Surely not." Of course it might be another girl. But somehow she didn't think so – Bob seemed too keen on Opal. So what was his real reason for not taking her home? Brenda hoped it wasn't because he knew that his mother wouldn't approve of his girlfriend? If this was the case, Opal was in for a bumpy ride!

"I hope you're right. Anyway, I've got other things to worry about besides Bob. The exam that's coming up soon, for one."

"You'll sail through it."

"Sail through it! Perhaps? But I've still got to get myself a black skirt. We have to sit 'schools', that's what the exams called, wearing a white blouse, black skirt, cap and gown. I can hire a cap and gown. There's no problem there. It's the skirt. As you know, all my clothes are in bright colours as well as being short. I tried Marks and Spencers, Ellistons and Cavells, too. All their black skirts only come to my knee. I thought I'd get one made by a dressmaker, but when I found out what it would cost, I changed my mind."

"I'd lend you my black skirt, but it wouldn't be the right length. Look, why don't you try a second-hand shop, you might be lucky."

"I don't fancy cast-offs."

Brenda laughed. "I suppose they could be flea-ridden or something. I've had a marvellous idea, why don't I run you up one on the Singer? I could slip down to the Cattle Market at the Oxpens on Wednesday and get some cheap black material."

"Oxpens?"

"You know, the weekly open market near the station. They sell everything, including dress lengths."

"But Bren, can you spare the time? I don't want to impose on you. You're so busy already, what with the children and your novel. What chapter are you on now?

"Four. Look, don't be silly, I'll be glad to do it. You've done enough for me. And as for my novel, to tell the truth, it's sending me silly. I'd be glad of an excuse to forget it for a bit. Though I don't think I'll be able to, it's got into my very blood. Do you know I sat for two hours last night just staring at my typewriter."

"Writer's block, that's what you've got."

"But what can I do about it? Will I ever write again?"

Opal smiled. "Of course you will. Now how about me making us some tea? Then you can tell me all about your difficulty. Perhaps I can help you iron it out."

* * *

Brenda was on her eighth chapter. She stared at what she'd already put. She smiled. Yes, Yes! She typed the phrase that she'd just thought up. Her fingers inadvertently touched a wrong key. "Drat!" A typing error. She rubbed it out, retyping the words in correctly and then read the piece through again. "Oh, God!" This wasn't what she wanted to say at all. Muttering under her breath, she ripped the sheet from the machine, screwed it up and flung it in the bin, where it joined others. She glanced at the unused sheets beside her. She was nearly out. Could she squeeze the price of a new packet from her housekeeping?

* * *

Brenda was on her eleventh chapter - this writing was harder than people imagined - she'd shed a bucketful of sweat, blood and tears. Nibbling her plait, she frowned at what she'd got so far.

The door opened and Miranda appeared. "I can't sleep, Mummy."

"Get back to bed immediately," Brenda snapped, her nerves in shreds.

Miranda's face puckered and she began to cry.

Brenda reached out to comfort her. What was she doing to her children? – taking out her frustrations on them. She would have to watch it. She mustn't let them think for a moment that she didn't love them. This writing was really getting her down. Was it all worth it? Whether it was or not, she felt drawn to give it her best. "I'm sorry sweetheart. It's Mummy's writing. It's driving her crazy. Look, I'll warm some milk, tuck you back into bed and stay with you until you've drunk it."

* * *

Brenda was on her eighteenth chapter. It was seven a.m. She sat on the edge of the bed, dressing. Suddenly an idea occurred to her. "That's it!" she exclaimed. She snatched up a notebook and pen to scribble it down.

The door opened and Melanie appeared. "I can't find any clean socks, Mummy."

Brenda put her notebook down guiltily. "There's some downstairs on the clotheshorse, darling."

Melanie went. She snatched up the book and pen, but, sighing, laid them down again. She'd forgotten what she'd wanted to write.

* * *

It was the beginning of the Michaelmas term and Opal's second year in college. Fourteen months had passed since Brenda had first made the acquaintance of Opal, and been encouraged into writing. She typed the last word, on the last page of her manuscript. "I've finished," she marvelled, straightening with difficulty, and flexing her fingers. "They feel like they belong in a box of chalk!"

The mantelpiece clock chimed midnight. Brenda had been typing without a break since putting the children to bed, determined to complete the revised version of her novel, all three-hundred-and-fifty double-spaced pages of it.

"Here," said Opal, pushing a mug in front of her, "drink your cocoa. I've warmed it up again. You're wearing yourself out. Think of the children."

"I know, but I just couldn't stop. I seem to have become addicted."

She had been working every minute she could squeeze in to complete her novel, which she had, at last, decided to call 'The Devil in the Flames.'

"Take a look at my synopsis. Have I cut it down enough? How does it sound?"

Opal reluctantly ran her eyes along it.

She handed it back. "Sounds OK. Now, come on, put it all away. It's time we were both in bed."

Brenda fingered the list of publishers that she'd made. "I wanted to decide which ones to approach first."

"Enough is enough. I need my sleep, if you don't."

“Sorry. You’re right,” Slowly she put the lid on her typewriter and placed her manuscript into its folder.

“I am,” said Opal.

“Wouldn’t it be wonderful to see ‘The Devil in the Flames’ at WH Smiths? First in a trilogy, by that up-and-coming novelist, Brenda Bellinger.”

Exasperated, Opal turned at the door. “It’d be more wonderful to see my bed. If I’m half asleep tomorrow at lectures, it’ll be your fault.”

CHAPTER 6

Brenda threw the rejection slip onto the kitchen table in disgust. Thirteen months had passed, months in which she had become steadily disillusioned. She was beginning to dread the rattle of the letterbox. It was not easy to take. Handley and Co was the ninth publisher contacted. 'The Devil in the Flames' was costing her a fortune in postage. Not to mention envelopes.

Every time she sent her synopsis and sample chapters off, she'd been uplifted by hope, thinking that surely this time it would be different, that this publisher would like her novel, would make her an offer for it. But it never happened. She was becoming really dejected. Was all her hard work destined to end up forgotten at the back of a drawer?

"I've told you before; you need an agent," said Opal. They'd just finished their evening meal and were discussing their day over a pot of tea.

"Will that be any better?"

"If you can get one to take you on, it could be. Quite a few publishers will only consider material sent in by an agent. It's worth a try, surely, the addresses of agents are in the 'Writers and Artist Year Book' at the library."

"I know that! I never told you," said Brenda, "but I have looked through that book. I picked out a couple of agents and sent off to them. I never got a reply from either of them – not even my return postage back..."

"Well, try again. It is worth trying again, isn't it?"

Brenda chewed the end of her pigtail. "I guess so. I do need to change the girls' books. I suppose I could visit the library and make another list of agents while I'm there."

"I should. Don't give up yet. Not after all the work you've put in."

"And the work you've put in. You helped me tremendously. I've not forgotten that."

"It was nothing."

Brenda gathered the cups together. "It certainly was. I couldn't have done it without you. I will give the agents another twirl." She picked up the crockery and left the room.

* * *

Opal sighed. It was getting a bit much, this fixation of Brenda's. She had problems of her own. The main one Bob. Although she pointedly took him past all the jewellers shops on their walks around town; hovering in front of the displays of diamond rings in their windows, he hadn't taken the hint. Neither had he taken her home to meet his mother. He always made some excuse or other as to why she couldn't accompany him. She thought of those magical moments on top of Shotover, a secluded, wooded area at Headington, and wondered if she hadn't made a mistake in letting their relationship go so far?

They walked arm in arm from Brenda's, enjoying the warmth of the September evening. Reaching Shotover common, they looked around, admiring the beauty of the place; the late flowering king cups; petals shimmering like scraps of yellow satin; a tangle of blackberry bushes, denuded of their fruit by birds; jam-making housewives and children's hands; the hazelnut and beechnut trees, heavy with their bounty; other trees, aflame with autumn's reddening tints. They took great gulps of fresh air that was free of traffic fumes and smoky chimneys and as invigorating as wine. As they picked their way beneath a cavern of tightly-knitted branches, the ground (thick with undergrowth and moss covered tree stumps) Opal was glad she'd put on her flat walking shoes instead of her usual high heels. But despite sensible footwear, she tripped over a tree root and went sprawling.

Bob knelt beside her, his face concerned. "Are you all right, darling?"

She winced. "My ankle. It hurts!"

He carefully removed her shoe and felt her foot. "I don't think there's any bones broken. It's probably just bruised." Suddenly his hand seemed to burn through her stocking.

She looked up, seeing a certain gleam in his eyes. His fingers crept up her leg and began to caress the flesh above her stocking top. She moaned; desire swamping pain. "Oh, Bob," she murmured, her arms reaching around him. Their lips met in a passionate kiss, his fingers tangling her black corkscrew curls. "Oh, Opal, my beauty."

She felt his hands moving down to unbutton her blouse. At

this, her childhood Sunday School teaching returned. Lovemaking before marriage was wrong, she knew that. But her senses were too stirred up to care, and she never made any move to deter him. With his tongue's tip, he traced a trail from her throat to her breasts. His mouth fastened on a hardened nipple, nuzzling until she gasped with pleasure. With her skirt, by this time around her hips, she couldn't help but respond. She just couldn't deny him. Her feelings for him were too strong....

He pierced her body - thrusting again and again within her, his lovemaking causing ripples of feeling that became sweeter and stronger with each stroke and more pleasurable than anything she had ever imagined. She cried out, willing it to go on forever, her fingers beneath his shirt, clawing the skin of his back in her excitement.

"I'm sorry," he said afterwards. "I've taken advantage of you."

She halted in the act of picking grass from her clothing and hair. What did Bob mean?

"No, you haven't. We're in love, aren't we? You do love me, don't you?"

He kissed her for an answer.

But ever since, she'd wondered why he'd spoken as he had? Surely if he was genuine, if he intended to do the right thing by her, he wouldn't have? What would have happened, if she'd become pregnant? She'd not gone on the Pill like so many of her friends. It was common practice amongst students living-in at Lady Margaret Hall to leave a bathroom window open on the first floor, so that boyfriends could climb in. She expected any day to hear that someone had been found with a man in their room and sent down by the Dean. She herself had really wanted to wait until marriage for lovemaking, so had been unprepared for events getting out of hand. She supposed she was lucky that she'd not got a baby on the way. But if she'd been 'caught', what would have been Bob's reaction at finding he was to father a half-caste child? Would he have dropped her?

* * *

Seated at his desk in his digs just off the Iffley Road, Bob was writing his weekly essay, but he couldn't concentrate. He laid his head in his hands. What on earth was he to do? He knew Opal was angling to be taken home to Tunbridge Wells. He'd been more than once with her to Birmingham and knew it was his turn, but he just couldn't face it. No way could he let her be hurt, for once his mother saw Opal, this is what would happen.

He recalled, how when he was twelve, he had brought home his best friend, Ranju. A boarder at his private school, Ranju's father was a diplomat at the Indian Embassy. His mother's manner had been icy. Later when Ranju had left, she'd told Bob in no uncertain terms that he must drop him.

He'd been shocked and confused. "But why? I like Ranju."

Tightening her lips, she turned away. "Because I say so."

Bob's mother was rather haughty to those whom she considered inferior to herself, although passionately devoted to her only son, who resembled her in colouring and build. He knew she would be willing to make an allowance for most foibles as far as he was concerned, except one. For his mother, Belinda Lou, had been born in Montgomery, Alabama - the Deep South of America.

She'd met his father, Alfred Brown, when he'd attended a medical convention there in 1938. They'd been introduced at a dinner party at a friend's house. Alfred had fallen for the eighteen-year-old Southern Belle. After a whirlwind courtship, they'd married. He had brought her back to England. Dominating their drawing room was his mother's portrait, painted for her eighteenth birthday. Smiling aloofly, she wore a royal blue ball gown, her fair hair dressed in ringlets, and with a white rose tucked into the bosom of her dress.

His mother's fine skin was now lined and her hair greying, but she still dressed in haute couture, as apart from her own fortune, his father had left her extremely well off.

Bob frowned as he visualised his home, Larks House - the large, high-ceilinged rooms, the elaborate and costly furnishings. He compared it to Opal's parents' semi. Although their home was small, it emitted a warmth that was missing from his own, despite all the creature comforts. He thought of Opal and her mother sitting companionably together, a skein of orange wool dangling between Beulah Walker's wrists, as Opal wound the wool for her into a ball. The older woman, plump and jolly, her complexion resembling plain chocolate; Opal's more like milk. If his mother could have seen him with them she would have been outraged. But he supposed it might not really be her fault that she thought in this way. From an early age she had been encouraged to think of her family's Negro servants, as well as her 'Mammy', who had done more for her than her own mother, as worthless. Such ideas disgusted him. But he was not a strong person; he didn't know how to cope with such a problem. His mother had guessed, some time ago that he'd a girlfriend in Oxford. She was always hinting about when was he going to bring her home.

So although Bob was in love with Opal, he just wasn't brave enough to admit to his mother the colour of his girlfriend's skin. Or to Opal, the fact of his mother's prejudice.

* * *

After the girls had left for school, Brenda tucked Mark into his pram and set off for town. Despite being early November, it was a pleasant day. The fresh air and exercise will do me good, she decided. Walking briskly over Magdalen Bridge, she glanced down at the river, which glittered in the pale winter sunlight and was overhung by weeping willows. The towpath, thickly carpeted by the red-gold leaves of oaks and elms, their bare branches reaching to the sky like sentinels, was deserted today, apart from a grey squirrel who scampered along the ground, disappearing up the trunk of a tree, its upright bushy tail resembling a lavatory brush. She remembered a hot summer's day in June when she and John were courting. As they strolled hand in hand along the towpath; he in flannels and rolled-up shirtsleeves, she in a lacy blouse, waspi-waist belt and pencil skirt, with sunshine, warm on her neck and shoulders; the grassy bank beside the river had been dotted with couples prone and entwined. John had pulled her to him in a passionate embrace, saying, "Darling Bren, will you marry me?" In his hand, a small box that contained an engagement ring.

On the bridge, a red bus moved heavily past her. Behind its grimy windows she noticed passengers, their faces just pink smudges.

She jumped as several boisterous students ringing their bicycle bells speeded by; their long scarves flying behind them like banners in the breeze.

In the busy High Street, she passed the massive colleges; their familiarity rendering them almost invisible. She had to weave her way in and out of the chattering throng of young and old who pointed eagerly at the ancient buildings. Many were Japanese tourists with cameras slung around their necks. She turned into St Aldates. Parking the pram, she went into the high-ceilinged library, found the book she was looking for and made her list.

* * *

That evening she ticked off four agents' names - addressed four envelopes - and popped four copies of her synopsis and sample chapters into them.

* * *

The waiting and agonising began again - the pacing up and down the passage, listening out for the postman's step.

One brown envelope flopped onto the mat - no good - the agent had written on her rejection slip that she was too busy to take on any new clients. A couple of day's later number two envelope appeared - this time nothing was written on the slip. Number three was another rejection, but with a note from the agent saying, 'Sorry, but I've retired.'

Three weeks passed and there was still one envelope unaccounted for. Brenda had begun to wonder if it had gone astray? After all, the Post Office wasn't infallible. She decided to take Opal's advice - forget 'The Devil in the Flames', consider it as apprentice work and start another novel. A contemporary theme might be more successful. That evening she drafted a rough synopsis of an idea from her own experience that had been buzzing around in her brain. The story's background, the Publicity Department of Morris Motors in the 1950s. The main characters, two teenage copy typists.

Her head was full of her new novel the following morning. The girls had left for school, woolly-hatted, scarved, wellington-booted and squealing excitedly – there'd been a heavy fall of snow during the night - a bad start in her opinion to 1970, if not in theirs. She had just put Mark in his Baby-bouncer while she did the washing up when the letterbox rattled. She took no notice. She expected it was the gas bill. She continued scraping cornflakes off cereal dishes. She'd no intention of hurrying to the front door for a bill.

On her way upstairs to make the beds, she spotted a brown envelope on the mat. So it had turned up after all. She almost felt like putting it straight into the bin; it would only be the same as the rest, 'Thanks, but no thanks'.

Half-heartedly she opened the envelope. To her surprise a letter was fastened to her material with a paper clip. A letter - she thought - don't get too excited - not yet - it'll probably say no more than the rejection slips. But despite herself, her fingers trembled as she held it up to read:

Rose Cottage,
Clifton Hampden.
29th December, 1969

Dear Mrs. Bellinger,

Thank you for the synopsis and sample chapters of your novel, 'The Devil in the Flames'. I'm sorry to have kept you waiting so long, but I have been away in America. I read your material with great interest. In fact, I could hardly put it down. I should very much like to see the complete novel. Please send it to me by return post.

It was signed - David Certes.

CHAPTER 7

Brenda plumped up a cushion on the settee, straightened an ornament and wiped a speck of dust that she had missed from the edge of a picture frame - was that better? She didn't want to let herself down. She winced, as her eyes fell onto some scuff marks on the skirting board. His home was probably larger and no doubt, smarter than hers.

She went to the window, but there was no sign of her expected visitor.

She returned to the tea tray, fidgeted with a teaspoon and altered the arrangement of her freshly baked shortbread biscuits on the paper doylie. She glanced at the clock - he'd said two p.m. - it was that now - he should be here at any minute.

Brenda had despatched her novel as requested. A month later, when she'd given up all hope, she had received a letter from him saying that he would like her to visit him to discuss the details of his taking her on as a client. She was to ring Clifton Hampden 7070 so that they could settle a time and date to suit them both.

She had rung his number. When she'd explained her situation, that she had three young children and no transport, he'd kindly offered to call on her instead.

A car droned in the distance. It grew louder, turned into her street and purred to a stop.

A car door clicked, steps sounded, followed by a rat-a-tat.

She jumped; David Certes?

What would he be like? Young, or maybe not so young? It was difficult to tell over the phone. Nervously she smoothed her skirt, patted her coiled hair, hurried to the door and opened it.

"Mrs. Bellinger?" queried a cultured voice.

"Yes."

"I'm David Certes."

She 'took in' a dark-haired man in his early thirties. He smiled crookedly, a smile that somehow stirred her senses. She sharply brought herself under control and channelled her mind to the manuscript he had come to discuss. This inexplicable feeling was no doubt due to the thought that the publication of her novel was now a possibility.

They sat around the tea tray, talking about her book and the legal contract she would need to sign. He pointed to a photograph on the mantelpiece. "Your family?"

"Yes."

"Three children and a husband. How on earth do you find the time to write?"

"Just three children. I'm a widow."

"Sorry," he said awkwardly.

"That's all right, you weren't to know. John, that's my late husband, has been dead for over three years. An accident at work..."

He attempted to say something, but she went on; "As to how I find the time for writing, well, it's not always easy, but when you love doing something, you can always find the time."

"That's true."

Outside a lorry rumbled past causing the windowpane to rattle.

"And have you been writing long?" he asked.

"About two years. Of course I've always loved reading. As a girl, I must have got through nearly everything in the junior section of the library, and perhaps writing is a natural progression. It was my lodger who started me off. She's an English student – was a reporter - and in fact has had some literary success herself. She's helped me quite a bit."

"Even so, it's unusual for someone to reach such a high standard so quickly."

"Thank you." He really thought her writing outstanding! This was great! Just wait till she told Opal. Thank goodness she had listened to her and not given in when it all looked so hopeless.

He took a bite from the shortbread biscuit on his saucer. "These are delicious. I can see that writing isn't your only talent."

"Have another. Yes, I do enjoy baking, but not as much as I do writing. To think that for so many years I never realised what I really wanted to do. I was a shorthand typist before marriage, but I can't say that the work ever really gave me much satisfaction, Mr. Certes."

"David, call me David," he replied warmly.

"David, a nice name. I've always liked it a lot. You must call me Brenda." She halted, feeling foolish; her face as pink as her tray cloth.

He appeared not to notice. "I've read several other manuscripts recently, but I must say that none of them were as fresh or as exciting."

Their eyes met and a spark seemed to pass between them. What on earth could it all mean? Could she really put what she was experiencing down to the excitement of getting somewhere with her book? "That's kind of you to say so."

"Not kind at all, just truthful." He stood up reluctantly. "I'm afraid I'll have to go. I've an appointment in Abingdon in forty-five minutes. I only hope my Morris Oxford doesn't break down on me, she can be temperamental at times, and especially in this frosty weather."

They shook hands. Did she imagine it, but was he reluctant to break contact?

Brenda listened to his car start and set off down the street.

She glanced at herself in the passage mirror and was startled to see her face was soft and dreamy. She grimaced. Best not to get carried away! She was only a housewife of no particular looks. There were millions of younger and prettier girls than herself. Why, she was thirty next month. She patted the skin beneath her chin. Could she really be that old, almost middle-aged? It was daft to imagine that there had been a mutual attraction between them. It would be unfair, too, to John's memory to encourage anyone else so soon.

She relived the last half hour, seeing David Certes smiling over the teacups. Besides someone so good looking would be sure to have a wife. She remembered his waistcoat's missing button. Perhaps not.

* * *

Ten days later she received a contract, which she signed and sent back post haste. Things were starting to look rosy. David was definitely top of her list of names.

* * *

Brenda had to peg her washing firmly on the clothes line to combat the March winds. In fact a couple of Mark's nappies were blown away into Mrs Brigg's garden. Unfortunately they were ripped to shreds by her fox terrier. Mark had recently returned from a week's stay in the Children's Ward of the Churchill Hospital, their family doctor thinking it was time to reassess his condition. She'd missed Mark terribly. And with all the travelling to and fro to the hospital, had had less time than ever. The specialists' conclusion had been that there was no actual physical improvement in him. Should there ever be, which in their opinion didn't seem likely, it would be a very slow process indeed.

* * *

During the intervening weeks, since meeting David Certes, she'd received a letter and had a couple of visits from him. So far, it appeared, he hadn't been able to place her novel. But her supposition had been right, he was in fact a widower; his wife having died from cancer a year earlier.

"I'm so sorry," she'd said, but secretly she'd been relieved that there was no Mrs Certes at home. The conversation had returned to her manuscript and his lack of success.

"Don't lose hope, Brenda. It can take some time. But in the meantime, it would be advisable to start another. Many publishers like to know that there is a further book in the pipeline."

She refilled his cup. "I have thought along these lines, but Mark's been ill again with his chest, so I've had no time to write."

David frowned sympathetically, eyeing the child on the rug. "Is he often poorly?"

"He has quite a few coughs and colds in the winter, but the doctor reckons he could outgrow them. At least, I hope so."

David leant over to tickle Mark's tummy, the boy gurgling at the attention. "I second that, for his sake, as well as yours." He looked serious. "Is there nothing the doctors can do for him?"

"Nothing! It's unlikely there'll be much improvement in his physical condition. In fact, just the opposite. He could go all twisted as he gets older and suffer a lot of pain."

"But surely in the future…? I mean, they're making discoveries in the medical field all the time."

"Not as far as brain damage is concerned. I've got to face it; it's possible I could still be doing everything for Mark when he's thirty."

"It won't be easy for you coping on your own."

"No, but what other choice do I have?"

"You could remarry... I'm sorry, I shouldn't have said that."

"That's all right."

"So have you got another novel in mind?" he asked, changing

the subject.

"I'd thought I'd try one with a more contemporary theme. What do you think?" She outlined her idea.

He rubbed his chin. "No, it would, I think, be best to do a sequel to 'The Devil in the Flames'; carry on from where you left off. Sagas are what people want these days. You can always come back to the other idea later, when you're established. Though, Brenda, I may be jumping the gun!"

"I'll go by your advice."

The conversation turned to other matters. He asked her if she had any other interests besides writing and the family. "I play the clarinet myself, I find it very soothing after a hard day," he said and then chuckled, "Of course, my parents, when I was living with them and learning it, didn't find it so."

"I don't play myself, but I do like music."

"What kind?" he asked.

"Mainly classical. My favourites are Tchaikovsky's 'Overture to The Storm', the Strauss waltzes, 'Roses From the South' and 'Die Fledermaus', and of course Mozart's 'Concerto for Two Pianos'."

"They're amongst my favourites."

"You know, I first got my love of classical music at school. They took us to the Town Hall for a concert. The other girls weren't at all keen; called me a lark listener, 'highbrow', you know, for enjoying it."

David laughed. "Did your husband share your taste?"

"Not really, he preferred a diet of pop and military marches. Well, I don't mind a little pop, I quite like the Beatles. I sometimes listen to their stuff on Radio Oxford. But I much prefer classical music. I used to play my records while John was at work on the old gramophone that we bought from Taphouses when we were courting. Mark must take after me. He loves it too; my records send him off to sleep when he's fretful."

"Soothes me too, when I'm feeling tense. Failing that, watching a good play. I used to act myself in the college drama group."

"What a coincidence. I was in the Co-op Amateur Dramatic Society when I was seventeen. Loved it too, although I never had a big part. I left when I met John at the Carfax Assembly Rooms, near Carfax Tower. He'd come along to keep a mate company, but wasn't much of a dancer." She laughed. "He said doing the 'Gay

Gordons' with me was worse than going on a route march - he'd done a stint with the Oxford and Bucks - National Service."

"But why stop acting?"

"It wasn't John's thing. I suppose I wanted us to find an interest we could share."

"That's understandable."

"But I still love a good play. Though I haven't been to the theatre or playhouse for ages. I don't really fancy going on my own. I suppose Opal, that's my lodger, could come with me, but then we'd have the problem of finding a baby-sitter."

"I imagine that isn't so easy."

"It's got to be someone trustworthy and used to dealing with children. My neighbour comes into that category, but I don't like to put-upon-her too often. Although I'd really love to visit the theatre again," she added wistfully.

Opal came into the room. "We ought to make the effort Bren, you hold me to it, and I'll hold you to it, then we'll be sure to get there."

* * *

On Easter Sunday, Brenda, Opal, Bob and the children attended morning service at St Mary and St John's Church on the Cowley Road. Grey-stoned and lichen-covered, this was the church where Brenda had been confirmed, married and her babies christened. She was extremely grateful, too, for all the support given her by the vicar and the caring church members when John died. The church was bright with flowers, particularly lilies (they, being in season) and the glow of candles. Its high-ceiling curved and buttressed with oak beams, embellished with sacred carvings, resounded to organ music as the congregation lustily sang God's praises. The very air alive with a feeling of hope and rebirth.

Brenda carved the joint of roast pork, placing generous slices onto plates that already contained, golden potatoes, buttered carrots and petit pois. Around the table, the others watched, salivary glands working double time.

There was a knock at the door. She frowned. "I'm not expecting anyone."

Melanie leapt from her chair and ran to answer it. A man's voice was heard in the passage.

"Whoever can it be?"

Melanie reappeared. Behind her was David Certes. "I hope you don't mind me popping in, I've some chocolate Easter eggs for the children," he said, proffering three brightly-coloured boxes.

"You shouldn't have. How kind of you. Say, thank you to Mr Certes, girls."

"Thank you, Mr Certes."

"Not Mr Certes, David."

"I don't think that it would be polite for them to call you by your Christian name," said Brenda.

Melanie and Miranda, eyes gleaming in anticipation, shot out their hands. "Can we have them now, Mummy?"

"No, not until after dinner," she answered firmly.

She turned back to David. "Do stay. There's plenty."

"I don't think..." he replied awkwardly.

"Oh, come on," she said, pleased by his unexpected visit; her feelings for him having become stronger each time she saw him, although she wouldn't admit it, not even to herself.

Opal raised her eyebrows, but added her entreaties.

He sat down at the table. "Have you started your new novel yet?"

Brenda smiled. "I have, but Opal's a writer too, you know, she's just had three of her poems accepted for an anthology called 'New Lines'."

David turned to her. "Good for you."

Opal shrugged her shoulders. "I'll be lucky to see any cash for them. I've just got to be satisfied with the glory, and that doesn't keep my purse filled, I can tell you."

"No, it's a pity, but poetry is never well paid." He turned back to Brenda. "Well, go on; tell me about your new synopsis."

She needed no second invitation. "It's set in the reign of William III and is the story of two beggar sisters and a rich lord."

"Sounds interesting, tell me more?"

"There isn't any yet. Look, what about 'The Devil in the Flames', have you had any success in placing it?"

He hesitated. "I'll be frank, Brenda. I've tried several publishers, but no, I'm afraid I've still not managed to find one to take it as yet," he answered apologetically.

Her lips quivered.

"Don't give up though. I haven't," he added.

Brenda spooned a mouthful of dinner into Mark's open mouth. She'd quite lost her appetite for hers. She'd thought, in her ignorance, that getting an agent meant she was on the first rung of the ladder to becoming a published author, not realising that the rungs were so far apart. She'd half expected to be signing copies of her books before very long – and making enough money by her pen to be able to put by a considerable sum to pay for the expert care that Mark would no doubt need at some future date when she could no longer manage him at home.

* * *

"'A Midsummers Night's Dream' is on at the New Theatre next week," said Opal, a couple of weeks later, looking up from the 'Oxford Mail.

"I love Shakespeare."

"So do I."

"I've seen 'King Lear' and 'Romeo and Juliet' and a film of 'Hamlet', with Sir Lawrence Olivier at the Ritz cinema as a schoolgirl. We did act out 'A Midsummers Night's Dream' at school, but it's so long ago that I've forgotten the plot. What's it about?"

"What isn't it about! It's got Kings, carpenters, fairies, and even a man wearing an ass's head, it's hilarious! When I saw it, back in Birmingham, I couldn't stop laughing. We ought to make up a party and go to see it."

"But the cost of the tickets? Then there's the children?"

"Don't worry about the tickets. I'll ask Bob. He'll be only too pleased. As for the children, surely Mrs Briggs would be happy to mind them?"

"Maybe. But a party, you said. Who else are you planning on asking to join us?"

"Bob, of course."

"Of course. But who else?"

Dark eyes twinkled. "I did wonder if we could ask that agent of yours, David Certes?"

"No!"

"Why not?"

"I'd just rather we didn't."

Opal grinned. "I've got a feeling he'd jump at the chance to get to know you better."

"I'd rather keep things as strictly business."

"I don't believe you."

"Well, I'm not going to ask him."

"I'll do that, give me his telephone number and I'll ring him."

Brenda frowned. "Anyway, I've nothing suitable to wear to somewhere like the theatre."

"Rubbish! You're not wriggling out of it like that, Brenda Bellinger. I bet you've got a dress or two in your wardrobe that could be adapted. You're clever enough with your needle for other people, so why not for yourself? I'll not take no for an answer. We'll go upstairs this very minute and look to see what you've got."

* * *

Opal pulled a grey dress with a tight pencil skirt from the wardrobe. "No, I don't think so, it's far too drab." She laid it on top of Brenda's bed, along with several other rejects.

She removed a rather faded blue dress with a pleated skirt, pulled a face and placed it on the bed.

A red-check and a mauve dress followed the blue onto the reject pile.

Brenda smiled wanly. "See, I told you. I've got nothing."

Opal ignored her. She'd found a yellow cotton dress decorated with tiny white flowers.

She examined it carefully. "What about this one?"

"Hmm. That was my favourite in the fifties, but it's so outdated now."

"Maybe, but couldn't it be modernised?"

Brenda looked thoughtful. "I suppose if I was to shorten the skirt and move the waistline. Yes, it shouldn't be too difficult to do."

"There you are then. Now, all I've got to do is find something suitable in my wardrobe."

* * *

It was the evening of the theatre trip. Mrs Briggs, who'd been only too pleased to baby-sit, was watching the television with the girls. Mark being already snugly tucked up in his bed.

"Don't worry, Mrs Bellinger," she'd said, "I'll have these two upstairs by seven-thirty at the latest."

David, who hadn't needed urging to agree to Opal's invitation, was to call for them in his Morris Oxford at seven. They were to meet Bob in the foyer at seven-fifteen; curtain up being twenty minutes later.

Brenda sat before her dressing table in the altered dress. It had turned out far better than she had hoped. She powdered her face and coloured her lips with strawberry-pink lipstick.

"Are you nearly ready, Brenda?"

"Yes, come in."

Opal entered the room and stood behind her. She was wearing a turquoise mini-skirted dress, with a rope of white-beads wound about her throat, and white earrings, shaped like seashells. She picked up Brenda's comb. "Let me do your hair differently," she said, "I think it'd suit you piled up on top in the style of a coronet."

Humming to herself, she combed, plaited and pinned.

She stood back, pleased with the finished result. "What do you think?"

"I certainly don't look like the everyday, Brenda Bellinger."

"You certainly don't." Opal studied Brenda's reflection in the mirror. "It just needs a finishing touch." She took a posy of artificial yellow rosebuds from her handbag and fastened it just above Brenda's ear. "There - Grace Kelly to a 't'."

"I could never look as good as her."

Opal laughed. "We'll let David be the judge of that."

* * *

Brenda looked around excitedly. She was seated in the Circle of the New Theatre. On her right-hand side was David, on her left, Opal, with Bob beside her. High above them stretched row upon row of purple plush covered seats; their occupant's features, indistinct. The auditorium hummed from the combined clamour of conversation as the audience eagerly waited for the orchestra to tune up and the safety curtain to rise.

She inhaled the perfume of the white rose pinned to her dress. To her surprise, and secret delight, David had presented it to her when he'd arrived at her house. She flushed, remembering Opal's raised eyebrows and knowing smile.

"Would you like a programme?" he asked, breaking through her thoughts.

"Thank you."

He fetched one, and they sat studying it, dark and fair heads close together. His fingers inadvertently touched hers, sending a thrill running through her. He began to explain the plot. Brenda had found her school copy of Shakespeare and had gone through the play earlier that day; she didn't want to appear an ignoramus. After all, David was extremely literate. Even if he found her attractive, he could soon get bored if he thought she wasn't, at least, quite intelligent.

The lights dimmed. The safety curtain began to rise. A discordant din, trombones and tubas, clarinets and cornets, broke out from the orchestra pit. All tongues stilled. The curtains parted, revealing a woodland glade...

* * *

The play was over. They made their way out of the theatre. "What did you think of it, Brenda?" asked David.

"Wonderful, far better than I expected. All the actors were very good, but the fellow who played Puck was brilliant."

"I told you that you'd enjoy the play," said Opal.

"It's not that late, why don't we go round the corner to the Red Lion in Gloucester Square for a drink, finish off the evening properly?" suggested David.

Brenda smiled. "I'd like that."

But Opal had caught Bob's eye.

"I'm afraid I've got some college work that must be done tonight," he said.

"I'm rather tired," put in Opal. "Besides, I've got an early lecture tomorrow. I'll go and relieve Mrs Briggs. I'm sure she must be longing for her bed. Bob'll see me home. You both go and enjoy yourselves."

"I'd rather you came too," said Brenda, suddenly feeling awkward. This was obviously a put-up job to get her and David together. Having a drink with David, Opal and Bob was one thing. David on her own, quite another. It would seem like being on a date. It was a lifetime since she'd courted. In fact she hardly knew how to act with a member of the opposite sex anymore. Could she say she'd changed her mind? No, there was no way she could get out of it.

CHAPTER 8

David led Brenda into the crowded interior of the Red Lion. He found her a seat. "What would you like to drink?" he asked.

She hesitated. "A shandy would be nice."

He smiled. "I'll have the same." He shouldered his way through the press of patrons around the bar to try to get served by the landlord; a beefy looking individual, with thinning hair and a bulbous nose; his sleeves rolled to his elbows; his tattooed arms like ham joints.

Brenda looked around. She admired the deep mullioned windows and the wood panelled walls that were hung with prints (copies of old masters she assumed); the plush red carpeting; the wall lights; the imitation candelabra, that shed their mellow glow onto the small blackened oak tables, the tops of which were hidden by empty bottles and glasses and around which, seated on three-legged stools, were people of all ages, from a toothless old man who dribbled in his beer to two teenagers holding hands. She briefly wondered about their lives. Her glance moved to the bar and David. What on earth could she find to say to him when he came back with their drinks? She couldn't keep talking about her book, even though it was of great importance to her. She had to think of some other topic of conversation or he'd think her a bore. But even as she puzzled this over, she kept asking herself the selfsame questions that women since time immemorial have asked. Was he attracted to her as much as she hoped? When he drove her home, would he expect to come in? Should she ask him in? And if she did, what if he should want to kiss her? She didn't think he'd expect more than a kiss, not yet at any rate. He'd have too much respect for her to rush things, of that she felt fairly certain.

"Sorry I've been so long," he said, setting down the drinks.

"That's all right. I've enjoyed looking around. I've always found it interesting, studying people and guessing who they are and what they do for a living."

He laughed. "The hallmark of a true writer."

This started the conversation off on the subject of writing in general - famous authors - the books she most enjoyed.

To her shame, Brenda hadn't read quite so much since television. With the children, home, and now writing, there wasn't much time anyway. She had attended Cowley St John's Girls, a church school; its foundation stone was dated 1850, and surrounded by prefabricated classrooms on the Cowley Road. A knowledge of literature had not been considered so vital. Although she did remember reading George Eliot's, 'The Mill on the Floss' with the class. Recently, since making David's acquaintance she'd been borrowing Dickens, Thomas Hardy, and the books of several other authors from the library and reading for thirty minutes before sleep in an effort to further her education.

"I like Thomas Hardy's, 'Far From the Madding Crowd'," she said.

He mentioned a few others, such as Mary Webb's novels. Luckily she'd recently read 'Gone to Earth' and 'The House in Dormer Forest', so was able to comment.

"What about Dickens?" he asked.

"Oh, I'm very fond of his works too, especially 'The Tale of Two Cities' and the 'Old Curiosity Shop'. I'll never forget the first time I heard the 'Christmas Carol' on the wireless; one Boxing Day it was. I'd have been about fourteen - the ghosts sent icicles down my spine. I got it out of the library recently, but this time it made me cry. I suppose I was identifying Tiny Tim with my Mark."

He nodded. "How is Mark? Has there been any improvement in his condition?"

"No, perhaps there won't be, but I keep hoping."

"I think you're very brave."

She blushed. "It's nothing."

"He's such a lovely little chap, your Mark. He always has such a big smile."

"Yes, he has. I wouldn't be without him, despite all the problems. Anyway," she added brightly, "they're getting him a wheelchair with a hood and apron. The Health Visitor arranged it. The springs have completely gone on my pram and Mark's getting too big for the pushchair. I had to take him to the Wingfield Orthopaedic Hospital at Headington to be measured for one."

"That's good."

She nodded. "But I still don't know how long it'll be before I get it. But I suppose I'm lucky to be getting one free for him. Anyone needing a wheelchair would have had to pay for it when I was a child."

"Have you always lived in Oxford?" he asked.

"Yes, Oxford born and bred. We lived in Charles Street, just a short distance from the house we're in now. It doesn't sound very adventurous, does it?"

"Oh, I don't know."

"And you, have you always lived in Clifton Hampden?" asked Brenda.

"No. I've only been there twelve months. I was born in Ilford, Essex. When the war started we moved to Reading. My dad's sister came and got me and my mother out of the air-raid shelter in the middle of a raid. She took us back to Reading with her."

"And was your father away fighting?"

"Yes, in the Army. He served in the desert with Montgomery. He was one of the 'Desert Rats'. But it wasn't as exciting as it's painted. He was bitten by mosquitoes, covered in dust, and the majority of the time, bored stiff."

"I don't suppose it was. My dad died at Dunkirk."

He patted her hand sympathetically.

"And have you any brothers and sisters?" she asked.

"No, my mother wasn't able to have any more after me. But that's enough about me and my family. Tell me more about you and yours, Brenda."

He seemed to be interested in everything that had ever happened to her, beginning with her childhood and early teens, leading up to the present day...." so with Miranda having ripped off a large section of wallpaper," she said, "and being unable to afford a decorator, I had no option but to re-paper the front room myself."

"Time!" called the landlord.

They looked up.

"Goodness, is it that late?" she exclaimed, in astonishment.

David consulted his watch. "It certainly is."

He drove her home.

Her eyes were drawn to his masterful hands on the steering wheel. Idly, she wondered what it would be like to have those strong fingers caress her? She blushed, as realisation hit her that she didn't want the evening to end - for them to have to say good-night. Suddenly her bed seemed very lonely.

She made up her mind. She would ask him in for coffee. "Would you...?" she began. He turned to her, his expression unreadable in the dim interior of the car. "I've got to go," he apologised, "I'm leaving for London first thing. I'll let you know how I get on as regards your book."

She swallowed her disappointment. "Thanks."

Brenda watched his car disappear. Why hadn't he wanted to come in? He'd seemed to enjoy her company earlier. She told herself that he must have had second thoughts. After all, her girls, and especially Mark, were a responsibility that few men would be keen to take on. He'll have decided that it was best not to get too friendly.

* * *

As regards her writing, Brenda was losing heart again. "I don't think David Certes is ever going to find me a publisher."

Melanie and Miranda, wearing summer frocks, were enjoying their Weetabix. It was the first of May. Although barely nine a.m., it was already warming up and outside birds were twittering.

Opal took up her mail from the kitchen table. She'd just returned from town where the Morris Dancers had traditionally heralded in the month of May, or 'May Morning', as it was commonly called. Over hundreds of years, as was the custom, students at the Oxford colleges had watched the antics of the Morris Dancers on Magdalen Bridge, as with bells jangling, the men leapt high into the air and crashed their beribboned sticks together, their clogs clattering on concrete. Afterwards, she and Bob, along with their friends, had breakfasted at one of the town cafes.

"Why should you think that?"

"I've neither heard nor seen anything of him for a fortnight."

"That's not long."

"It seems a long time to me. I've a good mind to write and tell him not to bother with my book; it's just not worth the hassle."

"Don't be so silly. He's a busy man. You're not his only client. He must have dozens. You've just got to have patience."

"It's easy for you to say."

Opal grinned. "I know what it is, it's not just your book that you're worried about, it's David."

"Don't be so ridiculous!"

"I'm not. It's written all over you."

"You're imagining things."

"I reckon he fancies you, too. I've seen the way his eyes rarely leave you."

"You're just talking nonsense. He'd never fall for someone

like me." She turned her head, listening, "Mark's crying. I must go to him... get him up."

She ran up the stairs. She couldn't really hear Mark crying. But she just wasn't going to listen to any more of Opal's romanticising. Of course she didn't fancy David. And it was obvious that he didn't fancy her. Yes, it was purely business on both their parts. She tried to summon up John's features, the way a lock of dark brown hair fell over his brow - the merry blue eyes - the sensitive mouth - the firm chin, but somehow those dearly loved features had become rather hazy.

That night she had a vivid dream. She and John were strolling down a country lane. Birds were singing in the hedgerows. The trees above them, shady and green. With her holding onto his arm, John pushed Mark's pram, whilst behind them, dawdled Melanie and Miranda, scuffing their shoes and arguing as usual.

They approached a cottage with roses around the door. Suddenly the door opened and out came David. She gasped in surprise. "I didn't know you lived here?"

David smiled a welcome and stretched out his hands. She turned to John, intending to introduce the two men. But John had disappeared.

* * *

As Brenda dreamt, Opal was lying sleepless in her bed, as she worried about Lady Margaret Hall's ball, that was fast approaching and the fact that she could not afford a ball dress to wear to it. Bob had promised to accompany her, so she really wanted to shine, but what chance had she compared to students whose wealthy fathers were buying them model gowns.

She confided her problem next day. "I really don't know what to do, Bren."

Brenda was quiet for a moment. "I've got it," she said, "you could go in my wedding dress."

"A wedding dress, would that be suitable?"

"It would if it was worn without the jacket, and I did a few alterations."

"But surely you don't want your wedding dress used in such a fashion?"

"I want to help you. It'll take my mind off my book. Besides it's only taking up space in my wardrobe."

"But won't your dress be too short?"

Brenda laughed. "It was always too long for me. I almost tripped over the hem coming out of church. It was made by my mother-in-law, so I had to wear it."

"I see."

So the dress, a froth of white satin and tulle was brought out of mothballs and Opal tried it on. Brenda, with a mouthful of pins, set about the alterations. She made some darts in the waist. "I'll take this in a couple of inches; let out the bust about the same. Then I'll sew red, green, gold and blue sequins onto the bodice. What do you think?"

"I think it's very good of you." Opal studied her reflection in the wardrobe mirror, visualising herself in the altered dress, enfolded in Bob's arms as they danced a dreamy waltz together. Surely he'd be so taken by the sight of her that he'd just have to pop the question?

* * *

Brenda was washing a pile of Mark's terry nappies when she had an unexpected visitor. She'd sewn the final sequin onto the dress the previous evening and it now hung in Opal's wardrobe, awaiting the big event.

She lifted out a sodden nappy with the end of her copper stick and deposited it in the spinner of her twin tub. "Drat! Who was that knocking?"

She wiped her hands on her pinafore.

At the door, to her dismay, was David.

He smiled crookedly.

What on earth was there to smile about? It had rained all day and there was no way she was going to get her washing dried outside. Not to mention the fact that her oven seemed to be going wonky, the fairy cakes she'd made that morning had burnt and, they would need a scrape. A wail came from the pram in the kitchen; Mark wasn't so well. He had a runny nose. Besides that she looked a mess, her hair wanted washing, she was wearing her old slippers with a hole in the toe, and to cap it all, she'd a spot on her chin – the size of a mountain in her imagination.

"I can see you're busy, but can I come in?" he asked.

"I suppose so," she said, embarrassed at being caught at a disadvantage. Why hadn't he written first? She'd have had a chance then to put on her best dress and her high-heeled shoes and arrange her hair in a becoming coil behind her head. She led him into the front room. “Did you want to see me about anything in particular?” she asked, her mind half on the million-and-one chores that needed to be done before the girls returned from school. An idea, one that didn’t please her, surfaced. Was he here with bad news? Suddenly she felt that he was about to say he could no longer be her agent, that her book was unpublishable.

She felt sick. Was her book really so important? Why, she might never see David again. Despite all her denials, she knew she would miss him. More than that! She was in love with him.

She ventured a quick look at his face.

It couldn’t be that. He’d surely have more tact than to look pleased at the prospect.

“I had to tell you straight away,” he said.

“Tell me what?”

“You’ve done it.”

“Done what?” she asked, exasperated.

Barely able to contain his excitement, he fumbled in his briefcase, and held out a letter. “This was in the morning’s post.”

With a trembling hand, she took it from him. She began to read – her heart leapt – surely the letter couldn’t really say what she thought it did? She rubbed her eyes and looked again – she’d not been mistaken. The words that she’d longed to read were there in front of her, in black-and-white!

* * *

Opal entered the house. For once, everything seemed quiet. Too quiet, she thought, perplexed. She heard from the direction of the dining room, suppressed giggles, followed by a loud, “Shush!!”

What was going on?

Opening the dining room door, she gasped.

Brenda, dressed in her best, her face wreathed in smiles, grabbed at her arm. The girls, also in festive attire, leapt up and down excitedly. While Mark, seated in his special chair, waved his arms and chuckled; Opal could swear that there was a glint of understanding in those warm brown eyes. She saw that the table was set as if for a party, with a plate of sausage rolls; a large pork pie, cut into quarters; a bowl of nuts; a packet of cheesy biscuits; several bags of crisps; two bottles of lemonade and a bottle of Tarragona port.

"What's all this in aid of, Bren? Have you won the pools?" asked Opal, perplexed.

Brenda hugged her. "Better than that. Ten times better than that. And it's all thanks to you."

"You've not?"

"I have. My novel's been accepted by Smyth & Sons, Publishers. It's just got to be edited."

Opal hugged her. "I can't tell you how pleased I am. But I didn't have that much to do with it." You did all the hard work.

"Oh, yes, you did. I'd have given up on several occasions if it hadn't been for you. Now, let's crack open this bottle of port. This is a celebration."

"But when did you hear this marvellous news?"

"David Certes came round this morning. Caught me on the hop. I looked a real sight."

"Bet that didn't please you?"

"No, but I soon forgave him, bringing the news that he did. Smyth & Sons' cheque's in the post. Even allowing a percentage for David, it should be a tidy sum. I get the same again when the book is published, in about nine months."

Opal eyed the spread, "so you thought you'd spend some of the money in advance."

"Why not? I think we all deserve a party." She opened the port and poured out a generous glass. She lifted it high, the liquor, (where it caught the light) winking like rubies." Here's to you, Opal Walker." She passed the wineglass to her. "May all your dreams come true."

Opal laughed, her earrings jangling, and taking the glass toasted her in reply, "And all your dreams too, Brenda Bellinger."

* * *

Opal handed Brenda a magazine. "Just look at this Bren," she said, "it's a short story competition. First prize one-hundred pounds and publication in their magazine - second and third prize, twenty-five and fifteen pounds, and a ballpoint pen for the four runners up."

Brenda waved the magazine away. She picked up a bottle of Calamine lotion and some cotton wool from the kitchen table. "I haven't got the time or the energy to bother. I've enough to do with working on my second novel and looking after Melanie and Miranda, both as you know, with the German measles. Do you think that Mark looks peaky? I hope he doesn't catch it too. If he did, well…"

The excitement of hearing that she was to be published had somewhat paled in the event of St Mary and St John's school suffering an epidemic of Rubella and both her girls coming down with it.

"Don't worry. Mark's stronger than you realise."

"I only hope you're right!"

"Of course I am, Bren. Look, this is a very prestigious literary magazine. You've got to be a really outstanding writer to get in it."

She rubbed a weary hand across her brow. "I'll think about it later."

"Later could be too late. Look, you don't need to write anything fresh," argued Opal, "haven't you got one about the land-army girl and the airman. You never did send it away anywhere, and it's just the right amount of words."

Brenda hesitated. "No I didn't, but I just can't get up enough energy to do anything about it."

"But surely you'd like a hundred pounds?"

"Well, yes, but there's sure to be thousands of entries. I wouldn't stand a chance."

"You don't know that. I've always thought that story very moving."

"It's just too much of an effort."

Opal smiled to herself. If Brenda wouldn't do anything about it, she would. Surely she wouldn't grumble at being the recipient of a hundred pounds. Of course she might, if all she received from the magazine was a ballpoint pen.

CHAPTER 9

"Good grief!!" exclaimed Opal, "you'll never guess who's written to me."

Brenda looked up from her own mail. "Can't say that I can, but by the look on your face, I'd venture a guess and say that it was the Queen of England."

Opal laughed, her earrings jangling. "I'd not be any more surprised."

"Well, who has then?" asked Brenda, becoming curious.

Opal handed over the letter. "Well I never, fancy Bob's mother writing to you."

"Evidently, Mrs Brown's as curious about me as I am about her. She noted my address when Bob dropped a letter that I'd sent him. Fed up with waiting for him to bring me home, she's decided to do something about it. She wants to meet me. She's coming to Oxford for a few days, taking the Trinity suite at the Randolph Hotel in Beaumont Street."

"Gosh! She must be extremely well off if she can afford to stop at that posh place. They sit down to dinner in evening gowns and dinner jackets. What wouldn't I give for a few days of being waited on there."

Opal smiled. "Me too. And as for her being wealthy, I rather suspect you're right. I've seen the Randolph's guests through their dining room windows when Bob and I were on one of our walks; the women with a fortune in jewellery round their throats and fingers."

"We don't know how the other half live, do we?" reflected Brenda, glancing ruefully down at her floral pinafore.

"No, we don't. I wonder if they have satin sheets on their beds at the Randolph?"

"Satin! I'd love to sleep on satin."

"Would you?"

Brenda laughed. "Not really. I was only joking."

"I'm relieved! Aren't satin sheets considered rather amoral?"

"Are they? How exciting. But as for the Randolph Hotel having satin sheets on their beds, I couldn't say. I don't suppose we'll ever find that one out unless we win the pools, and I never do them. I've got better things to do with my bit of money than to waste it gambling."

Opal grinned. "That's not the only way to come up with a fortune. Your novel might turn out to be a best seller."

"And pigs might fly!"

"You never can say. It's pretty good, I reckon."

"Thanks for all your faith Opal, but I think I know my limitations. Now, getting back to your Bob's mother. Does she want you to go to the Randolph to meet her?"

"No, she suggests the Cadena Cafe in Cornmarket. Says their cream horns are not to be missed."

"I agree! How will you recognise Mrs Brown?"

"Bob did once show me a photo of her. But anyway she says she'll be wearing a red rosebud in her buttonhole; and that she hopes that three p.m. next Tuesday afternoon will be convenient for me. I'm to let her know if it isn't - she sounds really nice, Bren."

Brenda hugged her. "I'm glad. I'm really pleased for you. Perhaps if you can get her on your side, it'll bring you and Bob closer. But will you tell him of his mother's letter, and that a meeting between you has been arranged?"

"I don't think so. Mrs Brown's going to invite him along to the Cadena as well. She wants to give him a surprise. I can't wait to see his face when he finds me and his mum taking coffee and cakes together."

As Brenda busied herself with her chores later that morning, she tried to quell the uneasy feeling that kept rising to the surface. She didn't like to say it, but she had her doubts about this meeting with Bob's mother that Opal was so looking forward to. She only hoped that it wouldn't turn out to be too much of a surprise for those concerned. After all, she reflected, Bob must have some good reason for keeping the two women in his life apart.

* * *

Opal got off the bus at the Carfax Tower and made her way along Cornmarket Street, dodging the crowds of shoppers. There were middle-aged women in floral frocks, teenage girls, leggy in miniskirts. She passed more than one harassed husband, laden with purchases, trailing wearily behind his wife. She had to smile at the sight of toddlers in pushchairs; their faces smeared with biscuit or ice cream; ejecting bottles or dummies onto the pavement. She pitied the long-suffering parents of older children who whined and wanted and clutched at their hands or clothing.

She felt the sun warm on her arms and neck. It was a lovely summer's day she reflected and pleasant to be out and about. Feeling slightly apprehensive, she glanced at her reflection in a shop window. Did she look all right? Was her skirt long enough? Taking Brenda's advice she had decided to wear more muted shades than usual. She had on a grey skirt and white short-sleeved blouse. In her ears she wore small conservative pearl studs instead of her usual dangly earrings.

The clock of the Saxon church, St Michael's of the Northgate, chimed the hour. She quickened her step, not wanting to get off on the wrong foot with Bob's mother by being late. She thought of her own parents and the letter she would write to them later, describing this meeting. Her own mother, especially, had been concerned on her behalf about Bob - she'd let it slip that, so far, she'd not been invited to his home. Beulah Walker's dark eyes that glinted with merriment in her round, jolly face became unusually serious. "He seems nice enough, but I don't know… there's something that puzzles me about him. It's as if he has something to hide. Do be careful, love. I don't want you getting hurt."

Opal shrugged away her mother's misgivings. Everything would be all right after today. The Cadena Cafe came into view. Her nostrils twitched pleasurably at the wonderful aroma of coffee that the place was famous for. She only hoped that it would taste as good as it smelt.

She entered the cafe, blinking at the gloom after the bright light outside. Readjusting, she saw several tables covered by gaily-checked cloths, each with a three tiered cake stand, and a selection of mouth watering cakes and pastries. A dozen ladies, of all ages, shapes and sizes were being served by waitresses in black satin dresses, white lace aprons and matching caps. But which of these ladies, with laden shopping bags beside them, indulging in cakes and tea was Bob's mother?

Opal's eyes moved questioningly around, coming to rest on a well-padded woman with snow-white curls and a round, pink, unlined face - a walking stick propped beside her. This couldn't be her. She was far too old.

Another, thin and angular, who reminded her of her headmistress in Birmingham, was dividing a chocolate éclair into minute pieces. Definitely not, Opal told herself.

A smartly dressed woman, who seemed vaguely familiar, caught her attention. Aged around fifty, she wore a veiled hat perched on top of hair, once fair, now greying. Around her lined neck was slung a fox fur. And pinned to her green velvet jacket was a red rosebud.

Opal moved towards her. "Mrs. Brown?" she queried, "I'm Opal Walker."

The woman looked up. Recognition dawned. Her grasp tightened on the handle of her coffee-cup, some of the hot liquid splashing onto her lap.

"Oh, no! Are you hurt?" Opal cried, aghast.

She received no answer.

She grabbed up a napkin from the table. "Let me help you."

"I can manage," said Mrs Brown frostily, her voice, despite many years in England, still retaining a hint of a Southern drawl.

"But your skirt?"

"I'll see to it myself!" she half turned her back, dabbing at her skirt with a napkin.

"I was only trying to help," said Opal. All the stories her mother had ever told her came flooding back. In South Africa, a black man had been horsewhipped for having the audacity to raise his eyes to a white woman. Two white men had raped a black woman but the police had done nothing about it. Bile formed in her mouth. She tried to swallow, but almost choked. She looked up, Bob was at the door. Mrs Brown had seen him too, her expression saying, how dare he not warn me about you! How dare he let me be shown up like this! She waved an imperious hand in his direction. The horrified Bob stumbled towards them, his face the colour of putty at having recognised his mother and girlfriend together. The slowness of his steps revealing that he felt like turning tail and running.

He reached the table. "Hello Mum," he mumbled. He turned to Opal. "I didn't realise that you were going to be here..." his voice trailed off.

"Obviously not!"

"Well, what have you got to say for yourself?" said Mrs Brown coldly. She lowered her voice, "I don't know how you have the gall to subject me to this!"

"It isn't my fault."

"Isn't it?" said both women together.

"Perhaps we should sit down quietly and talk about it?" he suggested.

His mother's eyes hardened. "How can you ask of me such a thing. Why, your granddaddy would turn in his grave if he knew." Her voice came out louder than she intended and the clatter of crockery and low hum of conversation ceased. A waitress, attending to a nearby table, looked over, frowning.

"But Mum, that was Alabama and years ago. We can't… we shouldn't think like that now. Opal is an intelligent girl..."

His mother cut him short. "I know what she is, and it's not someone I should want to mix with. And unless you've got no feelings for me at all, you shouldn't either."

"Of course I care about you, Mum, but.."

"I think I'd better go," said Opal. She had to get away from this bigoted woman or explode. She'd thought that maybe Bob might have another girl, and all the time... It just never occurred to her that the problem might be racial. What a fool!

"No, no, stay and talk."

"There's nothing to be said. It's best that we don't see each other again."

"No, Opal, no! Please don't say that."

"It's no good, Bob."

"Let her go, son."

Bob ignored his mother. "But Opal, this can't be the end. I love…" But she had already turned and was walking from the café, struggling to keep her dignity.

He made to go after her, but grabbing his hand, his mother clung to him. "No," she said, "it's best to end it now. She's not for you. She'll be far happier with one of her own kind."

* * *

The front door opened. Brenda looked up. She glanced at the clock - three forty-five - Opal was back early. She threaded the needle through the material of the dress she was mending and rose to her feet. Could something have gone wrong at the Cadena? Had she been right all along to feel doubt about this meeting with Bob's mother? Were those ragged gasps she could hear, crying?

She hurried into the passage.

Opal, in a daze was attempting to climb the stairs.

"Are you all right?"

She turned, her face confirming that she'd been crying.

"What on earth's happened?" Brenda asked.

The explanation was incoherent.

"Come into the kitchen and I'll make a cup of tea."

Opal let herself be helped along. In the kitchen, the kettle was put on, tea made, and a dash of whisky added to it.

"Now tell me all about it," Brenda encouraged gently. Was Bob ill? Has he had an accident? Something terrible must have happened to get her in such a state.

Opal swallowed. "It's Bob," she said, "we're finished."

"Finished. Surely not. You're both so much in love."

"I thought so too, but that was before I met his mother."

Brenda frowned."What do you mean? I thought you said she sounded nice?"

"Nice! That's a laugh."

"Look, Opal, what has Bob's mother got to do with all this?"

She gulped. "I must have been blind. I should have been warned when he put so many obstacles in the way of our meeting. Of course, he daren't take me home, not with her being so colour-prejudiced."

"What!!"

"It's obvious that Mrs Brown was born and brought up to think the white race superior and people like me less than dirt. You should have seen the way she looked at me, as if I was some worm that had crawled from beneath a stone. I felt about one inch tall. Then Bob appeared and began pleading with her. I was so embarrassed. Everyone in the cafe was looking on, enjoying it no end, I reckon. But what is worse, what really hurts, is that Bob didn't tell her where to go. I never realised, until now, that he is so spineless. He's completely under her thumb."

"Hmmm. I've had my misgivings about you and him. I couldn't help but think it fishy that he's never taken you to meet his mother, especially after your parents had welcomed him into your home. But he is such a pleasant fellow that I've tried to give him the benefit of the doubt."

"'Was," said Opal pointedly, "not 'is'."

"You're talking as if he's dead."

"Bob's definitely in the past tense. To think I swallowed all those tales about a sick mother. He must have thought me an idiot."

"I suppose he should have told you the truth."

"Yes, he should!"

"But if he had, what would you have done then? It would have made things really awkward between you. Perhaps you'd have felt that you couldn't go out with him any more?"

"Yes, I definitely would."

"Maybe he couldn't face that. Look, all this must be extremely difficult for him. Perhaps when he's thought seriously about what has happened, he'll stand up to his mother. Tell her that he loves you and she's just got to accept the fact."

"I can't see him doing that. Besides, even if he did, there's no way I could stomach having someone like Mrs Brown as a mother-in-law. My life wouldn't be worth living .No, this has got to be the end. I'm just going to have to grit my teeth and forget Bob."

CHAPTER 10

Brenda was fetching in the milk. The girls had left for school, Opal for college and Mark's breakfast was next.

Bottles in hand, she looked up, startled by the screech of a motorbike turning the corner. She at once recognised Bob. He gave a tentative wave. The bike slowed and shuddered to a standstill. Seconds later he'd joined her on the doorstep. "Can I come in? I must talk to you. I know Opal's not here. I passed her at the bus stop."

Brenda hesitated. "I don't know how you've got the cheek to show your face. Opal's dreadfully upset."

"I know. I am too. Look, please let me come in and talk to you?"

"I can't see it'll do any good. It's Opal you need to make it up with. How on earth could you treat her like you have? You should have been open with her from the first. Let her know how prejudiced your mother is."

"That's why I haven't taken her home. I just didn't want to hurt her."

"So you just left things, until you hurt her ten times more."

Bob's eyes fell.

She noticed the smudges beneath his eyes, and felt almost sorry for him. Opal probably wasn't the only one who hadn't slept a wink last night. Maybe he couldn't help being weak. And how would she have felt if her mother hadn't approved of John? Bob was in an awful position. She made up her mind. "I suppose I'd best ask you in, we can't talk out here."

He sighed with relief and followed her into the front room.

"You may as well sit down. I'll make a cup of tea. You look as if you could do with it."

"That's very kind of you."

She left the room, calling back from the kitchen, "Have you eaten?"

"Thanks, but I couldn't stomach any food," he answered.

She returned. "Kettle won't be long."

"Look, I love Opal, but I love my mother too. What a mess. Do you think Opal'll ever forgive me?"

"I couldn't say. She seems set at the moment that everything is over between you. But she might come round later."

"Do you think that's possible?"

"I don't know. You'll just have to give her some proof that she comes first. You've got to be willing to stand up to your mother. Tell her that if she can't accept Opal, she can't have you."

"I won't find that easy."

"I don't suppose you will."

There came a wail from upstairs.

"Mark's awake, I'll have to fetch him down."

"I'm sorry, I'm holding you up."

"It can't be helped. I'll just get him. Won't be a tick."

Seconds later, she returned, carrying the four-year-old in her arms. "You are getting a lump," she said to him, laying him on the rug.

Mark gurgled and flailed his arms, as if in reply.

"He likes to keep me in view," she explained, fastening Mark's fingers around the string of a brightly-coloured balloon. "There you go sweetheart."

Chuckling, his brown eyes followed the balloon as it floated above him.

"You've got enough problems of your own without me adding mine," Bob reflected, shamefaced.

"Think nothing of it. Opal's been such a good friend to me, that there's nothing that I wouldn't do for her. Besides I know she'd really like to get back with you. "

"Would she?" he asked eagerly.

"I think so, but she's been very hurt by your mother."

"I know."

The electric kettle whistled.

She hurried out. As she poured the boiling water onto the tea-leaves, she thought of Opal's and Bob's problem. Why was it necessary for people to make so much of it? John's family hadn't. John's sister's GI had turned out to be a negro, but neither of John's parents had thought that this mattered one way or the other. They had accepted Reuben because their daughter loved him. They'd thought that if she did, it was because he was worth loving. It had been as simple as that. John's mother, who was not an educated woman by any means, having left school and gone into Service at twelve, had insisted that she couldn't see that a black person was any different to anyone else - after all the colour of their skin was only pigment. Surely they were identical to whites on the inside.

Brenda couldn't help but agree with her late mother-in-law's reasoning. Especially as all human life could have originated from Africa anyway. Although she could see that the differing cultures might cause some problems.

She returned with tea and bourbon biscuits on a tray.

Bob took the cup, sipping gratefully, but declined the biscuits.

"Something to eat might do you good."

He shook his head.

"Mark'll have one, won't you, darling?"

Mark's eyes glowed in anticipation, as Brenda fastened the fingers of his other hand around a bourbon and put it to his mouth.

"He can manage to feed himself with a biscuit," she confided proudly.

Bob nodded, too full of his own problems to be interested in anything else. "Would you put in a good word for me with Opal?" he pleaded.

Brenda's brow furrowed. "I could try, but I can't promise anything. I certainly don't want to end up piggy in the middle. You need to have it out with your mother. Has she gone back to Tunbridge Wells yet?"

"No, not until Friday."

"Then get off to the Randolph and have it out with her. What can she really do? She might blow her top. But if you show that you're adamant, surely she'll come round?"

"But what if she doesn't?"

"She will, take my word for it. I'm a mother, I know. Mother's always come round as far as their children are concerned." Behind her back she crossed her fingers.

Bob groaned and put his head in his hands. "I feel like I'm being torn in two."

She went over to the settee and put an arm about his shoulders.

"Pull yourself together Bob. I know it won't be easy, but if you really want Opal, you'll have to do it. And before very long too."

"Mother's so strong-willed. I suppose she's never been thwarted. Father always gave in to her."

* * *

In the street, a Morris Oxford turned the corner. It stopped outside the terraced house. A car door clicked to. Footsteps sounded. Being so deep in conversation, neither Brenda nor Bob heard anything. A few minutes later, the vehicle started up again and moved off.

* * *

David Certes' car was thirty minutes from the noise and bustle of Oxford's city centre. The houses had thinned out to fields, green as viridian, rich pasture for sheep and cows; the soft grey of the sheep contrasting with the sheen of the brindled cows lying closely together on their stomachs.

He changed down, grating his gears, pulling the wheel around only just in time to avoid collision with an approaching bicycle. He glared at the old man in rough clothes; (trousers fastened by bicycle clips), much to the man's fury. In David's mind's-eye burned the cosy picture that he'd recently witnessed. What a fool he'd been. He'd thought that the student was interested in the black girl, but all the time he'd been after Brenda. And obviously, being successful, if their closeness on the settee was anything to go by.

David had called to see how she was getting on with her second novel, and to make arrangements for them to edit 'The Devil in the Flames' together. That very morning he'd received a letter from Smyth & Sons saying that they hoped to see the revised novel shortly.

Combing his hair carefully and patting aftershave over his chin, he had put on his best suit, which he'd first brushed, although it was immaculate; eyeing himself critically in his wardrobe mirror. With a spring in his step, he'd set off, eagerly anticipating this meeting with Brenda.

Then he'd spotted the motorbike outside her house. It didn't need a genius to know that Opal would be in college. Warning bells rang in his head. Through the open window he'd heard voices. And peeking through saw Brenda and Bob, having a tête-à-tête.

He thought back to the evening of the play. How he wished now that he'd gone back with her for coffee. He had hesitated because of Angela, his late wife, feeling somehow disloyal at being so attracted to another woman.

He'd met Angela, a dental receptionist, and a blonde like Brenda, at a dance in Reading where he'd been brought up. He'd recently finished his two years at St John's College, Cambridge and begun working for a well-known literary agency. His parents, both schoolteachers, had taken to Angela immediately. They'd been married six months later. Life had been good. They bought a flat in the town centre. He'd started his own agency, which flourished. Soon he was becoming increasingly well-known in literary circles. All that was necessary to complete their happiness was a child. After two years of trying, unsuccessfully, she approached their doctor. A smear test revealed cancer. Despite all the specialists could do, Angela had died sixteen months later.

He'd never expected to find love again. He cursed under his breath. What an idiot he had been. If he'd only taken up Brenda's invitation, this other thing probably would not have developed. After all she was a lovely young woman who had been on her own for over three years. She would be vulnerable. He wondered how her friend, Opal would react when she found out about the situation. He shrugged his shoulders wryly, well, their private life was none of his affair. From now on he would concentrate solely on being Brenda's agent; his percentage, his only concern.

* * *

Bob parked his motorbike as near as he could to the Randolph Hotel. He had made up his mind. Opal had to come first. He just couldn't let her slip through his fingers, not even to please his mother.

He approached the hotel's main entrance, and was almost knocked over by a uniformed commissionaire, chest bristling with medals, who dashed to open the door of a limousine that had just drawn up.

Bob went through the swing door and into the plush foyer. He approached the reception desk.

"Can I help you sir?" asked the receptionist, his manner somewhat intimidating to Bob, despite the fact that he was used to staying in such classy places. He tried to catch his breath. Now that the moment was almost upon him, he felt that an iron band was squeezing his chest. Could he really do it? Could he really say what he had set out to say?

"Mrs Brown. Is Mrs Brown in her suite? I'm her son."

"I've not seen her go out." The receptionist studied the keyboard. "Yes, her key's not here," he said. "Trinity suite. Third floor."

Bob made his way to the lift, not certain whether he was pleased or not. It would be better to get it over with on the one hand, but on the other, if she'd been out, well, he could have put it off with a clear conscience. He wanted, more than anything, to get back with Opal. But how was he going to find enough courage to tell his mother, that this time, he wasn't going to be browbeaten into her way of thinking?

He summoned the lift.

The shaft shuddered, followed by a soft humming. A few seconds later, doors slid open. He pressed the button marked 'Third floor'.

The elevator set off on its ascent.

Bob stepped out. A corridor lay ahead of him, richly carpeted, its walls, mirrored and hung with gleaming prints. Along the corridor were tubs of exotic plants, some in vivid flower. He caught his reflection in a gilded mirror and was startled. He looked like someone about to be shot. With dragging steps he made his way along the corridor. At the end, was a door. A plaque said, 'Trinity Suite'.

He raised his hand to knock, then froze, as he anticipated the next few moments. In his mind's eye he saw the inside of the suite, his mother seated with a tray of afternoon tea beside her. He saw her face brighten at his unexpected visit. Heard his hesitant words. Saw her expression change as he spoke, her mouth tightening into a slit of displeasure.

His hand fell to his side.

He just wasn't brave enough to face her, at least, not yet.

He turned and crept back to the lift and descended.

CHAPTER 11

Opal removed some textbooks from the kitchen table, pushing them into her briefcase. She glanced at the wall calendar, and the date that she'd ringed in red. Lips tightening, she hastily turned away. The all-night ball at Lady Margaret's Hall was a mere three days off.

"I don't suppose you'll be going now?" said Brenda, having followed the direction of Opal's eyes.

"I've no partner. I'm sorry about all your work on the dress."

Brenda wrinkled her nose. "Toast!" she exclaimed, jerking the smoking grill pan from the electric cooker. "Do you think I could scrape it?"

"You could use it for shoe leather."

"You're right, perhaps I'd better put some more on. Now, where was I? Your dress."

Opal sighed. "It seems a shame not to wear it. You spent hours and hours sewing on all those sequins."

"That doesn't matter. But, perhaps you should go. You've got to get on with your life, that's if you really are finished with Bob?"

"I am."

"If that's so, couldn't you find another dance partner?"

"Perhaps."

"One of your friends at college might know someone."

"They might do."

"Think about it then. It does no good to mope. If anyone should know, I should."

Brenda had decided to stop languishing over David. She'd spent quite enough time on him. It was obvious that she meant nothing to him. At least, not in a personal way. She'd not set eyes on David since the evening of the play, having received from him only one letter; a very stilted, businesslike letter at that, saying that Smyth & Sons would require 'The Devil in the Flames' to be edited shortly. No, she'd made up her mind. It was time to move on, as far as he was concerned. She'd seen a Writers' Circle mentioned on a poster in the library. They met once a fortnight. If she could get Opal or Mrs Briggs to baby-sit for her, she could go. Meet new people, people who were interested in writing, like herself. Maybe make new friends. Definitely, this is what she needed to do. Opal ought to do the same.

She put fresh slices onto the grill pan. "I hope I can do these without burning them." She turned back to Opal. "Do think over what I've said."

"I promise I'll think about it." Opal picked up her briefcase. "See you later."

* * *

"I've found a partner for the ball," said Opal, the following evening.

Brenda looked up from spooning mashed potatoes onto plates. "That's wonderful. Who is it? Where did you find him?"

"He's the roommate of Gillian's brother. You've heard me mention Gillian, haven't you?"

"I think so."

"Humphrey's studying History at Keble."

"So what's he like, this Humphrey? How old is he for a start?"

"Gillian says he's twenty-six. She showed me a photo of him, but it wasn't that good. He's five-foot-eleven, so he's taller than me, and at least I'll be able to go to the ball, and wear your dress."

"Goody! I can't wait to see you in it. Maybe as well as being tall this chap'll be dark and handsome?" She laughed inwardly. Perhaps he'll have a dishy friend. One interested in a widow with three children? Someone who could take her mind off David!

Opal laughed. "Not with my luck. He'll probably have buck teeth and a squint."

* * *

Miranda and Melanie, giggling excitedly, bobbing around Opal, as Brenda fastened back her corkscrew curls with the sequinned hair band, that exactly matched those glittering on the dress's bodice.

"Opal looks like a princess," exclaimed Miranda.

"Cleopatra," said Melanie, airing her knowledge, recently got from watching a programme on television about ancient Egypt.

"Yes, Opal looks very nice," agreed Brenda, "those coloured stones in the earrings blend well with everything else."

Opal smiled with satisfaction. "Shall I give you a twirl?" Not waiting for an answer, she twirled, eyeing her mirrored reflection delightedly, as her tulle overskirts billowed about her, bell-like. Her smile quivered and disappeared like a cloud masking the sun.

She's thinking of Bob, thought Brenda. No doubt wishing that he could see her like this.

A knock came at the front door. She hurried down to answer it. A gangling young man stood on the step. He beamed at her. "I'm Humphrey, Opal's partner," he said. In his hand, he carried a corsage of red carnations.

Brenda's heart sank. Though pleasant, and no doubt clever, this unprepossessing man, with a large Adam's apple, was hardly likely to turn Opal's head. Still he did make it possible for her to attend the ball. But with such a partner, would she have a good time?

* * *

A large marquee festooned with fairy lights, had been erected on the field adjacent to the grounds of Lady Margaret Hall. It was reached by means of a little bridge.

In the entrance, colourful pot plants had been arranged to form a grotto reminiscent of the Botanical Gardens. On a flower-decked dais, members of a band, dressed in evening attire, played a quickstep. At one side of the marquee, the Dean, in her wide shouldered forties style dress smiled benevolently. She was accompanied by middle-aged academics in drab evening gowns and three-piece suits. And no doubt brought out of mothballs, once a year by the tutors, especially for this occasion.

Opal felt Humphrey's hand stickily through the thin material, as he attempted, ineptly, to lead her around the floor. She only hoped his clammy fingers weren't soiling the back of Brenda's dress. She'd feel awful if she had to return it in less than a perfect condition. But apart from this worry, she was extremely satisfied as to how her appearance compared with those of the other students. Many of the gowns were obviously far dearer, but few looked as eye-catching.

A size eleven dancing pump came down onto her foot. "I'm sorry," he said.

"Don't mention it," she replied graciously, gritting her teeth. She'd attempted the foxtrot, the tango, the waltz and now the quickstep with Humphrey, and he was hopeless at all of them.

She spotted Gillian. Her partner, a wide-shouldered six footer with Greek godlike features, was also a proficient dancer. Opal grimaced, comparing him to Humphrey. It didn't appear she had a lot to thank Gillian for. Although Humphrey was a decent sort, he could badly do with dancing lessons. She thought of the popular School of Dancing in Broad Street. It was above Boswell's, a drugstore and was run by a refined middle-aged lady. She wondered if she could suggest that he go there for some tuition without hurting his feelings? She decided that she didn't really know him well enough. She sighed. At least he wasn't racially prejudiced!

The compere, a dapper man with brown hair slicked over a bald spot, announced the supper dance.

Taking the floor once again, she thought, with relief, that at least she would soon be gaining some respite while they ate.

The supper, a lavish affair, was laid ready at one end of the marquee on white-clothed trestle tables and consisted of minute sandwiches, sausage rolls, hors d'oeuvres, iced fancies, and fruit punch in a massive silver bowl. No doubt this contained something stronger than just fruit juice!

Humphrey proved to be as clumsy at eating as he was at dancing. He talked with his mouth full, and flakes of sausage roll spurted everywhere. The sight of this didn't help Opal's appetite. He had, she thought wryly, the makings of a full-blown egg-head or absent-minded professor.

The table was littered with dirty plates, glasses and half eaten sandwiches. When the dancing was about to restart, she turned to Humphrey and asked whether he would mind if she sat out for a while, explaining that she was developing a headache. It was only a little white lie, and she was desperate!

His face dropped.

"There are some partnerless girls here. If you like, you can ask one of them to dance."

"But I don't like to leave you..." he began.

"I don't mind, honestly."

After a token hesitation, he went off, and was soon on the floor once more; his partner, a plain-looking girl, gazing at him with an ecstatic expression on her face.

Opal sighed with relief, easing off her shoes under her chair and rubbing one foot against the other. Amidst the dancers she spotted Cynthia Forbes, a girl she wasn't keen on. Cynthia was wearing an off-the-shoulder gown of thick cream satin. A gown that seemed to exude 'Paris'. Suddenly Opal's ball gown showed for what it was, a made-over wedding dress. Her eyes shifted to Cynthia's partner. She gasped, something twisted within her, as she recognised the features and fair crew-cut. How could Bob do this to her? How could he come here with someone else? She averted her head. Willed herself invisible. She sensed dancing feet coming nearer and nearer. Bob and Cynthia? She tried to rise but was frozen to her seat. The footfalls receded. Was the danger over? She ventured a hasty glance, but it was the wrong couple. For at that very moment they danced past her, Cynthia with a smirk on her face, Bob horrified.

* * *

In the makeshift cloakroom, Opal rummaged amongst the pile of coats and wraps on the window seat for the leopard skin jacket that she'd borrowed from Mrs Briggs. But where was it? She had to get out of the place. She couldn't stay a moment longer.

With relief she found the jacket, and was just about to put it on when the door opened and Cynthia and two other girls entered.

"Not going already?" said Cynthia.

Opal didn't reply.

She came nearer. Her lips stretched in a spiteful smile, "Lost your tongue?" Cynthia turned to her friends. "She's upset because I'm here with her ex-boyfriend."

Opal tried to edge past, but Cynthia blocked the way. How could Bob go out with someone like her? Someone so talked about, so tarty. She recalled the episode of the bathroom window at college and how Cynthia had been caught with a man in her room. She'd been strongly reprimanded, and the window nailed up. Opal imagined that if it had been somebody poor, like herself, she'd have been 'gated', at least. Later, the newly installed, oak main doors, costing a thousand pounds or more had been paint-daubed with the words, HER MAJESTY'S PRISON. No one had ever admitted to doing it. Opal, and everyone else knew who it was. She remembered, too, just after this, overhearing Cynthia laughing with her cronies about the workmen who were putting right the damage, "Well, it gives the working man something to do."

Opal had been disgusted at her attitude, thinking of Brenda's late husband and her own father, 'working' men both. It was men like these who'd kept this country going in the past – for hardly a 'living' wage. They were worth, in her opinion, a dozen of Cynthia's stockbroker father whom she'd seen calling for her in a flash Rolls Royce.

Cynthia snatched the jacket from her hand. "What a tawdry bit of tat," she said, dropping it to the floor. She grabbed Opal by the shoulders, digging in her long painted nails. She laughed. "Let's see if your blood's red like the rest of us or the colour of tar."

"How dare you!" Opal wriggling from her grasp, kicked her sharply in the shins.

"Ouch! You black bitch, I'll..."

Footsteps clattered outside. But they passed by.

Cynthia spat out, "He's had enough of black meat, keep away from him, he's mine now."

"I'm sure I don't know what you mean."

She laughed. "You know all too well. I mean Bob Brown. Keep your hands off, or I'll pull out those stupid curls of yours by the roots.

"Leave her be, Cin," said one of the girls, "we don't want any trouble."

"Yes," said the other girl, whose hair was backcombed into a fashionable beehive, "let's get on with what we came here to do, powder our noses."

She ignored her. "I know just the fellow for you, Opal," she said, her eyes glittering,

"He stokes the boilers. I expect you've seen him about, Jimbo, his name is. He's one of your sort. He's got muscles on him like duck eggs. And a big you-know-what, by the bulge in his overalls. They reckon they can keep going for ages. You'll get ten times more fun in the sack with him."

Her friends laughed coarsely.

"Don't be so foul."

"Foul am I?" Cynthia shot out a hand and attempted to drag her nails across Opal's face.

She backed hastily, but Cynthia's foot was on the hem of her dress. There was a sound of ripping as the delicate material came away at the waist. "Oh, no, look what you've done!"

Furious at having Brenda's dress ruined, she stamped hard on Cynthia's toes; at the same time slapping her hard across the face.

She shrieked. The other two girls shrank back.

Opal ignored them. Picking up the leopard skin jacket, holding the dress to her, and with head held high, she walked from the room.

Down by the front entrance Bob was waiting.

He turned. “Opal, I must speak to... Good God, whatever’s happened to you? Your dress is torn.”

She didn’t reply, and brushed past him.

He called after her. “Come back!”

Her steps never faltered on the gravel path and she was soon lost from view amongst the blackened foliage of trees and bushes.

He ran after her. “At least let me call you a taxi?” he panted.

“I can manage, thank you,” she replied stiffly, shrugging him off, “you’d best get back to your Cynthia - she’ll need your shoulder - or maybe even a crutch.”

He frowned. “It isn’t like you think. She means nothing to me. I only agreed to come with her on the off chance of bumping into you.”

But Opal, glimmering like a moth, had disappeared through the gate and into the darkness of Norham Gardens.

CHAPTER 12

Brenda covertly studied David's strong profile and his firm hands manoeuvring the steering wheel, she, refusing to acknowledge the stubborn leap of her heart. She was beside him in the front. Behind, counting the passing sheep and cows were Melanie and Miranda, with Mark held upright between them.

Having left Oxford on the A 423, they were making for Clifton Hampden and David's cottage. He had invited them for the weekend so that he and Brenda could edit her book. There'd not been enough room in her house to accommodate him. Reluctantly she'd agreed, knowing his help would be invaluable. 'Don't worry about the children,' he'd written, 'my housekeeper, Miss Tribble will be only too pleased to keep them amused while we get down to work.'

Brenda only hoped that Miss Tribble knew what she was letting herself in for.

It was a fortnight since Opal had returned to James Street from her College ball, several hours earlier than Brenda had expected her, and in a dishevelled state. She'd almost had to prise the sorry tale from her. Evidently Bob had been there with another girl. And if that hadn't been bad enough, this girl had then assaulted her.

Brenda had tried to persuade Opal to report the incident to the Dean. She went over in her mind their conversation.

"Would she believe my word against Cynthia's?"

Brenda frowned. "Why shouldn't she?"

"Why indeed - because Cynthia's got a rich father - because she's white."

"That shouldn't make any difference."

"No?"

"She shouldn't be allowed to get away with it."

But all Opal wanted to do was to forget the incident. In the end, Brenda dropped the subject.

The Morris Oxford took a corner sharply, causing the girls to giggle and jerking her back to the present.

"Who assaulted Opal?" asked David, his eyes concerned in the driving mirror.

Brenda realised that she'd been thinking aloud.

She explained.

His manner seemed to alter at her words. "But, I thought.." he began.

She turned to him. "Thought what?"

He flushed darkly. "I thought that you and Bob.."

"You thought what about me and Bob?" she asked in disbelief.

"I thought... I thought.. that something was going on between you and him.."

"What!!"

"I called around to see you about your novel, and to make arrangements for us to edit the first one. A Wednesday morning, three weeks ago, it was. I saw the two of you seated closely together in your front room."

"And you read something into that?"

"Well, yes."

"What on earth do you take me for? Do you think I'm the sort who'd try and steal her friend's boyfriend?"

"Well, no."

"I was just attempting to console Bob. You see he and Opal had just spilt-up. His mother's fault. She's colour prejudiced. I suppose that's understandable with her background; she's from the Deep South of America. Anyway, she treated Opal like dirt when they met. I was telling him that he'd have to stand up to his mother if he wanted Opal back, and even then she mightn't come round. He was pleading with me to put a good word in for him. That was all there was to it!"

David smacked his brow with his palm. "I have been an idiot!"

"You can say that again. And get both your hands on that wheel!"

The car turned right onto the B 4015. They approached a long narrow bridge with a one-way traffic sign. They drove onto it. Beneath, flowed the river Thames, sparkling like cut-glass in the sunshine. On the opposite side, thickly bordered with Weeping Willows could be seen the steeple of the village church, and the tops of beetle-browed thatched roofs. From many chimneys, despite the warm weather, white ribbons of smoke wound through the sky.

The church, its stones black with age, came into view, surrounded by a graveyard with yew trees and lichen covered tombstones that leaned drunkenly. Melanie pressed her nose against the glass, "Bet that churchyard's haunted," she said, "and at midnight those graves'll open up and ghosts in sheets'll come out and float about." She began to wail hollowly.

"Stop that!" chided Brenda, "you'll frighten Miranda."

Miranda looked indignant. "I'm not a scaredy-cat."

"You're scared of that picture book with a witch in it," retorted Melanie.

"Oh, no, I'm not!"

They neared a two storey inn. It had a picture book thatched roof, and walls of dazzling whiteness. Hollyhocks in tubs framed the door. "The Barley Mow," said David, "it's world famous."

"It looks very old."

"Fourteenth century."

"As old as that!" said Brenda.

"Is your cottage fourteenth century too?" asked Melanie.

"My cottage is almost modern compared to the Barley Mow," he laughed, "the landlord reckons that there's been an inn on this very spot since 1352; not only that but it was featured in the book 'Three men in a boat' by Jerome K Jerome. I'll take you there for a drink while you're here."

"I'd like that," smiled Brenda.

"Us too," piped Miranda, "can we have lemonade and crisps?"

He smiled. "Well, maybe, but children your age aren't allowed inside, so you'll have to have them in the garden."

"I'd rather, anyway," put in Melanie. She pointed to the gaily-striped parasols sheltering the wooden tables and benches, "It'd be fun sitting under one of those umbrella things."

They drew up at a rather spacious whitewashed cottage. Also thatched, it had mullioned windows and a bright blue front door with red roses around it. Above this was a weather-worn stone plaque with 1630 engraved upon it. The cottage was surrounded by a rambling garden, brilliant with pompom asters, red, yellow, white and lilac, that had thin pointed green leaves and yellow centres. Chrysanthemums, silver, pink, lilac and yellow. Six-foot high larkspur, flowing with fine deep blue effect. Gladioli, orange flame, apricot and shrimp pink, flowering shrubs.

"What a beautiful garden," said Brenda.

"I can't take all the credit." David indicated an elderly man with rolled up sleeves and a cloth cap on a thatch of greying hair who was weeding a flower bed. "Ned comes from the village twice a week."

Two apple trees, their twisted branches resembling stags'

horns were heavy with nature's juicy bounty. Between the trees, a swing was suspended.

Spotting the swing, the girls began swaying back and forth on their seats.

"Careful of my springs," he chided playfully. He hooted his horn.

The front door opened and a woman with a white cottage-loaf hairdo and a wrinkled rosy face, like a well-kept apple, emerged. She was wearing a smart floral overall.

David turned to Brenda. "My housekeeper, Miss Tribble."

They got out and he introduced them.

Miss Tribble, her face wreathed in smiles, shook Brenda warmly by the hand. "Pleased to meet you and your little darlings, Mrs Bellinger," she said. "I've got tea all ready. I do hope you all like home-made scones and cream?"

Melanie and Miranda licked their lips.

"They certainly do," laughed Brenda, as, with David pushing Mark in his chair, they followed the housekeeper inside.

* * *

That evening, after several goes each on the garden swing and a game of Happy Families with Miss Tribble, the girls settled down for the night in their bedroom under the eaves. The room, papered in a delicate pink with a pattern of tiny red flowers, contained three narrow beds, each with a colourful patchwork counterpane. Mark was already asleep, Brenda having got him undressed and to bed an hour earlier, he being tired out by the journey and fresh country air.

"Miss Tribble says she will take us for a picnic tomorrow, Mummy, while you and David are working," enthused Melanie.

"Mr Certes to you, Melanie, I've told you enough times."

Miranda smirked at her sister's ticking off. "I never forget," she said smugly.

Melanie ignored her. "I'm going to push Mark's wheelchair, and..."

"And me, I'm going to push it too."

"All right, we're going to push his chair, and Miss Tribble's going to carry the picnic basket. She's really nice, isn't she Miranda? She says she will take us to Hawthorn Farm first; to show us where there are some baby rabbits."

Miranda's eyes gleamed. "Can we have a rabbit to take home,

Mummy?"

"I don't think so. They're a lot of work. You have to clean out the hutch regularly and I really haven't time."

"We'd do it, wouldn't we, Melanie?"

"Yes."

Brenda sighed. "Until you get fed-up. I'm sorry sweetheart, but I don't think it's a good idea." She bent and kissed her.

"Miss Tribble's promised to take us to see a peacock and peahen too," put in Miranda.

"You're not going to want them?"

She giggled. "No, of course not, Mummy. The peahen is the peacock's wife, you know. Miss Tribble says she might be able to get us a feather each from the peacock's tail. If we're good, of course."

"Make sure you are then."

She looked indignant. "I'm always good," she said.

Melanie raised her eyes to the ceiling.

Brenda laughed and smoothing Miranda's golden hair, kissed her.

She closed their bedroom door. The children were all so excited about this trip to the country. But what did she feel about it? Or rather, what did she feel about being in such close proximity to David? Although she was determined to keep things on a business level, it wasn't so easy. In the last few hours, since putting him 'in the picture' about Opal and Bob, his frigid manner had radically changed. She was tempted to see him once more, in a romantic light. She glanced at her reflection in a mirror on the stairs, seeing herself as he would see her as they edited her novel later that evening. Was her newly acquired blue dress smart enough? Was that slight flush on her cheeks becoming? She had worn this dress to the Writers' Circle meeting the previous Wednesday, but she may as well have been wearing an oily boiler suit, for all the good it did her.

Making up her mind, she had attended one of the Circle's fortnightly meetings in the centre of Oxford; Mrs Briggs minding the children.

She'd been very disappointed. The majority of the members had been women and elderly women at that. She had never before seen so many tight pepper-and-salt perms, crow's-feet and crepey necks in one room. The men were no better, in their case, with thinning hair and paunches. After a lot of waffling by the

Chairwoman, the minutes were read. Then came the real business of the evening. Member's own work. These mostly consisted of chunks of indigestible verse or long-winded, unpublishable articles read in thin reedy voices or mumbling monotone, that had had her yawning in her seat. The highlight of the evening was the tea and chocolate biscuit. The meeting, thankfully, ending at nine-fifteen.

She entered the drawing room. David, attired in a dark dinner jacket, white shirt and red bow tie was stood before the French windows through which could be seen (the blue velvet drapes being drawn back) a well-rolled lawn, its emerald smoothness dotted with white daisies.

He smiled and handed her a tall crystal glass of red wine, which catching the evening light, glittered like rubies.

Brenda looked around, admiring the sumptuous couch and armchairs, considering that their upholstery exactly matched the drapes. Her eyes were drawn to a portrait in a silver frame of a fair young woman, a single rose in a glass set before it. She bit her lip as something akin to jealousy stirred. Was this his wife? If not, who was this picture of? And more importantly, what did she mean to David?

He'd followed her gaze. "Angela, my late wife," he said briefly, "taken on her twenty-third birthday."

She noticed a muscle throb in his throat and that his voice had become strained. "Angela was very pretty," she said, relieved that the photograph wasn't that of a recent girlfriend.

"Yes, yes she was. Come on, I'm hungry." He took her by the hand, ushering her into the adjoining dining room. The oval table was covered with a white lace cloth, and set for two, and a silver candelabra with red candles cast a soft glow. Beside it, on a heated trolley were several covered dishes. He smiled, and pulled back a chair for her. "We're to help ourselves," he said. "Miss Tribble has gone to her own quarters. She'll have her feet up now, watching the television, so she won't disturb us."

The meal that he served, started with creamy chicken soup, followed by roast duckling and green peas; apple charlotte and cream completing it. Despite her nervousness, Brenda savoured each mouthful. "Your Miss Tribble is a marvellous cook," she enthused.

He smiled. "She certainly is; keeps this house like a little palace too."

"I could do with someone like her to give me a hand."

"A few more blockbusters and perhaps you'll be able to afford a housekeeper. How's your second novel coming on? No sign of Writer's Block I hope? I really enjoyed those chapters that you sent me, when am I going to be able to see some more?"

She laughed. "No, I've not suffered from that affliction recently. I've just finished Chapter Twelve. I'll give you it, and Chapter Nine, Ten and Eleven when you take us home."

"That's great. Smyth & Sons have been worrying me again about your second novel. If I can set their minds at rest, they'll probably fix a date for the publication of 'The Devil in the Flames' as soon as they receive the revised copy."

"I can't wait to see it in 'WH Smiths."

He reached across the table and laid his fingers lightly over hers. "That'll be quite a moment for both of us," he said, looking deep into her eyes.

They returned to the drawing room with their coffee.

Reluctantly David laid down his empty cup. "Well I suppose we had best get down to work."

"I suppose so," replied Brenda, following suite.

From a drawer, he produced a manuscript she recognised only too well and a big black pen. Sitting side by side, they began.

* * *

She closed the children's bedroom door. They were tired out. They had gone on their picnic with Miss Tribble, which they said had been in a field covered with cowslips, and coming back at four o'clock, full of excitement with grass in their hair and clothing and each clutching a silky-blue peacock's feather each.

She and David, after spending all morning with the novel, had snatched a quick sandwich for lunch. At six p.m. he'd taken them all, as promised, to The Barley Mow, for lemonade and crisps. It had been a long but rewarding walk, pushing Mark in his wheelchair up and down the winding lanes. The original plan was that they go by car, but unfortunately, it refused to start. They'd all enjoyed themselves, none more so than Brenda. She shivered pleasurably reliving David's warm glances over his pint. If only this weekend could go on for ever.

The evening progressed in the same way as the previous one. But this time the covered dishes had contained vegetable-soup, lamb cutlets, sauté potatoes and asparagus, followed by jam sponge pudding and custard. "I shall be putting on weight," she smiled ruefully, as they left the table, "and I could do with losing some."

David refuted this with an admiring look, that made a flush of rose stain her cheeks.

"Well, back to the grindstone," he said, putting down his coffee cup and reaching for the manuscript.

At ten p.m. he laid down his pen and smiled. "That's it, I think."

Brenda stretched. "Thank goodness for that. I'm shattered."

"So am I. How about a nightcap?"

"Nightcap?"

"A drop of brandy."

"All right."

From a decanter he poured liberally into the two glasses. He handed one to Brenda, his fingers inadvertently touching hers. She almost swooned with pleasure, but he pulled back as if stung, the drink spilling. "I'm sorry," he said, "I hope it won't stain?" He dabbed at her skirt with his napkin.

"If the worst comes to the worst, the dry-cleaners'll get it out," she murmured, overcome with emotion.

His hand slowed, his breathing becoming irregular. Dropping the napkin, he took her glass and placing in on an occasional-table, pulled her to him. Her heart thudded so hard, she felt it would burst from her chest. Was her secret wish about to come true? A wish that she would hardly admit, even to herself. Did he feel for her as she did for him? And if he did, would he ask her to marry him? Make her mistress of all this? It was obvious the children liked him, he was especially good with Mark, bonding with the boy and feeding him with his crisps at the Barley Mow. To have a father to take an interest in him was what he needed. The girls too.

She felt David's fingers tangling her hair, drank in his whispered endearments, felt his butterfly-kisses on her brow. Then his lips closed to claim hers, in a kiss so sweet, so passionate, that desires, dormant so long, began to reawaken. She felt his fingers unbutton the bodice of her dress; caress the smooth flesh of one breast. She moaned as he teased a hardened nipple.

"I'm sorry," he said, breaking off; pushing her away.

"Whatever for?" she asked, confused.

White faced, he was staring at his wife's portrait. He turned back to Brenda. "I can't," he said in a strangled voice.

"I don't understand?"

He had already left the room.

* * *

David sat on his bed, his head in his hands, his thoughts in chaos. "Oh, Angela, Angela!"

He felt like a betrayer. It was barely eighteen months since he'd held Angela's hand in the hospital; had finally kissed her goodbye. A frail shell of the woman whom he'd adored. He had loved her so much, so very much. He thought back to some three years earlier. It had been a cold winter's day, but in their flat, with the velvet curtains drawn against the darkness outside, it had been cosy and warm. Angela's fair hair had tumbled from the pins securing it, as she bent over the fire, a toasting fork in her hand, her face rosy from the heat. She'd turned and given him the slice of toast to butter, her blue eyes soft with love in the mellow glow of the firelight. Then she had told him.

David thumped his pillow. Angela shouldn't be dead! She was too young. It was so unfair. From beneath his bedside-table, he drew out a photograph album. He opened it, lifting aside the tissue sheets that covered the black-and-white snapshots. Angela in a bathing suit smiled up at him. Beneath, in her handwriting was written, Brighton, August 1964. He remembered that holiday well. It was three months after they'd been married. They'd stayed in a small guest house, not far from the front. Their room had been rather cramped, the brass bedstead creaking every time one of them turned over, but they hadn't cared. They were together, and that was all that had mattered. He turned the pages. Here was a photograph of them both, taken at a friend's wedding. He frowned. The snap didn't do Angela justice; the black-and-white not being able to show off her lovely colouring; her corn-yellow hair, her brilliant blue eyes. He bit his lip - colouring that so resembled Brenda's. Further on in the album were some photographs that he and Angela had tried to paint in with Photo Tint. But the final result hadn't been really successful.

He pushed the album back beneath his bedside table, flicked out the light and moved to the window. He stared down into the garden; the flowering-shrubs, so bright during the day, appeared black and rather sinister. Was he confusing Angela with Brenda? His emotions seemed to have gone haywire of late. But the ghostly bushes conjured up no answer to his dilemma.

CHAPTER 13

Brenda stared at the closed door. Whatever could it all mean? she thought, puzzled at David's behaviour. She looked at the photograph of Angela. She supposed eighteen months was not so very long. Perhaps it was a bit soon for him to 'move on' and think of love again. He was most likely still grieving. After all, she herself was often distressed when thinking of John, despite the passage of three years.

Mark started to cry. She went up to him. His legs had been playing him up a lot recently, he, getting muscle spasms. Very few nights went by that she didn't have to rub his legs with embrocation and dose him up with a baby Aspirin. David might well have heard her at 3 a.m. the previous morning, although she had tried to be as quiet as possible, as she moved around and endeavoured to settle Mark back down again.

She halted, her hand on the doorknob. That could be it, her earlier supposition, correct. It wouldn't be because of his late wife that he was holding back. Loyalty didn't worry the majority of men. At least she thought not. Men were not like women, who, in most cases, were more sensitive about such things. The reason was more likely to be that he didn't want to get too involved because of Mark. After all she had made no secret of all she had to do for him, and that some of the things weren't too pleasant. Mark's bowels caused him constant problems due to his inactivity. Brenda had to dose him with Syrup of Figs or Senocot, and even this, sometimes didn't work properly. She'd spent more time than she cared to remember, holding him over a potty and encouraging him to evacuate.

Cleaning his teeth was another difficult task. Mark would chew on the brush. "Come on, Mark, open your mouth," she would plead, exasperated. There would be quite a sloppy spluttering as she tried to get him to rinse his teeth, she, holding a small kidney dish, supplied by the Health Centre, beneath his chin. Sometimes, due to muscle spasms, his arm would jerk the cup from her hands, sending water and cup flying. On one occasion, after a particularly messy teeth cleaning, she'd remarked to Opal, "I don't know what I'm going to do when I need to shave him."

Opal had replied. "Just be glad he's not a girl, like our thirteen-year-old neighbour, back in Birmingham. At least you won't have to contend with 'the curse' each month. Not like her mother."

Brenda opened the bedroom door. By moonlight, she could see that the two girls were fast asleep, Miranda with her thumb in her mouth. But Mark, sobbing, his brown hair wet on the pillow, was writhing in pain.

She hurried over to him and pulled back the bedclothes. "Mummy's here darling, she'll soon make you better."

* * *

Brenda entered the breakfast room, which was just off the kitchen. It had red chintz curtains at the windows, whilst on the tiled windowsill stood several pot plants, tawny-yellow, pink and white chrysanthemums; a botanical garden in miniature, she thought.

David, apart from offering her the butter dish and the milk jug, hardly addressed her at all. She was glad of the children's and Miss Tribble's presence, as well as having something to busy herself with in feeding Mark with his Weetabix.

The children didn't seem to notice anything amiss, as they enjoyed cereal and toast.

Miss Tribble passed Brenda her home-made marmalade. "Did he take much 'getting off', dear?" she asked, her grey eyes concerned. "I heard his cries. It's such a shame he should have to suffer so, can't they do anything?"

Brenda took the china pot and spread a spoonful of lemon marmalade over a slice of toast. "They've told me of an operation to release the tendons behind the knee, but he would have to be in hospital with his legs in plaster for months. I've heard, too, that in cerebral palsied cases, such as Mark's, it mostly doesn't make much difference anyway; so all I can do is give him Aspirin."

Miss Tribble shook her head. "Poor mite."

"Yes, it's bad enough not being able to do what other kiddies can, without being in pain all the time."

"What can he do, my dear, if you don't mind me asking?"

"No, I don't mind. Not much really. Not much at all. He has no use in his right hand and only a small amount in his left. It's always difficult to buy him toys at Christmas and birthdays. I got him a hand-controlled car, hoping he could manage it, but he has never been able to."

"What a shame."

"I lay him on the floor by the shoe cupboard sometimes. He has a whale of a time pulling out shoes and boots with his good hand. You should hear him chuckle."

"It's nice to think he can get some fun out of life."

"I agree."

David pushed back his plate with a half-eaten slice of toast on it. "I'll just check the car. It might start now. If not, I'll try and hire one to take you home." He hesitated, "It's a pity you can't stay a little longer, there'd be no problem then, but I suppose that the girls…"

"Yes, they've got to be back at school," said Brenda, grabbing at the excuse not to extend their stay, her discomfort in his company growing by the minute.

He left the room.

Brenda turned to Miss Tribble who was piling the crockery together on a tray. "Can I give you a hand with the washing- up?"

She smiled pleasantly. "No, dear, you have a rest while you can. I'm sure you don't escape the washing-up very much at home."

"Opal, that's my lodger, does it with me after our evening meal."

"I help Mummy wash the cups sometimes," put in Melanie.

"I dry the spoons," chirped Miranda.

Miss Tribble, carrying the tray, turned at the door. "You two girls can help me dry the cutlery if you like."

"Can we, Mummy?"

"Go on then."

Melanie and Miranda scampered after the housekeeper.

David returned. "It's no good. Car's as dead as a dodo. I'll have to see if the garage has got something I can hire while mine is being put right. This Morris Oxford has been nothing but trouble. I'll have to look out for another vehicle. I can't go on like this. I need a car I can rely on."

He left the room. She heard a 'ping' as the hall phone was lifted, followed by the sound of dialling...... "you'll come and tow it in.. good... something else, I need to hire a car immediately... you can't help me?.. too short a notice. Of course I realise that you're only a small concern... thanks anyway." The phone was put down.

"I'm sorry," he said returning, "but I can't get a car. I suppose I can't expect Clifton Hampden to be like Oxford." He paused. "I hate to have to say this, but I'm afraid you'll have to go home on the bus. I'll come with you and see you're all right."

"Thanks. But don't bother, I'm sure we'll be fine."

"It's no bother. Anyway it's the least that I can do." He took out a bus timetable from a drawer and consulted it. "Yes, there's a bus to Oxford in three-quarters-of-an-hour, ten-thirty."

"We should just get it then. Look, don't worry about the bus, I don't mind, really I don't. I'll just make sure I've not forgotten anything." She left the room, returning minutes later with all the various bags she needed when taking her family anywhere.

Miss Tribble, followed by the girls, came in from the kitchen carrying a neat pile of terry towelling nappies. "Oh, there you are Mrs Bellinger. Here's the nappies that I scrubbed out yesterday. They're nice and aired."

"Thanks very much." Brenda put them to her cheek." "You've got them really soft."

Miss Tribble smiled. "I always use Lux flakes."

"This'll be the last time I'll have to bring 'terries' when I come away. My Health Visitor is arranging for me to have some disposable pads that I can use as nappies for Mark. They're going to be delivered once a fortnight, so I shall keep them for emergencies."

"That's good, my dear. Someone like you deserves all the help she can get. I must say I really admire you."

Brenda reddened. "I'm just doing what any mother would."

"I wonder?" Miss Tribble patted the girls. "They've been very helpful," she said.

Melanie and Miranda preened themselves at her words.

"I put away all the crockery," said Melanie.

"Well I put away all the cutlery," said Miranda, "and hung up a saucepan and frying pan."

"I'm glad to hear it. I only hope you'll keep it up when we get home," she laughed.

The housekeeper smiled, and shook her hand warmly. "Here's wishing you all a safe journey," she said.

"Thank you. And thank you for looking after us so well," replied Brenda.

Outside David was waiting for them. Brenda's heart leapt as she caught sight of his strong profile and dark head, but she told herself not to be so silly as to harbour tender feelings for him, as it was obvious that they weren't returned.

He gave her a hesitant smile, "I'll push the chair for you," he offered, taking the handlebars, "it's not too far."

"That's all right, I've always been fond of walking," she awkwardly rejoined.

They set off, with the girls clutching their peacock feathers, giggling and chattering as they leapt about. Brenda was desperately trying to find some topic of conversation, in an effort to ease the tension.

"Miranda pointed. "What's those flowers?"

Brenda corrected her. "It's what flowers are they, Miranda."

In the hedgerows were purplish blossoms on stalks about a foot high.

David smiled. "Good thing I was top at Nature Study at school. They're called Devil's-bit."

"Devil's-bit! What a nasty name," chorused both girls.

A little further on they saw some leafless flowers like pale purple chalices. He smiled, "And those are Meadow Saffron, or another name for them is Autumn Crocus."

"And those golden flowers over there?"

"That's Hawkweed."

"What are those thimble shaped flowers?" asked Brenda, becoming interested.

"Oh, those are Foxgloves, some call them glove-fingers, and they're said to be devoted to witches."

Miranda shivered. "Ugh!!"

"Oh, don't be such a baby!" said Melanie.

"What's that?"

"What's what?"

This time it wasn't flowers that Miranda was on about. In a field on the other side of the hedge was an odd figure with arms stretched out at right angles, a piece of sacking pinned around its neck and a floppy hat perched over one eye.

David smiled. "It's a scarecrow, made of straw. It's there to frighten the birds."

"What for?"

"You are silly," put in Melanie, "don't you know anything? Surely you've heard of Worzel Gummidge?"

"Who's Worzel Gummidge?"

"A scarecrow, silly. Mummy read us a book about him once. He got fed-up of standing in a field and trying to stop the birds from eating the crops so he went off and had a lot of adventures."

"And does this one?"

"Does this one what?"

"Have adventures."

Melanie raised her eyes upwards. "Course not. That was only a story. "

Despite the awkwardness they were feeling, both Brenda and David had to laugh. They continued on their way - Miranda pointing out every second tree and bush and asking what they were. The bus stop came into view. It consisted of a small shelter made of glass and corrugated iron and was painted a sickly green.

David consulted his watch. "Ten-twenty-five," he said. "The bus shouldn't be long now."

Hardly had he spoken than the red single-decker came into view and rumbled to a halt beside them. "You get yourself a seat, I'll see to the children," he insisted.

With relief, she did as he said. He carried on Mark and placed him onto Brenda's lap. She positioned him with his face towards the window. "There darling, you can look out and see the scenery," she said. But he wriggled himself back around; more interested in the other passengers who smiled sympathetically at him.

David helped the girls on, they, immediately commandeering the seat in front of Brenda.

He then folded up the wheelchair and stowed it in the luggage rack.

Finally he took his seat beside Brenda.

The conductor rang the bell and with a lurch the vehicle set off.

Reaching Gloucester Green, he insisted on them getting a taxi.

"But the expense?" said Brenda, "I've not been in one since my wedding day." She felt embarrassed at being indebted to him – especially now.

"Well you're going in one now," he replied firmly.

The driver put the chair into the boot. They all piled in, the girls excited at their first ride ever in a taxi. They drew up at Brenda's house, but David refused to come in, saying he had to get back, that he was expecting an important phone call.

She lifted a tentative hand in reply as the vehicle drew away. Was that a forlorn look on his face? She shrugged the notion away.

But Melanie and Miranda, their grins resembling the Cheshire Cat from Alice in Wonderland waved enthusiastically until the taxi was out of sight.

* * *

That evening Brenda discussed her weekend with Opal over a pot of tea, "...his cottage was lovely. His housekeeper, Miss Tribble cooked like an angel. The children really enjoyed themselves. But.."

"But, what?"

"It's David himself. I can't make him out. We seemed to be getting on rather well, very well, in fact. He put his arms round me... we kissed... and then...we...." Brenda's cheeks became rather pink.

"I think I get the picture," smiled Opal.

"But all of a sudden he froze up, mumbled an apology and left the room."

Opal's face changed. "Without any explanation?"

"Yes."

"You say his wife's not been dead so long?"

"Well no, eighteen months, I think it is now."

"That'll be it then, he's not really ready for another relationship. It's too soon."

Brenda frowned. "I don't know. It could be because of Mark."

"It could be, but I don't really think so. A shallow person might be frightened off by a handicapped child, but what I can see of his character, he's far from that. And he seems to be genuinely fond of children - all children. When he came here that evening to take us to the theatre, he made quite a fuss of Melanie and Miranda. Didn't he seem disappointed that Mark was already in bed? Didn't he bring them all sweets? No, I reckon, if you want David, you just must have patience."

"Perhaps you're right."

"And how did you get on with your novel?" said Opal, changing the subject. "Did you get all the editing finished?"

"Yes we did. All I've got to do now is to retype it and send it back to Smyth & Sons."

"What a slog that'll be."

Brenda groaned. "I'm not looking forward to it, I can tell you. I'll not have time for novel number two while I'm doing the retyping. Wish I could afford to employ a typist, but those agencies are way beyond my means."

"If you like I could type-up some pages for you. I've got a few free periods coming up soon."

"That's very good of you. What on earth would I do without you?" she exclaimed, hugging her.

"It's nothing," Opal said.

* * *

Ten miles away in Clifton Hampden, David, seated at his study desk, stared at the blank sheet of writing paper. What a fool he had made of himself. Brenda must think him a real idiot. Although he was very attracted to her; possibly even in love with her, when it had come to it, he just couldn't do anything about it. He'd wanted to. God, how he'd wanted to! But he kept seeing Angela's sad and reproachful face. How could you forget me so soon her eyes seemed to say? How could you make love to another woman?

He groaned and put his head in his hands. In different circumstances, if he had gone first, would she have forgotten him so soon? No, he told himself. Angela had been too sensitive for that, too loyal. In fact, he couldn't imagine her ever putting another man in his place. Although to be fair, if she'd been alone, he'd have wanted her to find a decent chap who would care for her when he couldn't any more. He'd have wanted her to find love and happiness again. Angela had really needed to have children too. She was the sort who would only be half a woman without them. He couldn't have been so selfish as to expect her to miss out on that.

His thoughts swung back again to Brenda and the previous evening. He had ruined their blossoming relationship. How could he ever explain? It would be far too embarrassing. He didn't even know if he could face being her agent anymore. He frowned. Perhaps it would be better; certainly easier for him, if she got another agent. Or failing that, she could be her own agent. Work with Smyth & Sons direct. Yes, she didn't really need him, he convinced himself.

He unscrewed the cap of his Parker fountain pen and began to write.

CHAPTER 14

"What on earth is wrong?" asked Opal, seeing Brenda's woebegone face as she entered the kitchen.

It was two evenings later and Opal had just returned from college, tired out from her tutorials and hoping for a hot bath before going on a date with a student from Balliol, someone who might, or might not, be able to take her mind off Bob.

Without a word, Brenda handed her a letter.

She unfolded it and read.

"I'm sorry," she said, handing it back.

"As you can see he doesn't want to be my agent anymore. I didn't think he'd do that."

"Perhaps he'll change his mind?"

"Why should he?" She squeezed David's letter into a small ball and left the room. She lifted the lid of the solid fuel boiler and poked the paper ball down beneath the coals. She returned to Opal. "That's that," she said, brushing her hands.

"David could have had second thoughts by now. People often do when they've slept on it," reflected Opal.

Brenda sniffed. "Even if he did, I reckon that like most men, he'd be too proud to admit to it."

"That's a rather sweeping statement. Would John have been like that? How many men have you known that well? Anyway, you were married at nineteen, weren't you?"

"Well, yes." Her face puckered.

Opal put her arms about her. "Come on, here's my hanky. Have a good cry. Get it out of your system. You should be able to get another agent easily enough now, I reckon. Or you can do as he says; work direct with Smyth & Sons."

"Another agent wouldn't be David," mumbled Brenda from the depths of Opal's cardigan. "I don't know why he's acting like this."

"From what you've told me, embarrassment, I suppose."

"I don't know what I'm going to do without him. I love him. I didn't realise just how much, until he kissed me."

"Well I love Bob, but I'm having to learn to live without him.

Tearing up all those letters that he keeps sending hasn't been easy, I can tell you."

"I don't know how you can do it, especially without reading them. I couldn't."

"Oh yes, you could. You've got a core of steel when you need it. Look how you've managed to bring up three children on your own."

"I'd no choice."

"I don't know. A lot of widowed mothers would have given up ages ago, especially with a youngster like Mark to care for. Most likely they'd have considered that their only course was to have the children taken into care."

Brenda flinched. As a child, it had been a recurring nightmare of hers that she might end up in a home. Ann, her best friend at school, whose father, too, had died in the war, had been sent to a Girls' Village run by St Barnados Home when her mother was knocked down and killed by a bus. She'd never seen Ann again, although she'd received a few distraught letters from her, in which Ann said how unhappy she was and that her housemother was very harsh. Brenda shuddered. The discipline of such a place wouldn't go down at all well with her wayward pair, she was certain of that, and as for a home for the handicapped, one heard quite horrendous tales of such places. "I could never do that!"

"No, of course you couldn't. Now come on, pull yourself together. The first thing you're going to do now is to give your nose a big blow; the second is to drink a strong cup of tea. See, I'm getting to be just like you, recommending tea for every calamity."

Brenda laughed tearfully. "I can't stay miserable for very long with you around."

"That's the ticket," beamed Opal.

* * *

In the passage, just outside the kitchen door, Melanie and Miranda were playing Ludo.

Miranda rattled the dice and tipped them out. "Goody, two sixes." She moved her counters around the board. "Go on, it's your turn."

Melanie ignored her. "Did you hear what I just heard?" she said.

"David's not going to be Mummy's agent anymore."

"That's right. But I wonder why? Mummy liked him, I know she did. When we were at his cottage in Clifton Hampden she was really happy. She'd not smiled so much since Daddy died."

"I like him too," said Miranda.

"So do I. So does Mark."

"How do you know that?"

"He chuckled more. And when he saw David, his eyes lit up." She frowned, "I don't suppose he'll be taking us now."

"Taking us where?"

"You are thick! Surely you've not forgotten something like that? He promised to take us to St Giles Fair."

"It's you that's thick! Of course I've not. I can't wait to go on the roll-a-penny and the dodgem cars."

"Well, if he doesn't take us, you can forget the dodgems. I was hoping he might take us on the big wheel, too."

"Opal might."

"And she might not."

For hundreds of years a street fair, eagerly awaited by all the youngsters, had been held on a Monday and Tuesday in early September in the centre of Oxford. St Giles, Beaumont Street and some of Woodstock and Banbury Roads being cordoned off. Displacing the usual traffic would be an exciting world of rides and stalls. The very air would be alive with the belching of steam engines, churning barrel organ music, laughter and shrill excited voices, as young and old alike tried their hand on the shooting-ranges and the coconut-shies or took a breathtaking ride on the carousal's galloping horses. Melanie and Miranda had been eagerly looking forward to attending the fair with someone who would take them on all the rides; their mother being 'nervous' when it came to them.

"Do you remember the fun we had the last time Daddy took us to St Giles Fair?" asked Melanie reflectively.

"I'm not sure."

"No, of course you wouldn't. You were only a baby the September before he died."

"Oh, no, I wasn't!"

"Oh, yes, you were!"

"I wish Daddy was alive now," said Miranda wistfully.

"Well he isn't, and that's that. David could have made us a nice new daddy. But I suppose there's no chance of that now."

"Maybe he will change his mind?"

"Why should he?"

"I don't know."

Melanie nibbled the end of a stubby brown plait. "But perhaps we could change his mind for him?"

"What do you mean?"

"Come upstairs and I'll tell you. If Mummy or Opal overheard what I've in mind, they'd stop us."

* * *

Melanie poked a knife down into the money box and turning it upside down, shook it vigorously onto her bed.

"There's a shilling," squealed Miranda.

"Shush!"

"Sorry."

Melanie shook again. This time a half-a-crown slid down the knife blade onto the pink counterpane, followed by two sixpences, a brass threepenny bit and a blackened penny.

"Is that enough for our fares?"

"I don't know. What did our half price tickets from Clifton Hampden to Gloucester Green cost?"

"I never saw. David got them anyway."

"I know that, silly." She shook again and a two shilling piece joined the small pile on the bed. She shook the money box again, but this time it didn't rattle.

"It's empty," said Miranda.

"Clever." Melanie totted up. "Six shillings and ten-pence," she said, "that ought to cover it, I reckon."

Miranda giggled. "Are we going to sneak off now?"

"Don't be daft; it'd be dark before we got there. We hardly know Clifton Hampden at all. We need daylight to find David's cottage. There are no street lights down those country lanes."

"I suppose so. Do you think he'll be pleased to see us?"

"More likely, surprised."

"What about Miss Tribble, will she be pleased to see us? I like her, she's really nice."

"You like her cakes and tarts."

"Well you do too. You ate enough of them on the picnic."

"Not that much, you're exaggerating."

"When are we going then?"

"Tomorrow morning."

"But, school?"

“We’re not going to school.”

“Not go to school?” gasped Miranda.”

Melanie laughed. “No, we’re not.”

“But playing truant… I don’t want to get the ruler on my hand.”

“You won’t. I’ll say that it was all my idea if there’s any trouble.”

“Promise?”

“I promise.”

“You’ll blame me, I know you.”

“I won’t. Now shut up and listen. Tomorrow morning, we’ll kiss Mummy goodbye as we always do, but instead of going to school, we’ll get the bus to town. I’ll check Mummy’s timetable when she’s out of the room. There’s sure to be a bus that leaves Gloucester Green for Clifton Hampden in the morning. All we need to know is exactly at what time. Now let’s go back down and finish our game; pretend everything’s as usual. It wouldn’t do for Mummy or Opal to suspect anything. Mummy’d probably lock us in our bedroom if she knew what we were planning.”

“What on bread and water?”

“Where do you get your ideas from!”

Footsteps sounded on the stairs and Brenda called, “Melanie, Miranda, are you in your bedroom?”

“Yes, Mummy, just coming, Mummy,” replied Melanie, “we’ve been tidying it.”

Miranda giggled. “She’ll not believe that one if she comes up here. It doesn’t look very tidy.”

“It looks as if a bomb has hit it, at least, your side of the room does. Fancy leaving your picture books open and your toys everywhere.”

Miranda pointed to a heap of comics on a chair. “And what about them?”

“I was just about to put them away. Come on, I’ll do my side, you do yours.”

She nodded.

They quickly straightened the bedspreads on both beds and pushed everything, books, comics, shoes and toys, beneath. Then fixing their faces into what they considered an innocent expression, they hurried down stairs.

CHAPTER 15

Opal flicked the lever and the typewriter carriage shot back for her to start the next line.

It was the following morning. Opal, having some free time was re-typing some of Brenda's edited novel.

A shout came from above, followed by hurried footsteps on the stairs. Opal paused and listened. Brenda had just gone up to make the beds. What on earth could be wrong?

The door burst open and she appeared, waving a scrap of paper. "It's the girls! They've raided their money box and gone to Clifton Hampden to try and make David change his mind."

"What!!"

Brenda handed her the note.

Opal read.

"That bus ride last Monday must have given them the idea."

"Yes. So what are we going to do? Phone the police or chase after them to the bus station?"

"We?"

"You didn't think I'd let you go haring off on your own? Let's see, how much of a head start have they had?"

"They left, supposedly for school, at a twenty-to-nine. It's now a quarter past, about a thirty-five minute start." Brenda moved hastily towards the door. "Come on, let's go."

Opal followed her into the passage. "But what about Mark?" she asked.

"Oh, God! I'd forgotten all about him. I'll have to ask Mrs Briggs if she'll mind him, but what if she's not in?"

"Let's hope she is."

Brenda hurried into the kitchen where Mark lay in his pram. "I'm sorry darling, but you've got to go next door."

Waving his arms, he gurgled unintelligibly, but his brown eyes looked puzzled. She lifted him up and carried him out. Minutes later she returned. "It's okay, she'll mind him."

"Thank goodness for that."

Brenda pulled on her coat.

"So you're not going to ring the police?" said Opal.

Brenda slammed the front door shut behind them. "No," she said, uncertainly, looking along the street and eyeing the phone box. "Surely it'd be best to try and catch up with the girls. Then if we don't, we'll ring the police."

"You're right," agreed Opal, "it might be frightening for them anyway if the police turned up at Gloucester Green."

Panting, they reached the Cowley Road bus stop. To their relief a red double decker bus was approaching.

It halted.

They jumped aboard and flopped down onto the nearest seat.

Opal tendered their fare. "Carfax, please."

"You ladies look rather flustered," the young conductor remarked cheekily as he wound a handle on his machine to issue their tickets.

Opal realised that in their rush to leave the house neither of them had fastened their coats, and Brenda, her face drained of colour, still wore her slippers.

"My friend's little girls have run off to Clifton Hampden. They're only ten and eight," she explained.

"Goodness! That's a long way for kids that young to travel on their own. Have you contacted the coppers?"

"No, we're hoping that there'll be no need. We're aiming to get to the bus station before the Clifton Hampden bus leaves, aren't we, Brenda?"

She didn't reply.

"Good luck!" He moved further down the bus. "Fares, please."

Opal slapped her thigh. "We should have got a taxi, Bren, it'd taken us straight to Gloucester Green and would have saved us precious time. It just never occurred to me. I'm so used to only going by bus. I was brought up to think that taxis were for the rich."

"Weren't we all, dearie," chipped in an elderly woman sitting opposite.

The bus moved along the High Street. Opal eyed Brenda apprehensively. Perched on the edge of her seat, she clutched her handbag to her like someone drowning without a life-belt. Opal patted her hand, "Don't worry, Bren, we'll make it."

She never answered; eyes sightlessly fixed to the grimy windows. Opal knew what she was thinking: Should I have called the police? Dear God, I hope I've done the right thing. Oh, hurry up bus, do!

With relief Opal saw Carfax Tower. "Come on, we're here,"

she said, nudging her.

The bus rumbled to a stop.

Off they leapt and dodging between crowds of shoppers, half running, half walking, they made their way along Cornmarket Street and into George Street where the bus station was situated.

"Not much further," gasped Opal, seeing a red single decker turn into the street that led to Gloucester Green.

Brenda suddenly bent double. "I've got a stitch," she sobbed.

"Touch your toes, like we did when we were kids."

She did just that, going red in the face.

"Is that better?"

She nodded.

"Let's go then."

* * *

The bus station, with its red corrugated-iron and glass shelters was laid out in an orderly fashion, each with a sign stating destination and times of arrivals and departures. The place seemed almost deserted. There were no other vehicles apart from the one that Opal had seen entering, from which mainly women, with pepper-and-salt hairdos and middle-aged spreads were dispersing. Clutching shopping bags, they were obviously intent on visiting the town centre and the large department stores.

Brenda and Opal's eyes darted this way and that, vainly seeking Melanie and Miranda.

"We really should have got a taxi. Though it mightn't have made much difference, unless we could have hailed one on the Cowley Road."

Brenda pointed to a bus shelter. "That's where you get the bus for Clifton Hampden. I remember getting off there on Monday."

"It's probably left, seeing as there's no one waiting," said Opal. "Let's go into the ticket office and ask." They made their way to a prefabricated hut.

Seated behind a counter was an asthmatic-looking individual in a uniform with rusty buttons, a peaked cap before him and a cigarette clamped between his lips - its long ash about to fall.

"Has the bus to Clifton Hampden left?" asked Opal.

He reluctantly put down his newspaper and consulted a docket. "That's right, ten minutes ago," he rasped, "the next one isn't till midday." He returned to his paper with a cough already in his throat.

Brenda's heart jolted. Taking a deep breath she said, "Excuse me."

The man looked up with a sour expression, he'd swallowed the cough.

"Were there two little girls on board?"

He looked from Brenda to Opal and back to Brenda. "Your little girls?" he asked.

"So they were on the bus?" said Opal, her mouth tightening.

"Now you come to mention it there was two small girls who were travelling on their own, who shouldn't have been. They're safely on the bus. That's all I can tell you." He returned to his paper, slotting his fag back into his mouth.

"What are we going to do?" asked Brenda, nibbling the end of her plait. "You'd think someone would stop them, realise that they were too young to be on their own," she looked meaningfully at the man.

He buried his head deeper into his paper.

"People are mainly too busy with their own affairs to bother," said Opal, purposely louder than necessary as they left the hut. "Look, I think we'd best phone David, ask him to meet them. There's a phone box just over there."

"I don't really..."

"You've got to, this is an emergency, Bren."

"But…" There were people around like those Moors Murderers', Hindley and Brady. A recent headline flashed through her head. A ten-year-old girl had disappeared while going to the sweet shop that was only at the end of her street. She'd been found strangled, amongst undergrowth a week later.

"You can't have two little girls being dropped off, miles from anywhere, and not being met. Anything could happen to them. I don't want to worry you…"

"You're right, Opal. I'll do it."

"You'd never forgive yourself if you didn't ring and something terrible happened."

They went into the phone booth and Brenda dialled David's number. "Come on! Come on!" she muttered, her fingertips dancing a frantic tattoo, willing Miss Tribble or David to be there, but nobody answered. She tried again and again, willing the silence to come alive.

Finally she put the phone down, forgetting to press button-B to get her money back.

"Wasn't he in?"

"No. What on earth can we do now?"

"Ring the police," said Opal.

* * *

Some miles away, Melanie and Miranda were excitedly looking through the bus window. Miranda tracing a picture with her fingertip on the smeared glass, as the houses thinned out and were replaced by fields and the occasional farm building.

"Look at that tumbledown cottage, it's got no roof."

"There's probably been a fire there," said Melanie.

"I wonder why all those cows are lying on their stomachs?"

Melanie disdainfully raised her eyes, "To digest their cud, silly, that's grass to you."

"I know that."

The bus rattled over a humped-back bridge.

Miranda pointed. "Look! That stream down there glitters just like the diamonds in Mummy's ring." She rolled up the bus tickets into a cone and blew through it as if it were a trumpet. "We had enough money for the fare to Clifton Hampden after all."

"There was no 'after all' about it, I knew we had enough for the fare."

"You always think you know everything."

"Well, I know more than you," replied Melanie smugly.

"Oh, no you don't!" Miranda frowned, "how will you know when to get off?"

She smiled. "Didn't you hear me ask the conductor? He says he'll put us off at the right stop. I told him about the huge oak tree by it and he said he knew where I meant."

"I don't remember any tree."

"You wouldn't."

Miranda looked around wide-eyed at the other passengers. The bus was fairly full. There were a dozen or so women, mostly plump, grey-haired and elderly like Mrs Briggs. Although there was one about Mummy's age. She had a small boy, who, squealing and chattering, bounced on her knee and pulled at her long black hair. There was also a sprinkling of men, of various ages. A youth with bright red hair and freckles had a bulging bag at his feet. While seated beside him was a lad, his brown hair uncombed, and roughly the same age as her friend, Susan's elder brother, Simon. Short trousers revealed scratched and grubby knees, and he kept pulling up his long socks that drooped about his ankles. On the opposite side of the gangway she looked into the friendly eyes of a rosy-cheeked man in a floppy trilby and a long black overcoat. He'd a fleshy nose that was covered in tiny red veins. She was fascinated by the white hairs that sprouted from his nostrils; they reminded her of a bunny's white whiskers.

He smiled and reaching across the aisle, offered a bulging paper bag. "Would you and your sister like a humbug? They're striped green and gold."

CHAPTER 16

Brenda put the phone down with a shaking hand.

"What did they say?" asked Opal.

"They said they'll contact the police station in Clifton Hampden and get someone to meet the bus."

"That's all right then, come on. Let's go home. There's less need to worry now."

There might be less need, but Brenda still felt uneasy. "But the girls, what will they think when they see a police car waiting for them?"

"Once they've got over the shock, I'm sure they'll be fine, probably enjoy a ride back home in a police car. It'll give them something to brag about to their schoolmates."

"I suppose you're right."

"I am, come on."

They made their way from the bus station. "Yes, we've left Mrs Briggs coping with Mark long enough, I reckon. After all, she's not getting any younger and he can be quite a handful at times, despite not being able to get about. He's probably pulled the bow on her pinny by now and untied it, like he does mine."

Opal laughed. "Yes, he's a rascal all right. There's definitely a lot of intelligence in him, if his mischievousness is anything to go by."

"Do you think so?" asked Brenda eagerly.

"That I do. Be careful of that wheelchair."

Just in time, she avoided colliding with it. "Sorry," she said to the middle-aged woman with fuzzy dark hair who was pushing it.

The woman smiled pleasantly. "It was as much my fault as yours."

She was pushing a spastic youth. He had a huge grin on his face and was in fact an older edition of Mark.

"I've got a son like this young man, he'll be five next January," said Brenda.

"Lenny's twenty. I'm his mother."

Brenda smiled. "Hello, Lenny."

"Hello, Lenny," said Opal.

"Lo," he replied, grinning even wider.

"We were just saying how mischievous my Mark is," said Brenda.

"If your lad's anything like mine, he'll get worse before he gets better. Lenny, although unable to do anything for himself, doesn't miss a trick. He's always organising raffles and tombolas for the church that I take him to. Friends and neighbours give me items for him – or else he gets the staff at the Day Centre he goes to, to go out and buy the prizes with his pocket money. That's where we've just been to, to church to set out his tombola for tomorrow's Garden Party. He gets all the praise, but I do all the work," she laughed ruefully. "I have to stick all the raffle tickets on the prizes and fold up the other tickets. But I don't mind, as long as he enjoys himself. I'm glad he's got an interest."

"I wouldn't mind either," said Brenda.

"Vicar's nicknamed Lenny, the Raffle King, isn't that right, Lenny?"

The child-man chortled. "F ther Ed din, F ther Ed din."

"That's right, darling, Father Edwin." She turned back to Brenda and Opal. "Lenny thinks the world of Father Edwin. He's such a kind man, nothing's too much trouble."

Opal saw a bus in the distance, and they hastily said their goodbyes to Lenny and his mother.

They climbed aboard. "It can't be easy coping with him," remarked Brenda.

"Lenny, you mean?"

"Yes. I wonder if Lenny's got a dad?"

"She'll be able to manage him for far longer if she's not on her own," reflected Opal.

Brenda saw David in her mind's-eye. He had been so good with Mark. She had hoped...She sighed inwardly. There was no chance of that now. "We'd best get a move on," she said changing the subject.

"Yes, I don't suppose it'll be that long before a suitably chastened Melanie and Miranda are delivered back to you."

"I can't tell you how relieved I'll be." Brenda felt as if a tight band had been removed from her chest. She felt so light-hearted that she could have sung.

"I can guess."

"Hello, ladies," said a familiar voice.

It was the same cheery conductor. "Haven't you found them?"

he asked concerned, as he took their fares.

"No, but we've phoned the police. They're picking them up," explained Opal.

"Good! That must be a weight off your minds." He carried on down the bus. "Fares please."

The bus encircled the Plain's roundabout-cum-war memorial and entered the Cowley Road. "They'll probably be starving after all their adventures," said Brenda. "I'd best do double the sausages for dinner."

"Good idea. We can pick up the extra from the butchers when we get off the bus."

* * *

Melanie and Miranda stared out of the bus window. Suddenly a large oak tree, its branches, heavy with leaves, came into view. "I think this is where we get off," said Melanie.

"This is your stop, girls," confirmed the conductor.

They jumped to their feet and holding onto the backs of seats, gingerly made their way along the lurching aisle to the exit. Miranda almost lost her footing and had to grab at her sister to save herself.

"Get off," grumbled Melanie, disentangling herself.

The bus halted.

"Thanks very much," said Melanie politely as she climbed down.

"Thanks very much," repeated Miranda, taking Melanie's outstretched hands and jumping from the platform.

Behind them came the man in the floppy trilby; the one who had offered them the sweets. They'd refused them, remembering that Mummy had said that they should never take sweets from strangers.

The bus started up. Away it went.

"Which way now?" asked Miranda, looking around.

Melanie's eyes swept over the surrounding scenery. She recognised the oak tree all right, but that was all she recognised. For the tangled blackberry bushes, the hedges and the field beyond that was occupied by a horse and its foal, seemed different from what she remembered.

She was puzzling over this when she realised that Miranda was picking blackberries and cramming them into her mouth. She pulled her away, "you shouldn't eat them without them being washed!"

"But I'm hungry," wailed Miranda.

"They could be full of creepy-crawlies."

"Yuk!!" She dropped the rest.

"You had some biscuits on the bus. Couldn't you have waited until we got to David's?"

"I'm hungry now!"

"Oh you're the limit, just look at you. You've got juice all over your mouth, hands and dress. What will he think when he sees you in such a mess. You look like a gypsy!"

Miranda pulled a face. "Anyway, you've forgotten the way to his house."

"Lost your way?" asked the man in the trilby.

Melanie remembered Mummy's warnings about strangers. She shouldn't really be speaking to him, but although she hated to admit it, they were lost.

"Do you know Rose Cottage?" she asked.

"Mayhaps."

"It's got a thatched roof."

He smiled. "Most cottages hereabouts have thatched roofs, m'dears."

"Well, do you know Mr David Certes?"

"Fancy you be wanting Mr Certes. Why, I deliver eggs to him."

"That's all right then," she said in relief, "do you think you could show us the way to his cottage?"

"I'd be pleased to, m'dears," he smiled, "just you be following me."

They continued along the country lane. He, naming the local landmarks.

"What's that?" asked Miranda, pointing to a tall tower with huge sails above it.

"The mill, m'dears. It's where Miller Matt grinds corn into flour."

"To make into bread?"

"That's right, m'dears."

"Windy Miller, Windy Miller, grinding up the corn.." piped up Miranda.

"That's a nice nursery rhyme," burred the man.

"That's not a nursery rhyme. It's from Trumpton, a children's telly programme that she always watches," explained Melanie loftily.

"I've not got a television – or a wireless. In fact, I've not even got any electricity or gas in my cottage."

"How on earth do you cook?"

"In a iron pot or in my side-oven. All my cooking is done on an old fashioned range."

The girls looked puzzled.

"Haven't you ever seen one?"

"I think I've seen a picture of a range in a schoolbook," said Melanie, "it had an open fire and a kettle sat on the hob."

He chuckled. "My old granny used to black lead her range at cockcrow every morning. I've never believed in these newfangled electric and gas cookers; what was good enough for m' gran' is good enough for me – even the privy out back."

"A privy – what's a privy?"

Melanie said smugly, "It's a kind of lavatory, silly, surely you know that?"

Miranda pulled a face. "Of course, I know."

"It's not one of them flush ones though."

"Not a flush lavatory? What is it, then?"

"It's a tea chest with a lid on top with a hole cut into it. When it gets full up, I empties it out and put its contents on the garden. Brings my veggies up a treat!"

"Yuk!" chorused both girls.

Miranda began to fall behind.

"Keep up, do," scolded Melanie.

"But my legs are aching."

The man looked concerned. "There's a short cut here," he said, "I'll just help you both over this stile."

They leapt down, he, steadying them.

On the other side was a field, overgrown with tall switch grass.

"Careful of the stinging nettles," he warned.

Hardly had he spoken when Miranda stepped into a clump. "Ouch! My ankle! It's burning!"

Luckily there was also a clump of dock leaves. He picked a juicy one and rubbed Miranda's ankle with it. "Is that better, m'dear?"

She dried her eyes, "Yes," she sniffled. With difficulty, they continued to cross the field, sighting at one end, almost hidden by bushes, a narrow track. He pointed along it. "We part company now, m'dears. You go that way. It leads to Mr Certes' cottage."

"Thanks very much," said Melanie.

"Yes, thank you," repeated Miranda.

"At the end of the track you'll see an old bunker."

"What's a bunker?" asked Melanie.

"It's a special wartime building that would have been used to defend us if ever we'd been invaded by 'Jerry' – the Germans, you know. It has slits in its sides for guns to be fired out of."

"Do you mean if that Hitler had got here? Mummy told me that when she was little she used to be frightened when they said his name on the wireless."

He nodded. "Thank God those days are long past. Look, m'dears, when you get to the bunker, you turn right. Oh, and don't go near it. It might be dangerous. Tramps kip… sleep in it. I don't know why they don't remove it."

"We won't," Melanie promised.

"Look you don't, m'dears." With a wave of his hand, he left them.

"Come on," she said, taking Miranda's hand. "Let's go."

They walked along the track, coming to a dingy concrete building with slits in its sides, which was wildly overgrown with weeds and bramble bushes. A thick flat slab of concrete reinforced with metal and partly covered with earth formed its roof. There were two large warped metal doors at the front, which were partly ajar. "This must be the bunker the man mentioned. Let's take a closer look."

"But the man said to keep away from it," said Miranda.

"Are you a scaredy-cat?"

"No, but…"

Melanie pushed her way towards the bunker. "Oh, flip, I've got my dress caught on the brambles. I can't get free. Come and help me."

Miranda tried to unhook her, but in freeing Melanie, only succeeded in ripping the material, as well as getting her own dress caught up and torn. Both girls examined themselves ruefully – their arms and legs were a network of scratches and pricks. "We won't half get it from Mummy when she sees the state we've got ourselves into."

"Well, it wasn't my fault."

Melanie rattled the broken, rusty padlock. "Let's go inside and explore."

"No, I don't want to. A tramp might be asleep in there. He

might shout at us for waking him up."

"Oh, look, there's a squirrel."

"A squirrel! – where?"

"There! What bright eyes and twitching whiskers it has: it's all furry and grey and just look at its bushy tail! Let's see if we can catch it. Oh, no, it's gone into the bunker. Come on, let's follow it. " And away she went.

"Don't leave me!" Miranda ran after her sister. Immediately, Melanie pushed the metal door to behind them. "It won't be able to escape us now." She made a kissing noise. "Don't be frightened, sweetie, I won't hurt you. I just want to stroke you. Keep still and let me." But the squirrel squeezed through one of the wall slits and was gone.

"Let's go," said Miranda. "I don't like it in here. It stinks!"

"All right, then. There's not much to see anyway. Only some old rags and straw, probably the tramp's bedding, and full of fleas!" She pulled at the door, but it wouldn't budge. "It's stuck. I can't get it to open again. Help me, won't you?"

Both girls pulled together as hard as they could, but nothing happened. They pulled and tugged 'till they were exhausted.

"We're trapped!"

"No we're not! We can get through the slits."

"They're too narrow," wailed Miranda.

"Let's shout through them." Both girls were soon voiceless.

"So we are trapped!" Miranda finally said.

"I'm sorry. But someone will come soon." In the dim light from the slits, Melanie looked around fearfully.

Miranda began to cry. "Mummy, Mummy."

They shouted again as loud as they could; kicking the doors with their shoes, the metal resounding with a clanging noise, but still nobody came. Sometime later, exhausted, they slumped down onto the concrete floor, and with Miranda sobbing and Melanie trying to console her, they eventually fell asleep in each others arms.

* * *

The door knocker thudded.

"That'll be Melanie and Miranda," said Brenda, catching sight of a black police car through the window.

"Don't grumble at them too much. All's well that ends well," said Opal.

"As if I would."

She opened the front door.

"Mrs Bellinger?"

Her eyes widened. The policeman and policewoman were alone. She tried to speak but failed. Her thoughts immediately returning to that awful day three years earlier. The day she'd lost her John. Her chest tightened. Was the same terrible thing to happen all over again? Please, God, no!

"Can we come in?" asked the policewoman gently.

"But... my girls... where are my girls?"

"Let's go inside, Mrs Bellinger," she urged.

"That'd be best," agreed her male counterpart.

Somehow Brenda put one foot in front of the other and led the way.

"I'm sorry," said the policeman, "but there was no sign of your little girls at that bus stop in Clifton Hampden. Unfortunately, our Clifton Hampden police were a few minutes late in getting there. But we're doing all we can to find your daughters, Mrs Bellinger. Our colleagues are at this moment contacting your friend, Mr Certes to see if they have turned up there. Also the bus driver. Don't worry. It is early days yet. We'll keep you informed."

"Yes, don't worry, Mrs Bellinger," added the policewoman sympathetically.

As if from a million miles away, Brenda heard Opal shut the front door after them and heard the police car start up and move off. Then she felt arms go around her, and a glass being put to her lips containing something strong that made her gasp. "Come and lie on the settee, you've had a shock. I'll see to Mark for you."

"But I couldn't rest."

Opal helped her over to the settee. "You must. Now lie down, let me put a blanket over you."

"But Melanie and Miranda… if something's happened to them." If they'd been taken off by someone; abused and murdered, she'd want to die too. But she couldn't, she had to go on living for Mark – he needed her and always would.

Opal patted Brenda's shoulder. "Don't think it. They'll find them, fit and well. I'm sure they will."

* * *

A tap came at David Certes's study door.

"Yes?"

Miss Tribble put her head around. "There's a policeman to see you."

"A policeman?"

"Yes, he wants a few words."

"Bring him in then."

Miss Tribble's light, brisk steps retreated. Seconds later they returned, accompanied this time by someone of a considerably heavier build.

"Constable Fowler," she said.

"Come in," said David rising, "bring us some tea, will you, Miss Tribble." What was all this about? He didn't think he'd been speeding, or parking in the wrong place.

The policeman put up a hand. "Thanks, but no tea. I've come about something potentially serious."

David frowned. "Serious?"

"Two little girls that I believe you are acquainted with may be missing. Your housekeeper says she hasn't seen them."

"Little girls, missing. What girls are you on about?"

"Melanie and Miranda Bellinger."

David gasped. Surely he couldn't be hearing right?

"It is understood that they were on their way to see you. I take it they haven't turned up?"

"No, no they haven't. I don't understand. You say they were on their way to see me? But why should they do that?"

The police officer shook his head. "They left a note for their mother stating this intention. They were seen at Gloucester Green Bus Station. We have also interviewed the bus driver. He claims he put them down a short distance from here. But he mentioned that an elderly man got off also. Whether this had any bearing ..." He left the sentence unfinished.

"How long ago was that?"

"Several hours ago, I believe. They should have been here by now, unless, of course, they have been prevented in some way or by someone."

"But, who?" And why? Bile rose in his throat as his mind supplied the answer. This couldn't be happening! Things like this are only read about in the pages of The News of the World.

"We don't know yet. It's just supposition. But you can rest assured that we will leave no stone unturned to find the children."

“Oh, poor Brenda, I mean Mrs Bellinger. She must be in an awful state.”

“What mother wouldn’t be, sir.”

“I’ll get my car out and drive around the lanes. Maybe I’ll find them.”

“It’s best you leave the police work to us, sir. We know the procedure. We are arranging to have tracker dogs scour the undergrowth.”

“Good! Yes, I suppose you’re right. I’ll go into Oxford and see Mrs Bellinger. She’ll need all the friends she can get at this moment, I reckon.”

“Yes, that would be best, sir. I take it that the lady who let me in, will be here to contact us should they turn up? Though it seems unlikely after so long.”

“Yes.”

The policeman left.

As David got behind the wheel of his car, he wondered why Brenda hadn’t rung him to tell him that the girls were on their way. He guessed that she might feel awkward with him after receiving his letter. But surely this was an emergency. Then he remembered that he had been out all that morning, collecting his car from the garage. Miss Tribble too, had been at the dentist. So maybe Brenda had rung, but there had been no one home to answer the call.

Ever since he’d posted that letter, saying that he no longer wished to be her agent, he had regretted it. No way would he have wished for something so terrible as this to happen. But at least now he would have an opportunity to reinstate himself with her.

CHAPTER 17

An owl hooted. Something rustled in the blackened undergrowth. A distant fox or badger called to its mate. It was past midnight. The moon slipped out from behind clouds to reveal the bunker.

Inside, the girls stirred in their fitful sleep. Melanie awoke. She rubbed her eyes. Opposite her, a ray of moonlight was striking through one of the slits, lighting up their prison, and revealing the curled form of Miranda asleep beside her. She shivered. She was freezing, despite being wrapped in a tramp's rags and lying on his straw. So it hadn't been a nightmare after all. They really were trapped in this horrid place. She moved stiffly. How she wished she were at home in her soft bed, with Jemima, her rag doll, beside her. She'd never dreamed how painful sleeping on concrete would be. What time was it? How long had they been here? Was it still today? Or was it now tomorrow? She listened. All was quiet. She willed footsteps to approach. None did. It seemed this short cut was rarely used. She swallowed. She might be the elder sister, but she was really frightened and wanted Mummy. Her tummy rumbled. Not only was she extremely hungry, she was thirsty too. How long could they go without eating or drinking? Would anyone ever come to rescue them? Or would they die of hunger and thirst before they did? She murmured the prayer that Mummy had taught them - "Our Father, who art in Heaven…"

* * *

Some miles away, in a large room filled with ringing telephones, and dominated by a map of Clifton Hampden, several officers sat drinking tea as they waited for it to get light. Since the Bellinger sisters had been reported missing, the police had been working non-stop to find them. Red Berets from RAF Abingdon had been drafted in to help with the search. They, and tracker dogs had combed the vicinity, but without result. The search had been called off once it had got dark. Chief Inspector Davies had had questions asked as regards the thickset man in a trilby who had left the bus with the girls, but had found out nothing. He'd put out an appeal on local radio. No one had responded. Of course that man could have parted company with them and gone innocently home. Nowadays, though, it was unlikely that he'd be totally ignorant of events, not after all the press and news coverage. The Chief Inspector checked his records. Again a blank. Could the man be a local? There were scores of elderly men in the area who wore that sort of headgear. A trilby hat, in itself, couldn't identify anyone. He frowned. And although, according to the bus driver he'd not been smartly dressed, that didn't mean to say that he wasn't from the professional classes. In Devon last year, a pervert preying on girls in parks had turned out to be a Bank Manager. Yes, they must catch him. If he got away with this once, he might try it again.

* * *

The mantelpiece clock chimed six. Brenda stirred on the settee and opened her eyes.

She'd never expected to sleep. She and Opal had sat up until past one, hardly speaking and drinking innumerable cups of tea, half hoping, half dreading a knock on the door. David had left just after eleven, saying he would get word to them should Melanie and Miranda appear. She'd been pleased, and not really that surprised to see him when he had turned up.

She eased herself up on her elbows and swung her feet onto the lino and looked across at Opal, sound asleep in an armchair. She began to shake, as the memory of the last few hours returned. Where were her girls? What had happened to them?

All the most horrifying tales she had ever heard or read about returned to torment her. She just had to get out of the house - walk the streets - do something - anything. She stood up, straightening the waistband of her skirt. She knew she looked a mess, but didn't care.

Careful not to disturb Opal, she crept upstairs, averting her eyes from the girls' bedroom, and looked in on Mark. He was fast asleep, with his favourite toy beside him; a lock of brown hair was almost in his eyes. She lightly brushed it away. He stirred and uttered a little moan, but settled back to sleep. Should he wake, Opal would hear him, she decided.

Downstairs she took her coat from its peg in the passage and slipped into it.

She pulled back the bolt carefully and let herself out of the house.

She walked towards the main road, too dazed to appreciate the crisp air. She turned the corner into the Cowley Road, her clicking heels disturbing the early morning silence. A milk float whirred. Bottles clattered and the milkman, whistling loudly, clicked open a garden gate some way behind her.

With a start she realised she'd reached Leopold Street. On the other corner loomed the blackened mass of St Mary and St John's Church. It seemed to draw her to it. She opened the gate and walked through the graveyard, a tombstone city of the dead, with its hundreds of occupants. Her eyes fell on a small marble headstone. An angel with folded wings leant protectively over it. Her eyes filled with tears as she read, 'Sacred to the memory of Emma - aged six - 1922.'

She pushed open the wide, iron-studded church door, and entered the carved, high-ceilinged interior, the only light coming from the stained glass windows on either side. She wrinkled her nose at the faint smell of incense. Passing the rows of silent pews, she walked down the centre aisle towards the altar. She knelt. "Please God," she prayed, "please let my girls be all right."

She rose and went to the statue of Our Lady. Clad in blue, and cradling the infant Jesus. Before Mary was a bowl of yellow roses still sleepy with perfume, and beside her, a prayer candle-stand. Brenda lit a candle. The flame flickered bravely in the gloom. Kneeling before the Virgin, she pleaded, "You're a mother. You too have suffered. Hear my prayer. Please bring my girls safely back to me."

Her thoughts turned to Aberfan. She knew how those mothers had felt now. Four years ago in South Wales, a mountainous coal tip, turned into slurry by torrential rain had slid down onto a village school and its surrounding houses. Out of one-hundred-and-forty-four dead a hundred-and-sixteen had been children. She remembered that she'd been listening to Woman's Hour when a newsflash had interrupted it. Later, the papers had been full of pictures of stricken parents waiting outside the school as they watched their children being dug out. She, like the majority of parents (she imagined) had really identified with those Welsh men and women. She'd read the newspaper accounts with tears in her eyes. Blue Peter had announced an appeal to send toys to the surviving brothers and sisters of the victims. She had bought a doll with the family allowance, even though she couldn't really spare the money, in thanksgiving that her children were alive and well. Attached to the parcel, a label, on which she had written, 'With love from Melanie, Miranda and Mark - Oxford.'

She heard footsteps. Looking up she saw an elderly man in a black cassock moving towards her from out of a side chapel. She recognized the vicar's bushy white eyebrows and thin features. He recognized her too, "My child, what is wrong? Can I help you?"

* * *

"A witch has me trapped by her pointed fingernails!" screamed Miranda, jerking awake and grabbing hold of Melanie.

"You know there's no such things as witches."

"But I saw her. She had a nose that reached to her chin and glittery eyes."

"You've just been dreaming." The realisation of where they were hit her. Melanie began to shake. "I'm cc cold...I... c... can...cana... stop my teeth.. cha...chat...ring."

"I'm cold too. I wish I'd got my winter coat."

"So do I."

"Or Mrs Briggs' electric blanket."

"Silly! Is there an electric point to plug it into?"

"N…no."

"Well, then!"

"And I'm awfully hungry."

"I know, I k…know," soothed Melanie. "I am too."

"I w…wish I had the tapioca pudding I left yesterday."

"So do I." What was that scratching sound in the far corner? A rat? Might it attack them? She looked around fearfully but couldn't really see anything, despite the daylight that now pierced the slits in the walls and lit up their prison.

"But I want Mummy." Miranda began to cry.

"So do I." They huddled together, pulling the rags over themselves.

* * *

There was a tapping. David went to the back door.

"Do you want any more eggs, Mr Certes?" asked George Farmer.

"I'm not sure? Just a minute - Miss Tribble," he called.

She appeared. "Yes, Mr Certes?"

"How are we off for eggs?"

She saw the egg-man. "Hello there, George. Keeping well, are you?"

He lifted his trilby. "Fair to middling," he replied. "And yourself, Miss Tribble?"

"Not so bad, George. Just a twinge of the arthritis in my knees. A sign you're getting old, I guess."

He nodded. "I get twinges too."

She went to a china dish on the dresser. "Yes, we could do with another dozen, I reckon."

"Right you are!" Eggs and money were exchanged.

"It's awful about those missing girls," said Miss Tribble.

"Girls – what missing girls?"

"Surely you've heard. It's been on Radio Oxford. And all the placards."

"I've no wireless. And I'm short-sighted."

"Two little girls are missing. Mr Certes knows them, don't you, Mr Certes? They were coming over here to see him. Then when they got off the bus, they disappeared."

George Farmer's eyes widened. "Disappeared! Never! How old are they?"

"Eight and ten – just little mites really." She pulled a handkerchief from her overall pocket, blew her nose, and dabbed her eyes. "I can't bear to think what's happened to them."

"And when was this?"

"About this time yesterday," put in David Certes.

"Yesterday morning!" George scratched his head beneath his trilby. "But I sees them. They were on the same bus as me when I comes from Oxford. They told me they were coming to see you, Mr Certes. I showed them the short cut. They never arrived?"

"No."

"No! That's awful. I should have brought them to your door. Made sure they got here, safe and sound."

"You weren't to know."

George slapped a hand to his temple. "I knows where they'll be. Well, I'm pretty certain they'll be there."

"You do, George. Where? Come on man, tell me?"

"The bunker. I told them not to go near it. Perhaps I shouldn't have drawn their attention to it, with little 'uns, being little 'uns. Curious as a cart load of monkeys my Poll were when she were a nipper. As sure as eggs are eggs, that's where they'll be."

Miss Tribble's eyes lit up. "Do you really think so? Oh, God, I hope so!"

David made up his mind. "There's no time like the present. I'll go and take a look."

"And I'll come with you," said George Farmer.

* * *

The two men approached the bunker. All was silent. Too silent. Were the girls trapped inside? And if so, what condition were they in? They'd certainly be hungry and thirsty after so many hours, if nothing else. David pulled aside the brambles which half-buried the place. What if George was wrong? What if this turned out to be a wild goose chase? No, he'd not think of that, not yet.

He eyed the closed doors. Rattled the broken padlock. "This wouldn't keep anyone out."

"No, I reckons tramps have been sleeping rough. Rather them than me. I likes my soft feather bed. Though maybe you don't notice the hard ground when you're 'high' on Meths."

"Maybe not." What if the bunker should turn out to be empty? It would mean that Melanie and Miranda must be elsewhere. But, where? Worse still, who could be keeping them there against their will? His hand tightened over the padlock. He felt so helpless. If only he could spare Brenda all this.

"Rots your guts, stuff like that." George paused. "What's that? It sounded like someone calling out from inside? And someone young at that."

"You're right. It's got to be them. Melanie! Miranda!" David called.

"Help! Help! The doors' are jammed. We can't get them open," shouted back Melanie.

"Don't worry, we'll soon get you out." He turned to George. "Give me a hand with this." They both pulled, and from the inside, the girls pushed – the doors shot open and an hysterical Melanie and Miranda rushed into David's arms.

They took off their jackets and placed them over the girls' shaking shoulders. With Melanie being helped along by David, and Miranda, by George, they covered the short distance to Rose Cottage.

As they crunched up the gravel path, Melanie began to scratch herself. "I'm really itchy! Something has bitten me."

"I've been bitten too," said Miranda, also having a good scratch.

"Don't worry, " David said, "we'll soon have you warm and comfortable, with a hot meal inside you."

"I'm thirsty," said Melanie, "I could drink a well dry."

"So could I," said Miranda.

David smiled. "We'll soon put that right – with a large beaker of drinking chocolate each – or you could have lemonade if you'd rather. " He turned to George. "Thanks for all your help."

"Don't mention it. I was glad to."

"I'm so relieved that all this has ended with nothing more serious than them being hungry and thirsty."

George nodded. "If it had, well, I'd never have forgiven myself for showing them that short cut."

An upstairs window jerked open. Miss Tribble's rosy face broke into a smile. She disappeared. Seconds later the front door burst open and she wrapped Melanie and Miranda securely in her arms. Thank God. Thank God you're safe!"

* * *

David drove the girls back to Oxford, they, huddled together on the rear seat, for once, having little to say for themselves. Neither was able to say much of what had actually happened to them after leaving George, a bare half a mile from David's cottage.

They had been questioned by a Chief Inspector and examined by a police nurse. The Inspector soon realised that he was wasting his time. "It's delayed shock," he said to David. "We'll try again later."

David had immediately contacted the police. They promised to inform Brenda that Melanie and Miranda were safely with him, and that he would bring them home just as soon as they'd recovered, had a bath, calamine dabbed on their flea bites and scratches, and something to eat.

Their clothing was ripped and filthy. He'd got Miss Tribble to take their measurements. Leaving her to look after them, he had gone into Abingdon and bought two completely new outfits.

The relief he'd felt on finding Melanie and Miranda unhurt, was immeasurable. He hoped that somehow Brenda could find it in her to overlook his letter. He regretted it bitterly. He wanted nothing more now, than to be her agent. Not for what he might make out of it financially, but so that he had an excuse to keep on seeing her. Would he ever be able to explain his actions of that evening at his cottage? Get her to understand his need to 'go slow' as regards their relationship - if there still was any relationship left?

The car turned into James Street. Before it had stopped outside Brenda's house, Brenda and Opal dashed out, tears in their eyes. There was a big emotional huddle on the pavement. He stood back, feeling awkward. Then Brenda disentangled herself and turned to him. She smiled, not only with her lips, but with her eyes. She took his hand. "Do come inside, we need to talk."

"I couldn't agree more," he murmured.

Their eyes met.

He followed her into the house.

CHAPTER 18

Several weeks had passed. David was once again Brenda's agent. The proofs of 'The Devil in the Flames' having arrived from Smyth & Sons, had been corrected and returned; now all seemed set for the publication date in February.

Miranda and Melanie were almost their old selves; they, both insisting they'd learnt their lesson. In Clifton Hampden, the bunker was in the process of being dismantled. Brenda was relieved that it would no longer be a danger to any other child.

David parked the car as near as he could to St Giles and the fair. He lifted Mark out and into his wheelchair. Mark waved his hands and chuckled, excited by the crowds. There was churning barrel organ music, loud laughter and shrieks and squeals from all around them.

Melanie and Miranda, their hands in Opal's, waited on the pavement - their smiles wide at the anticipated treat. They moved towards the brightly decorated stalls and rides. They stopped at the Coconut Shy where three coconuts in cups were set up on the top of poles. "I used to be good at this," said David. He proved he still was, when he won a coconut with a well-aimed ball. They all clapped. "Bags me the coconut milk," said Opal, "it's delicious."

"It's David's coconut. He might want to drink the milk himself?"

David tossed the coconut from one hand to the other. "We'll share it shall we? As long as I get a bit of the flesh I don't mind who has the milk, Brenda." He handed it to her and she put it into the bag on the back of Mark's wheelchair.

At the Rifle Range Opal won a big black-and-white china cat.

"A fluke," he teased.

"A fluke be blowed, my dad's got an air rifle and I've often taken pot shots at the target that he pins up on our shed door." She giggled. "He gets quite mad when Mum says that I'm a better shot than he is."

Brenda admired Opal's prize. "What are you going to do with it?"

"Don't know. One thing I do know, I don't want to be carrying something this size all around the fair."

"Give it here – It can go into Mark's bag with the coconut." Brenda eyed the bulging bag. "But you two had best not win any more prizes. If you do you'll have to carry them yourselves."

They spotted a Fortune Teller's booth.

"Go on in," encouraged Opal.

"If you go first."

"Okay then."

In she went.

Opal returned. "Well, what did she say?" asked Brenda.

"The usual thing – I'll never be rich, but I'll never be poor. After a setback, I'll find true love. Oh, yes, and I'm going to live 'till I'm ninety-two. It's your turn now."

In Brenda went.

The veiled woman who was seated before a crystal ball wore huge jangling earrings; Brenda did wonder if she'd borrowed them off Opal. She promised her great riches, a passionate love life and a half a dozen children. Brenda left the tent smiling. And although David pleaded, she wouldn't tell him what the woman had predicted, at least, not the part about the love life and the children.

At the Dodgems, David asked, "Who wants to ride with me?"

Both girls did. So he tossed a coin and Miranda won. Melanie pouted. Opal placed an arm about her shoulders, saying, "You come and have fun with me."

She cheered up, and eagerly clambered into a car, Opal following.

Brenda stood with Mark and watched as the cars bashed and crashed against each other. A terminal at the top of a pole at the back of each vehicle caused sparks to fly from the ceiling netting. The girls, their faces flushed, squealed excitedly. Brenda was glad they were enjoying themselves – even though she herself had never been keen on fairground rides. Not since… She shuddered.

Laughing, the girls ran to her. "Why don't you go on the Dodgems, Mum?"

"Yes, why don't you?" put in both David and Opal.

"No, thanks. I'd rather just watch the rest of you."

They walked on until they came to the Big Wheel.

Opal's more adventurous than me, she thought, as she craned her neck to make out the four, as they turned in a gigantic arc on the monster wheel that was lit up with coloured lights. As Brenda looked, the wheel shuddered to a standstill, leaving their two chairs swinging high and dry at the top. She gasped. Something was wrong! Melanie stood up and the chair she and Opal shared swayed precariously. "Sit down!" Brenda screamed, terrified – imagining Melanie plunging head first to the ground. These horrifying thoughts brought back bad memories. For several years, because of the war, there'd been no St Giles Fair. Then, a small travelling fair had come to the Cowley Marsh. Her dad, home on leave, had taken her. She'd gone on a roundabout. Her six-year-old legs clamped tight against the plaster flanks of the painted horse as it hurtled round faster and faster, she clinging on to its rough, thin mane, screaming hysterically, "Daddy! Daddy! I don't like it. Get me off! Get me off!"

With a creak the Big Wheel jerked, began to move round again and, with it, the past receded. Brenda heaved a sigh of relief. When at last, the Galloping Horses had halted and her dad had helped her off, she'd been violently sick and for days after had suffered from a terrible headache. After this, when St Giles Fair returned to Oxford and she'd gone with her friends, she had always stuck to trying her luck on the shove-ha'penny and roll-a-ball stalls. She grimaced – even the big slide at the park had given her the horrors - she would never go on it when the others did – though one day she had had to climb the steps to the top. She recalled the time she had taken her girls to Florence Park. Melanie had made a beeline for the slide and two-year-old Miranda, not wanting to be left out, had screamed to go on it too. Reluctantly, Brenda had agreed. Miranda, getting to the top had then refused to slide down. Brenda had feared that at any moment, she would fall. She would have been killed for sure. Sick and dizzy, Brenda had climbed up to get her down.

Safely back on the ground, and mimicking a sailor's gait, the girls begged for pink candy floss. They joined the queue. Soon, Mark included, was holding on to a stick and nibbling at the sweet fluff, stickying-up their clothes with it.

The girls insisted on riding the Helter-Skelter, a tall tower from which a chute spiralled down to the ground. Up the steps they clambered. At the top they sat on a square of mat before whizzing down to land in a giggling heap.

Miranda tugged Brenda's sleeve. "Our Mark's missing all the fun. He ought to go on a ride too," she said.

"It can't be anything dangerous."

"How about the Ghost Train?"

"Good idea, Opal."

David wheeled Mark over and lifted him into a carriage. Melanie and Miranda moved forward. "We can prop him up between the two of us," said Melanie.

David exchanged a glance with Brenda that said, 'It's not a good idea – two children can't really be expected to hold up another that's so badly handicapped?' She nodded back at him. He put his arms about the girls' shoulders. "Let's just watch this time."

"But I want to go on," insisted Miranda.

"I'll take you on something else," he promised.

Off went the miniature train, with Mark propped up between Brenda and Opal. The train, with its dwarf driver, quickened its pace; sounding its whistle, it chugged through a door into blackness. Ghosts wailed - cobwebs flapped in their faces - a phosphorous skeleton shot out of a cupboard in the wall, jigging the Dance Macabre - a headless torso threshing from side-to-side suddenly came towards them, and then retracted as if on elastic. Brenda, was startled and gasped. But nothing worried Mark, he just chuckled and waved his arms.

The carriages shot out of the tunnel, and stopped at the platform; Mark still laughing.

David and the girls laughed along with Mark. The two women joined in.

"I think we were more frightened than Mark – at least, I was."

"Me too," said Brenda. "Isn't Mark wonderful!"

The girls tugged at David's sleeve. "Don't forget you promised to take us on the Swinging Boats."

"I'd not forgotten," he winked, and led them towards the boats.

After laughing themselves silly in the Hall of Mirrors, tired and happy, they were heading back to the car when Melanie pointed at a stall set out with baskets of eggs, slabs of butter and pots of jam. The vendor, thickset and elderly, wore a white apron and a trilby. "Look, Miranda, it's that nice man."

"What nice man?" asked Brenda.

"The man who showed us the short cut to Mr Certes'." She pulled her over to the stall. "Hello," she said.

His face lit up. "Fancy seeing you again, m'dears. I hopes you've both recovered from your little misadventure?"

"Yes, we have, haven't we, Miranda?"

Brenda looked puzzled.

"It's George Farmer, my egg-man," explained David. It was he who led me to the girls."

He raised his hat, his face crinkling into a smile. "How do you do, m'dear."

Brenda also smiled. "Thanks, Mr Farmer, I'm very grateful."

"It was nothing. I was pleased to be of help."

"Can I buy some of those lovely eggs from you?" She fumbled with her purse.

"Buy! Certainly not! Have a dozen on me. As a little present for the kiddies."

"I couldn't!"

"Of course - you could, m'dear." He began putting them into a box. "They're new laid," he said, "they'll love 'em with 'soldiers'."

"Well, thanks very much. But at least let me buy a pot of your delicious looking strawberry jam?"

"I'd be pleased to..."

"How about the blackcurrant jam, Mummy? Can we have a pot of that as well? I love it on bread-and-butter – and so does Miranda and Mark."

"All right, all right, Melanie," sighed Brenda. "But you'll have to help carry them to the car." She turned. "I'll have a pot of each, Mr Farmer."

"Certainly. The fruits are from my own garden." He hesitated. "I know it's a bit of a cheek, and don't take me wrong, but you see, I really love kids, and I was wondering if the next time you visit Mr Certes at Rose Cottage, you could get him to bring you and the children round to see me?" He turned to Melanie and Miranda. "I've got some baby rabbits. You could help me feed them. You'd like that, wouldn't you? They're ever so pretty, with fluffy pink ears."

"Can we, Mummy? Please can we go to Farmer George's?"

George Farmer chuckled. "That's rich, that is. Farmer George, indeed!"

"I don't know, Melanie."

"My daughter married a GI So my grandchildren are in America. I can't make a fuss of them. I've never ever seen them," he said sadly.

"That's like our Aunty Ivy. She lives in Texas, where all the cowboys are."

"My late husband's sister," explained Brenda.

"My Poll's in Washington." He turned to the girls. "As far as I know there's no cowboys in Washington."

"Please, Mummy. Take us to Farmer George's to feed the rabbits."

"Yes, please, Mummy," repeated Miranda," we'll be good, we really will."

"That'll be a first," laughed Brenda. "Oh, I suppose I'd better agree. I'll never get any peace otherwise.."

"Great!" Melanie turned to George Farmer. "And you can be our honry…." She turned to Brenda. "What is the word, Mum?"

"Honorary."

"That's it. Our honorary grandad. As your grandchildren are thousands of miles away and we've not got one."

He smiled widely. "I'd like that very much."

The jam and money exchanged hands and Brenda turned back to the others and into the path of a young man. She recognised him immediately. It was Bob.

They chatted for a few minutes. "I heard all about Melanie and Miranda being missing on Radio Oxford. I can't tell you how shocked and upset I was. Thank God they were found safe and sound. I wanted to call, but... "he looked towards Opal.

"I understand, said Brenda."

Opal and Bob exchanged hesitant glances. "How have you been keeping?" she said at last.

"All right," he replied stiffly. They exchanged a few more pleasantries, then Bob said that his friends were waiting for him to catch them up.

Brenda had moved away to give them some privacy. From the look on Opal's face after Bob left, it was very obvious that she was still a long way from being over him.

* * *

Bob followed after his friends. How he wished he was in that agent's shoes and being made to feel like one of the family by Brenda and Opal. Seeing Opal again had intensified rather than lessened his feelings for her. He'd half hoped, half expected Opal to be at the fair with Brenda and the children. He had, so many times, anticipated getting a reply to his letters; the letters he'd written to her in the middle of the night when he couldn't sleep for thinking about her - but none had ever come. He couldn't blame Opal for not replying; she knew as well as he did that he'd not done anything about standing up to his mother. Opal had told him in no uncertain terms that unless he did, there was no way she would ever go back to him. Seeing her around town with other men had pained him. He guessed that as they were always different men, they couldn't mean that much to her, but that was small consolation.

He wanted to stand up to his mother. Oh God! Why was he such a wimp? He glared at a Hot Dog seller, much to the man's surprise. An idea flashed through his head. Should he visit a hypnotist? Under hypnosis people did things that they would never normally do. Could this be true? There was a hypnotist on at the New Theatre next week, perhaps he should be in the audience?

"Aren't you coming in, Bob?" asked Geoff.

They were outside the Fat Woman's tent.

"They say she's the size of a barrage balloon. Hope there's room for us!" winked Mick. "Anyway, it'll be a laugh."

Bob didn't really think so. There was nothing in his life at the moment or the foreseeable future to provoke the slightest laughter, and he couldn't see the fat woman changing that. Nevertheless, he followed the others into the tent.

CHAPTER 19

David drove them home to James Street; the children clutching the strings of coloured balloons. After a makeshift high tea, the girls watched television in the other room. Mark was asleep upstairs, tired out by all the excitement.

Opal smiling to herself, made an excuse and left Brenda and David alone together.

He grabbed his chance. "There's a dinner-dance on at the Randolph Hotel tomorrow evening. I wonder if you would like to come with me?"

"I'd love to," said Brenda. "Of course, I'll need to get a sitter." The Randolph should have the right atmosphere for their romance to blossom further. It seemed that at last, things were working out. Opal had been right all along. It couldn't have been because of Mark that he'd held back. It must have been that it was too soon after his wife's death. In that case eventually all would be well between them. She'd only one problem. What on earth was she to wear to such a classy place? There was nothing suitable in her wardrobe. She'd have to buy something rather different from anything she already had.

Satisfaction spread across David's face. "You will. That's wonderful. But the sitter? There won't be any difficulty getting one, will there?"

"I shouldn't think so. I'll ask Opal or failing her, Mrs Briggs."

"Good! I can't tell you how much I'm looking forward to tomorrow evening. Let me know when you've someone to sit with the children and then I'll ring up and book a table."

* * *

As he drove home to Clifton Hampden later that evening, warm thoughts of Brenda ran through his head. He knew now that he was definitely very much in love with her. At the dinner-dance he would be able, at last, to explain himself. He couldn't really say how soon it would be before he could carry their relationship further, but he felt sure she would understand and be patient.

* * *

Crystal chandeliers glittered overhead. Candlelight from wall sconces cast a romantic glow, as the Head Waiter pulled back Brenda's chair and she settled herself into it.

He did the same for David.

He handed them the menus. Made of stiff white card, they were so large when open that she could hardly cope with hers. Inside, the choice of dishes were in French.

"Don't worry, I'll choose for you," David said. "How about Fricassee of Lamb?"

"That's sounds fine."

He rattled off something in French. The man wrote it down on a pad.

Another waiter came with a silver salver of different coloured corsages. "A flower for Madam?"

"What a lovely idea."

"Which would you like?" smiled David, "a red or yellow rose, or maybe a pink or white carnation?"

"I think the white carnation would go best with my dress."

"A carnation it is then." He removed one and pinned it carefully to the front of her gown and she shivering deliciously.

The Wine Waiter appeared. He had a neat moustache and a precise walk to match. "Champagne, Monsieur?"

It came served in an ice bucket.

The waiter, with a flourish removed the champagne cork. It popped and he poured a taster into David's glass. David sipped and nodded and the waiter filled up his glass and then Brenda's.

He toasted her. "Here's to the most beautiful woman in the room."

She blushed feeling pleased. Glancing in the mirror that reflected their table, she admired her blue satin and white lace evening gown that she'd bought that morning from Paiges and which was set off by Mrs Briggs' string of pearls. Her hair too, that Opal had styled, was, she thought, just right. Opal had piled her fair hair high and finished it off with a blue satin bow. Her eyes moved on to David's reflection; his evening clothes were flattering. Their eyes met in the mirror, and within her, excitement stirred. When he took her home later that night, would lovemaking, at last, happen between them? Did she want it to? He reached across the white damask cloth to squeeze her fingers and she knew that she most certainly did. They were interrupted by waiters with tureens who served the meal with stainless steel tongs. Her plate began to fill.

He smiled conspiratorially. "Say, 'when'".

Hastily she did so.

They served David.

She spread her linen napkin over her knees and shot a look around the room in an effort to copy the other diners. How on earth did they know which knife, fork and spoon to use? She remembered someone once saying that you should start from the outside and work inwards. She took a deep breath and began.

He put down his knife and looked into her eyes. "I really don't know where to begin, but I must apologise for my behaviour back at the cottage. I did behave badly. I wanted to make love to you, but somehow, I couldn't. It was because of Angela. I felt so guilty about forgetting her so soon. Then later, of course, I felt embarrassed at how I'd treated you and what you must have thought of it all. So I sent you that letter, and regretted it immediately it was in the post."

"Did you?" she said with relief.

"I certainly did! I can't tell you how much."

"I didn't really know what to think. It did cross my mind that it might have been because of your wife. I mean, I've felt disloyal to John for having feelings for..." She stopped, blushing.

"For me?"

"Yes."

"But then I thought maybe it was because of Mark."

"Mark?"

"Well, he is handicapped."

"That'd never make a difference to me. He's wonderful," he said warmly.

"He likes you too. In fact, they all do."

"I'm glad," he said, "I really want them to like me. Look, Brenda, you'll always love John, and I'll always love Angela. We'll never forget them – wouldn't want to – but they're gone. They'd want us to get on with our lives. Be happy. They'd want us to find love again."

"Would they?"

"I'm certain of it. Now let's enjoy this evening."

After the delicious meal, eaten while serenaded by a violinist, coffee was served in minute cups, which the Head Waiter kept topping up.

Later they danced cheek-to-cheek to the music of a select

quartet.

David was an excellent dancer. He swept her smoothly around the floor in the foxtrot, tango and waltz. She felt as if her feet flew as they moved as one. She'd wondered if she had lost her touch, after all, it was years since she'd last danced. Would she remember the steps? She needn't have worried. In his arms all her old skill came back. It was an evening to remember and it wasn't over yet. She thrilled, thinking of the privacy of her living room, and his looked-forward-to embraces.

They danced the last waltz, the diners clapping them off the floor. She went to the cloakroom to fetch her things.

Her heart leapt as she saw him waiting for her in the corridor - the gilded mirror on the wall presenting him in perfect duplicate - two knights for the price of one!

"Happy?" he asked, settling Mrs Briggs' leopard skin jacket around her shoulders.

"Oh yes, I've not been pampered like this for years." She shivered deliciously. "Thanks very much." In fact, she had never before been treated as well as this, not even in her courting days. A painter and decorator could never have afforded to dine at such a swish place.

"It's me who should say thanks."

He drove her home.

The house was quiet. The children and Opal asleep upstairs.

He took her into his arms and their lips met in a long, lingering kiss. "Oh, Brenda," he whispered, "I'm madly in love with you."

"It's the same with me, darling," she breathed.

Brenda felt David's fingers tangling her hair, drank in his whispered endearments, felt his butterfly kisses on her brow. Then his lips closed to claim hers, in a kiss so sweet, so passionate, that desires, dormant for so long, began to reawaken. She felt his fingers unbutton the bodice of her dress; caress the smooth flesh of one breast. She moaned as he teased a hardened nipple.

Overhead a floorboard creaked – followed by the click of a light switch – footsteps – and the sound of the lavatory flushing. Brenda drew back. "Not here, not with Opal above us. I should be so embarrassed if she should walk in. And there's the children...."

"She wouldn't, I mean, surely she wouldn't come down?"

"No, but..."

He reached for his jacket, "I quite understand," he said slowly. "There's plenty of time for us; all the time in the world."

* * *

Brenda was singing as she hoovered the hall. Melanie and Miranda had returned to school the previous day.

She bent and picking up several handfuls of coloured plastic Lego, threw them into the cupboard beneath the stairs. She felt so happy that she didn't even frown.

As she dragged the vacuum cleaner into the dining room, her eyes were drawn to the vase of red roses on the sideboard. These roses had been delivered earlier that day by the florist, and with them had been a card saying: 'All my love, David.'

Life was rosy. Her girls safe and sound; Mark's new tablets were easing his muscle spasms; she had David's love, and in a couple of weeks, she would realise her ambition.

Through the racket she sensed a noise. She switched off. She was right. Someone was knocking at the front door.

She quickly patted her hair and went to answer it.

To her surprise, it was David.

"I never expected to see you this early."

His unsmiling face alerted her. "There's something wrong?"

He didn't reply. "Can I come in?" he asked.

"Of course you can," she said, "but whatever's the matter?" She made an effort to lighten her tone. "You look like you've found a farthing and lost a shilling."

"I'll tell you inside."

He followed her into the front room.

"Well, what is it?" By the expression on his face he had bad news for her. It surely couldn't be anything to do with her novel? She swallowed.

He handed her a letter.

She read slowly.

I don't understand?"

"It's clear enough," he said, "I'm sorry darling, but Smyth & Sons have gone bust. Old Smyth died recently and they found a lot of discrepancies in the accounts. Someone had been cooking the books and now they've gone bankrupt. They've got the culprit, a senior clerk. But that's no help to us. I feel really awful about this, Brenda."

"Why? It's not your fault."

"No, but it means that the 'The Devil in the Flames' won't be published."

CHAPTER 20

Brenda felt as if she'd been dealt a body blow. For so long she'd been buoyed up by the idea of being published. It had carried her along through all her trials and tribulations of being a one parent family. Now, it had all collapsed and there was nothing!

It was of little consolation that David promised to try and interest the American market in her work." I'm going to a literary convention in New York next week, so I'll see what I can do for you there, Brenda. I'll pull out all the stops."

"And what will that achieve? Even I know that they've got enough of their own writers and don't need English ones, not unknown ones, anyway."

"Maybe, but historical novels are on the up and up in the States. At least there's a chance. But if I can't get anywhere there, I'll try again here."

"Huh!! 'If at first you don't succeed, try, try again'. He moved to put a consoling arm around her, but she stiffened. "I've got to get on. I've a fair bit to do this morning."

Taking the hint, he reluctantly made his way to the front door. "Don't take this setback too much to heart, Brenda. How's the other novel coming along?"

But she was holding open the door for him.

* * *

"I'm so mad I could spit!" said Brenda through gritted teeth, rubbing furiously at the tanning in the cup she was washing.

"Hey, cool it, you'll rub away the pattern if you're not careful!"

Brenda pursed her lips. "If that old Mr Smyth wasn't already dead, I could murder him! David too, for finding me such a crackpot publishing firm."

Opal laid down a saucer. "I can understand your disappointment, but you can't really blame him."

"Can't I?"

"It wasn't him that did the embezzling."

"I know that."

"Then why blame him so much?" Opal hung up the tea towel.

"If I don't blame someone, I'll explode!" Though Brenda really knew she was being unreasonable, she just couldn't control the way that she felt at all. Everything was so mixed up between her and David again.

"Look, calm down. If David says he'll find you another publisher, then I'm sure he will."

Brenda slammed the saucepans down onto the draining board. "I only hope that you're right. But I'm not holding my breath."

* * *

Brenda stared at her typewriter. It was no good, she'd got that writers block again. It was days since she'd managed to write more than a paragraph. At this rate she'd never finish her second novel. What did it matter though? No one would want it! She'd no chance of getting this second one published, if David couldn't find her a publisher for her first. She had received a rather stilted letter from him some weeks back saying he was off to America the following day – since then only a postcard. She guessed he'd had no success is finding her a publisher in the States and was too embarrassed to admit to it.

Brenda missed David so much; hated the barrier that had suddenly sprung up between them. Not only couldn't she write, she was far too stressed out even to read a book, or watch television. The girls and Mark were missing him too. They kept asking when he was coming to see them again.

She could give them no answer.

* * *

Brenda stared at the letter in her hand. Outside the window, the bright autumn sunshine somehow appeared flat and grey.

Who on earth was this letter from? And what were they on about? 'We're delighted to inform you that you have won first prize in our short story competition.'

What competition? She didn't remember entering a competition. She racked her brains. No, she'd not entered any such competition, of that she was certain. In disbelief she re-read the figure on the cheque, one hundred pounds - why, it was a fortune!

She checked it again, £100!

She studied the letter looking for clues. The magazine was a quarterly one called 'The Nightingale'. The Nightingale! Nightingale…? - now, where had she heard that name before? She remembered the magazine that Opal had once shown her. Surely, that had been called The Nightingale?

Opal had wanted her to enter their competition. Pleaded with her in fact, to enter a story that she'd completed and had never sent away. The children had been so ill at the time with German Measles that, she'd felt far too drained to bother. So how had the story got into their hands? She definitely hadn't sent it. It seemed a great mystery. It was to have pride of place in their Spring Edition. Like a lightning flash it came to her. Of course, how stupid of her – Opal! She must have sent it. But what a cheek! How dare Opal take it upon herself to send away her work. She'd certainly give her a piece of her mind when she next saw her.

* * *

Opal had hardly entered the house when Brenda tackled her. "I've got a bone to pick with you."

"What do you mean?" She put down her briefcase and flopped onto a chair, "I've had an absolutely rotten day!"

Brenda pushed the letter in front of her nose. "Read that!"

She read. "But that's wonderful news, you must be really delighted, especially after the disappointment. I always knew that short story had the makings."

"Maybe. But how could you send my work away without my say-so?"

"I'm sorry about that. I know I was wrong, but you had too much on your plate at the time, so I did it for you. Aren't you pleased about the hundred pounds?"

"Yes, but you really had no right."

"I know, but it was too great a temptation. I kept thinking of that wonderful story lying there in the landing cupboard. I'm afraid I succumbed. I typed it while I was baby-sitting for you. Don't you remember? You popped out for some shopping. I was so scared that I wouldn't get it finished before you returned."

There was no reply.

"I promise I'll never do such a thing again."

The room was silent, apart from a hissing from the dining-room boiler.

"Please don't be cross with me," pleaded Opal.

"I should be." Brenda's face broke into a smile. "I can never be mad with you for long, and I must admit that the money's a Godsend. Both Melanie and Miranda are needing new shoes. And winter coats. The way those two are shooting up is unbelievable. I've had to let down all the hems on their dresses."

"Have you seen this?" asked Opal suddenly.

"Seen what?"

"This, the small print."

"What small print are you on about?"

Opal pointed. "It says here that part of your prize is to have a novel-length piece of your work read by a multinational publisher, Matthew Heatherington and Boyce, with an offer of publication if up to standard."

"No!!"

"Yes!!"

"It's a miracle! Have you waved a magic wand, or what?"

"I'm your Fairy Godmother, didn't you know?" laughed Opal, "Send them 'The Devil in the Flames'."

Brenda grabbed Opal and the two of them waltzed round the table, "Yes, 'The Devil in the Flames'."

"Mummy! What on earth are you and Opal doing?" asked Melanie.

"The Highland Fling, sweetheart."

"Your mother's had some fantastic news as regards her novel," explained Opal.

"Thank goodness for that. Perhaps now Mummy'll be in a better mood."

"I haven't really been that bad, have I?"

Neither Melanie nor Opal replied.

"I suppose now," said Opal playfully, "you'll want to be off to tell David? Poor chap'll be delighted to be let off the hook."

"Will you mind the children?"

"Off you go. I'll pop our dinners into the oven under a low heat to keep warm."

Brenda almost floated along the street. It was a glorious evening. The yellow and red leaves murmured on the boughs. Humming, she dialled David's number, willing him to be back from America. She just had to tell him this marvellous news immediately.

She heard the click of his phone. "David Certes."

She hastily pushed button-A. "David! It's me Brenda. I've had some fantastic news."

"Hey, slow down." From his end of the wire came a crackling chuckle, "What is it? From the lilt in your voice I'd hazard a guess that it's something to do with your novel."

"You must be a mind reader."

"So I'm right. What's happened?"

"It's a long story. I'll tell you fully when I see you. You are coming over, aren't you? Matthew Heatherington and Boyce are interested in 'The Devil in the Flames' and I might just get it published. They want me to send it."

"That's wonderful, truly wonderful. I'm very pleased for you. But how on earth did all this come about?"

"It was through a competition in 'The Nightingale'. Look, I'm sorry I've been so rotten to you."

The line went quiet. "That's all right," came his reply, "I understand how fraught things have been for you."

"Yes, well, am I forgiven?"

"There's nothing to forgive."

"You do think those publishers will like my work?" she asked, desperate again to be reassured.

"Heatherington and Boyce are highly thought of."

"But you haven't answered me."

"I'd say you've got a more than average chance. I'll keep my fingers crossed for you. Now, do you think you can get a baby-sitter so I can take you to the Playhouse tomorrow evening?"

* * *

The manuscript was posted. The weeks passed. At the back of her mind lingered a niggling doubt. What if, after all, these publishers didn't like her novel? Just because one publisher had accepted it, didn't necessarily make it certain that another would. Each morning she half expected the postman to knock with her manuscript. How could she bear the slap in the face? The thick skin that all writers had to have was one thing when it wasn't needed, another when it was. She knew that other writers had taken dozens of similar rejections and despite their disappointment, got on with other work - but could she? To take her mind off whether or not Matthew Heatherington and Boyce would think her novel publishable, she decided to concentrate on making her girls pinafore dresses.

Brenda worried for nothing. On the mat was a letter with their logo on it. She picked it up with trembling fingers; that they'd taken the time to write was surely a good sign? She took the letter in to Opal who was getting ready for college.

"I've had a letter from them, Heatherington and Boyce."

"You want me to open it for you?"

"Would you?" Please God! Please God! Let it be good news!

Opal opened the envelope and read.

"Well, what does it say?" asked Brenda, dry mouthed, fingertips sticking to the tabletop. "Do they..?" She couldn't finish.

Opal smiled. "They most certainly do," she whistled, "and from what I can make out, they're willing to pay double the amount that Smyth would have done."

Brenda steadied herself.

"You thought...?"

"Yes."

"I didn't, not for a moment," said Opal.

"What faith! Thanks."

"Pleased about the extra money?"

"Of course. It'll mean a week's holiday away for us all. Perhaps a chalet at Pontins. Bream Sands, near Weston Super Mare sounds nice. Mrs Briggs went last year and has never stopped talking about it since."

"What me too?"

"If you can spare the time? It'd not be the same without you. After all, you're a big part of the story."

Opal hugged her. "Aren't you a darling? I'd love to come, but it depends on when you're thinking of going."

"We'll try and sort out a time to suit everybody."

Opal read on. "They want to know if you're working on anything else? Send them your second novel. It is almost finished, isn't it?"

"I'm typing the final draft. But I haven't thought of a good title as yet."

"That's nothing. You know what publishers are, they're sure to change it, whatever you suggest. They like their little moment. The thing to do is to get the novel off to them."

"I will do. I must ring David with the good news. He'll be so pleased for me. Could you hang on with Mark while I pop to the phone box?"

Hearing his name, Mark chuckled.

"Off you go then and give him my regards." Opal bent to where Mark lay on the rug and tickled him under the chin, which made him chuckle all the harder. She placed the dinky car back into his hand, "There you go, sweetheart." She turned back to Brenda. "If you go on like this you'll be able to have the phone put in yourself. It'll be more convenient; especially should you need to contact the doctor for the children."

"What me with my own telephone!"

"Why not?"

"I've always thought that such things were for the middle-class."

"It's your income bracket that decides what class you are," said Opal, "you'll be middle-class yourself when you get known as an author."

"I never thought of that."

"Besides," Opal said, "I shouldn't be surprised if in thirty years or so, all homes, even working-class ones, will have the telephone in. It'll be considered an essential and not just a luxury item."

Brenda nodded. "Yes, I suppose it'll be a very different world."

"I'm sure it will."

"People living in New York and working in London."

"Summer hols on Mars and Venus. They reckon space travel will be commonplace by then."

"Ready-made dinners that take two minutes to cook."

"Throwaway clothing."

"I wonder where we'll all be?"

"I wonder?" said Opal.

CHAPTER 21

The bells of St Mary and St Johns church rang out to welcome in 1971.

Lying in bed, Brenda sighed thankfully. Soon Opal and David would be returning. Opal had gone home to spend Christmas with her mum and dad in Birmingham. David had taken the 'high road' to his parents' croft in the outer Hebrides. Giles and Mary Certes had retired there two years earlier. David's father was a keen ornithologist. But his mother had become ill. A faulty heart valve had been diagnosed. She'd been advised not to travel. Brenda knew that David had intended to ask her and the children over to his house to meet them. She had read rather a lot into this, which possibly had something to do with her dejection.

On Christmas day, Brenda had taken the children to church and invited Mrs Briggs for dinner and tea. They'd opened the presents that lay beneath the tree's tinselled branches. The girls whooped with glee as they tore off the wrapping paper, disclosing the gifts that they'd written to ask Father Christmas for. Brenda, opening a heart shaped silver locket from David and a jazzy bracelet from Opal, suddenly came close to tears. She hadn't felt so low since that first Christmas without John. Through misty eyes, she saw Mark crooning happily as he fingered a net stocking full of chocolate bars that Melanie had unwrapped for him. Brenda smiled. He'd not be allowed to take that stocking to bed with him like the one the Mentally Handicapped Society had given him. Mark hadn't wanted to be parted from the stocking, and thinking he'd not be able to get the chocolate bars from it, she'd let him keep it in his cot when she put him to bed. Later, she'd looked in on him – there he lay, fast asleep, chocolate all over his smiling face; bits of silver wrapper everywhere. He had bitten at every single bar through the stocking – it was a wonder he 'd not choked.

Brenda removed the stocking from Mark's hand. "Would you like a Mars bar, sweetheart?"

He gurgled an answer that could have been 'Yes'.

Brenda undid the stocking.

His eyes brightened as he watched her unwrap the chocolate

bar. She chucked him under the chin. "This stocking will stay in the cupboard this time, sweetheart. And not only will you have one bar of chocolate at a time, but I'll feed you with it." And tying a bib beneath Mark's chin, and placing him on her lap, she fed him thin slices of Mars, as she half watched Bob Hope on TV in 'On the Road to Morocco'.

Opal returned on the 2nd of January. David, with a box of Highland shortbread, the following day. He'd kissed her tenderly and confessed that he had really missed her. "The next time I go to Scotland, I'll take you with me," he promised.

She'd glowed at his words. Did that mean a proposal of marriage?

But as the days of January sped past, nothing materialised, much to her disappointment. She tried to think of something other than David. Everyone would soon have to cope with this new decimal currency. She herself imagined (or hoped) she'd have no difficulty in adjusting to it unlike Mrs Briggs and David's housekeeper, Miss Tribble, whose adjustment would most probably be more difficult. Brenda shrugged and after all, she told herself firmly, David, she was certain, just needed a little more time.

Mark, celebrated his fifth birthday on the 9th of January with Melanie and Miranda and their friends. They'd jelly and blancmange, hotdog sausages, plus a Punch and Judy show, which had been arranged by David. But the star attraction had been the chocolate birthday cake that Brenda had made, with Mark's name and five candles on the top. Mark, hadn't the puff, so his sisters blew them out for him. Following his birthday he'd started at the Mabel Pritchard Training Centre in Littlemore, where he was in the Special Care Unit.

Each morning, he was taken there by ambulance. At first Brenda had wheeled him in his chair to a pick-up point on the Cowley Road. There a coach would halt for Mark and several disabled children. She'd found this arrangement exhausting and time consuming. This continued for several weeks until one morning during a blizzard, she'd hauled him in his chair over the hard-packed snow, and then waited. After three quarters of an hour, she'd trudged back home with Mark, feeling more like a snowman than a woman. It turned out that the vehicle had broken down. But out of bad had come good. She'd complained about their cold wait, which led to him being picked up from the house itself.

Mark soon settled down at the Centre, but contrary-like she

wasn't really happy now that he was absent all day. The house was too quiet. She worried too, whether the staff at the Centre were caring for him as well as she did herself.

Melanie and Miranda joined the Brownie pack attached to St Mary and St Johns church. At the Scouts and Guides shop in Turl Street, Brenda bought their uniforms. Upon returning home, they clamoured to put them on. Arms swinging, they paraded proudly up and down the kitchen.

"I was no different to them when I joined the Guides back home in Birmingham," smiled Opal.

But being a Brownie meant that the Scouting anthem was forever being warbled by one girl or the other.

"Ging gang goolie goolie goolie goolie watcha, ging gang goo, ging gang goo," piped Miranda as she got ready for school.

"I think I'll have to get earplugs," winced Brenda.

If the girls weren't singing 'Ging gang goolie', they were singing the praises of Brown Owl. It was a case of, "Brown Owl says this, and Brown Owl says that," all day long. So much so that both Brenda and Opal became heartily sick of the poor woman. And if it wasn't talk of her, it was of how they intended to earn those highly prized Brownie badges.

"One girl has them all up both arms," remarked Miranda.

"Well, I'll soon get more than her," retorted Melanie.

"How can you? There's not an inch of space left on the sleeves of her tunic."

Melanie smirked. "I've got longer arms!"

* * *

It was the Saturday afternoon of the eagerly awaited Jamboree, which was to take place on the Iffley Road running track.

Brenda smiled, remembering what the girls had said earlier, "Mummy, Brown Owl says we'll be having tea in a marquee - that's a big tent - and we're to have ice-cream."

"Tawny Owl told me that there's going to be an egg-and-spoon race and a donkey to ride on," added Miranda, jumping up and down with excitement.

"Yes, Mummy," said Melanie, "and there's going to be lots of prizes and I'm going to win them all."

Miranda, not to be outdone put in, "You're not. I'm faster than you. You're as slow as a cart horse. Besides, I'm in the three-legged race and you're not."

Melanie, though, had the last word. "So childish! It's me who has been chosen for the relay race. Anyway, I'm senior to you. I'm next in line to Snowy Owl, so there!" She stuck out her tongue.

Opal and Brenda, with Mark in his chair, along with a host of other parents and grandparents craned their necks. They stood opposite a grandstand in which the Scouting Commissionaires were seated. From the distance came the throb of a drum. Any minute now, led by a band and with flags flying, Melanie and Miranda would swing past to give the salute.

Brenda jogged up and down to keep warm. "Lucky it's fine."

Opal agreed.

A cheer went up. "Here they come!"

The Scouts and Guides first appeared, arms swinging, heads held high, followed by the Cubs and Brownies.

Brenda and Opal had to smile at the sight of a beefy bugler whose puffed-out cheeks resembled twin balloons, and beside him an even beefier scout, his face set in a grimace as he concentrated on bashing the big drum for all he was worth. A sudden gust of wind caught the St Mary and St Johns' banner and whipped it around a guide's face. She stepped out-of-line and accidentally kicked the shins of the girl next to her, who yelped in pain. A hissed "Shush!" sounded behind them.

"Eyes right!"

Hundreds of pairs of eyes swivelled in the direction of the grandstand; their owners saluting smartly and being saluted in return.

Brenda had picked out Melanie's face from amongst the sea of brown. "There's Melanie!"

"Where? Where?" Opal's head darted this way and that.

Brenda pointed. "Just there."

"Oh, yes. She's certainly swinging her arms well."

"I never realised until now just how tall she's grown," sighed Brenda, "why she's almost a young lady. It won't be long before the both of them have fled the nest."

Opal laughed, her earrings jangling. "Don't start worrying about that. It's ages away. Besides you'll always have Mark. And if he's suitable for Speech Therapy… well."

Brenda didn't reply.

Opal watched the marching girls. "I know why they all seem so tall. It's because their chins are stuck up in the air. It's a wonder they don't fall backwards. Anyway, as far as Melanie and Miranda growing up and leaving home is concerned, well, you're still young, you might have more children yet. You'd like more children, wouldn't you?"

"Maybe."

"It's only a matter of time, isn't it? - before David asks you to marry him."

"Sometimes I think it is. There's Miranda! Doesn't she look smart? If only John…"

Opal took her arm. "Don't upset yourself."

"No, you're right. It does no good."

Opal looked over to where the girls were dispersing. "Are you staying for the games?"

Brenda smiled. "My life wouldn't be worth living if I didn't. Mark's wrapped up well. He won't take a cold."

Opal grasped the handlebar of the chair. "Come on, let's go and cheer them on then."

* *

It was a week after the Jamboree that the letter arrived.

Brenda fingered the envelope franked with the Education Department's logo. Miranda, eating a bowl of cornflakes, looked up as her mother returned to the kitchen. Her sharp eyes took in the envelope. "Bet I know what that is. Bet she's failed!!" she said.

"You know too much for your own good. Besides, they wouldn't bother to write in that case." Brenda slit open the envelope and read.

"Yippee!!" she called out. "Wonderful, wonderful. Your sister's passed the Eleven Plus"

She'd not expected her to pass when Melanie had sat this exam a week after the trauma of the bunker. It was too soon, and her daughter was still stressed out. She'd been proved wrong.

She shouted up the stairs. "Melanie!! You've done it!"

Opal appeared at the top of the stairs, pulling on her dressing gown. "What's all the excitement?" she yawned.

"It's Melanie. She's won the Scholarship! She's to go to Milham Ford Grammar in September!"

"Why, that's wonderful, Brenda." She came downstairs. "Can I see the letter?"

She handed it to her.

Melanie, rubbing her eyes, and almost falling over the hem of her long white nightdress, half stumbled downstairs.

Brenda hugged her. "You've done it!"

"Who's a clever girl then?" said Opal.

"You've won the Scholarship," said a begrudging Miranda. "It's in Mummy's letter."

Melanie's face lit up. "I've got it? I didn't think..."

"You certainly have," said Brenda.

"You'll be joining all those toffee-noses in their straw boaters," put in Miranda cheekily, flicking a spoonful of cornflakes at Melanie.

Brenda separated the girls. How proud John would have been at this moment. She wiped a tear from the corner of her eye. If only he were here. She bit her lip. But then there was David. Every time she saw him she felt all warm inside. She couldn't begin to count how much he meant to her. The stark fact was that David couldn't have come onto the scene if John had still been alive. As day followed day, she needed David more and more. And as she wouldn't have had Opal for a lodger, she didn't suppose that she would ever have started writing either. It was certainly peculiar the twists and turns that life could take. It was a far cry from what she'd imagined. If someone had asked her to foretell the future in the summer of '64 when she and John had been 'trying' for Mark, she never could have predicted what had actually happened.

1964 had been the year that she had attended Cowley St John's school reunion. After so many years it had seemed strange to enter the school hall again, where they had taken PT lessons with the muscular-legged Miss Baldwin.

All the teachers bar one were there, looking much older than she'd expected them to look. The headmistress, Miss Taylor's basin-cut was white instead of black. It was Miss Tallboys who was missing from the reunion. She'd gone to America, and finding a husband, had stayed there. Brenda was disappointed to learn this, for Miss Tallboys had been her favourite.

The teachers had organised children's games, seeming to forget that time had moved on, and that their former pupils were all now equally adults. Afterwards everyone had tucked into cake and sandwiches and ice cream cornets, a special treat from Miss Taylor. Only one 'old girl' from Brenda's year was there. She'd proudly shown Edie Daniels a photograph of John, Melanie and Miranda.

She'd rather pitied the plain woman who'd an overlarge chin, and at twenty-four was still single. Edie was already an old maid in her estimation. She'd confided to Edie that she and John were hoping to add to their family, never imagining that the picture of the future that she visualised, would all too soon be smashed to pieces. Brenda braced herself. It was best to think positive. No good dwelling on the past and what might have been. She thought about the famous Grammar school in Marston. She herself would have loved to have gone there. But she hadn't been clever enough. She'd envied those classmates who had won the Scholarship, who'd worn the Milham Ford's smart school uniform. At Cowley St John Girls, where she had gone on to at eleven, there was no uniform. This hadn't suited her. She'd been dying to swan around in a monogrammed blazer like the pupils at the Grammar. Still, the next best thing was to have a daughter who would wear it. And as she was about to get published, she couldn't have been so dim after all. She smiled to herself. A late developer, that's what she must be!

She realized Melanie was speaking, "Can I have a bicycle to go to school on now that I've won the Scholarship? My friend, Maisie has told me that she's been promised one if she passes it."

"But Maisie's got a dad," said Opal gently.

Brenda looked thoughtful. Milham Ford School was an awkward place to get to by bus. It would be easier for Melanie to ride across country on a bike; across the Cowley Road, through Pembroke Street, into St Clements and then along Marston Road; about a ten minute ride if there wasn't too much traffic. "We'll have to see," she said.

Melanie looked satisfied.

"Miranda will expect a bike too, if she wins the Scholarship," pointed out Opal.

Brenda didn't mind about that. The cost of a second bicycle should be no problem. As far as 'The Devil in the Flames' went, things were now really happening. The publication being set for the fourteenth of March. Her second book, to her delight, had also been accepted. This was to be published in twelve-months time.

CHAPTER 22

At last the moment had arrived. How proud she felt actually holding her book; despite its rather lurid dust cover.

The postman had delivered a large parcel. Guessing that these must be her complimentary copies from Heatherington and Boyce, she'd been so excited that she'd almost ripped the wrapping paper off the books, then and there. Somehow she had managed to contain herself, at least until back inside.

Opal was in college. Brenda bit her lip. She'd promised to open the parcel with her. It was no good, she just couldn't wait. With trembling fingers she tore away the covering. She gasped; there was her very first published book, with her name beneath the title. She stroked the letters reverently. To think that at last, all her hard work had actually paid off.

All day long, she kept popping back from whatever chore she was doing to gaze at and to touch the books. It was a dream come true. She, Brenda Bellinger had done it. She was a published novelist!

That evening, apologising, she'd shown them to Opal.

Opal laughed, "I knew you'd never be able to wait."

"I meant to."

"It doesn't really matter. Have you rung David yet?"

"What do you think."

Hardly had Brenda spoken, when there was a knock on the door. It was David with a magnum of champagne and a large box of fancy cakes. "To celebrate," he said. "Miss Tribble's in the car. I thought you'd want her in on this?"

"Of course," replied Brenda, excitedly. She hunted out her best wine glasses and started arranging the cakes onto a plate. "Well, don't just stand there, bring her in!"

He reappeared with Miss Tribble. She clasped Brenda's hands. "I'm so pleased for you, my dear. I expect you're dancing on air at getting published?"

"I certainly am." She settled Miss Tribble in the most comfortable chair in the front room.

"How about us asking Mrs Briggs in too?" suggested Opal,

"she likes a party and she's certainly been a friend in need."

"Good idea; pop next door and ask her."

"Right, but don't drink all the champers before I get back," laughed Opal.

Mrs Briggs was only too pleased to come. She brought a batch of sausage rolls that she'd made that afternoon. "It's odd," she said, "but I suddenly had this fancy to do some baking."

David went to the off-licence for some lemonade and crisps and cheesy biscuits for the children. The party got under way. Mark enjoying it as much as anyone as he was fed by David, a chocolate éclair, crisps and sausage rolls.

Melanie and Miranda both begged for a taste of champagne.

"It is a special occasion," coaxed David.

"Just this once then," agreed Brenda, "then straight up the stairs with the pair of you."

"I first drank champagne when I was sixteen," confided Miss Tribble.

"Did your boyfriend fill up your slipper?" winked David.

She wagged a finger at him. "Now, now, Mr Certes, that would be telling."

Brenda poured some into the girls' glasses.

Melanie pulled a face. "I'd rather have lemonade."

"I like it," decided Miranda, "can I have some more please, Mummy?"

"No, you can't," retorted Brenda, "I'm not having a teeny-tot champers-guzzler for a daughter. You shouldn't really have had what you did!" She turned to Opal. "She's too young, isn't she?" But Opal, nibbling a sausage roll didn't reply, being lost in thought. Brenda sighed. It'll be that Bob again. Would her friend ever get over him? She considered the small amount of champagne left in the bottle, "Do you want to finish this off, David?"

He put his hand over his glass. "Better not, I'm driving. I'll have some more lemonade though if I can, but after I've carried Mark up for you. He's nodding in his chair."

"Thank you." She turned to the girls. "I thought I told you ten minutes ago that it was time for bed."

"Sorry, Mummy," said Melanie.

"Sorry, Mummy," echoed Miranda. They politely kissed the cheeks of Opal and the two old ladies and disappeared.

David unfastened the strap securing Mark and put him over his shoulder in a fireman's hold. "Off we go," he said.

"Excuse me a minute," said Brenda, following.

Miss Tribble smiled knowingly at Opal and Mrs Briggs.

Both elderly ladies, having become rather tiddly as the evening progressed , began to sing songs from their girlhood. "Give me a little cosy corner and an armchair for two," wobbled Miss Tribble.

Mrs Briggs, equally wavery joined in, "Somewhere with somebody there, anywhere will do. Give me an evening in the twilight....." they finished off the song together, "and I'll find a little cosy corner in the arms of the boy I love."

"Good thing Mrs B only lives next door," whispered Opal. I'd better see if I can get her home while she can still stand." She helped her to her feet.

"Is it time to go?" asked a euphoric Mrs Briggs.

"Yes it is," replied Opal firmly, leading her out. But not before Brenda had hugged her neighbour soundly.

David winked, "Miss Tribble can sleep it off in the car." He fetched her coat from the hall. "Come along, Miss Tribble, time to go home."

"Whoops!" said Miss Tribble, almost tripping over the rug. I'm sure this rug's floating, or is it me?"

"No, it's not you Miss Tribble, it's the rug. Let's go." He helped her into her coat.

She clasped Brenda's hands in hers. "Thanks very much for the party dear. I've not had so much fun for ages."

"I'm pleased," she answered, kissing her on the cheek. Brenda turned to David. He took both her hands in his giving them a squeeze and looked deep into her eyes, before helping Miss Tribble to the car.

At last Brenda closed the door behind their guests. "I'll never forget today if I live to be a hundred," she giggled, picking up the plates and glasses and carrying them uncertainly into the kitchen.

* * *

It was arranged that she sign books at WH Smiths. One part of her was ecstatic at the idea, the other terrified. What if no one should want to buy her book? She knew there'd been considerable publicity in the Oxford Mail and Oxford Times - and she'd told them all at church, but that didn't mean anything. If nobody showed any interest, she'd sink through the floor.

They'd seated her at a table in an prominent part of the shop with her books arranged before her. At one end of the table, over which was spread a pink lace-edged cloth, was propped a poster with her photo, emblazoned with 'THE DEVIL IN THE FLAMES', and at the other, a cut glass vase containing yellow and white chrysanthemums. Pen in hand, she waited... and waited... and waited... At last, a white-haired woman approached and picked up a book. Brenda smiled pleasantly at her, trying hard to hide her apprehension as the woman flicked through the pages; shooting an uncertain look at Brenda as she did so. She frowned and laid the book back down again.

Brenda's heart sank. She wasn't going to buy after all. The woman hesitated. "Excuse me, I'm not sure if I want to buy this or not. It's not really for me you see, it's for a friend. It is a love story, isn't it? My friend only reads love stories."

Brenda reassured the woman that the 'The Devil in the Flames' was definitely a love story. But she still was unsure and finally wandered off.

Another woman approached, dark-haired and more forthright in manner. She picked up the book and read the blurb. "Great!" she enthused, "my mother will love this and so will my daughter." To Brenda's delight she bought two books and asked her to sign both copies.

A burly middle-aged man came up. He confessed with a sheepish grin that he read nothing but love stories, the soppier the better.

Several customers later, she thought that she recognised the young man before her. When he asked her to autograph a copy she became certain. This was one of Bob's friends. What was he doing buying a Romance?

Six foot tall, hair the colour of orange marmalade and worn in a pigtail, he was not someone you'd forget in a hurry. Yes, she decided, she had definitely seen him with Bob at the fair last September.

"You're a friend of Bob Brown, aren't you?" she asked.

"Yes, do you know him?"

"He's a friend of a friend," she replied. "What's your name?"

"Geoff Hallett, but the book's not for me. It's for my girl friend, Trish."

She wrote, 'Best wishes Trish from Brenda Bellinger,' proudly on the flyleaf. "How's Bob keeping? We've not seen him for a while."

"Haven't you heard?"

"No, what?"

He looked serious. "Bob's been in a crash. He's in a critical condition, unconscious in fact. He came off his motorbike in Broad Street, swerved to avoid a dog of all things. It was in the Oxford Mail."

"I don't always get it."

"He's in the Radcliffe Infirmary."

Brenda was shocked.

"A good mate," he continued, "it's a real shame. One moment everything before him, the next ..." He lifted his shoulders and gestured with spread hands.

"Are things that black?"

He nodded. "I guess so.. he's been unconscious for five days."

* * *

Brenda worried how this news would affect Opal. Although her friend professed to be over Bob, she knew different. She wondered what Opal would do? Would she be too proud to go and see him? Brenda knew what she would do if it were David who was lying there, even if they had quarrelled. She would drop everything and dash off to the Radcliffe immediately. But then, she wasn't Opal. Look how she'd managed to tear up all those letters from Bob without turning a hair. She seemed more in control of her emotions. Of course, there was his mother to consider. It would be very embarrassing for Opal to come face to face with her and she was sure to be there. Brenda had no love for the bigoted woman who had so hurt her friend, but she was a mother herself and could guess what Mrs Brown would be going through. She couldn't help but feel for her, hoping against hope that her only son would open his eyes.

* * *

Brenda laid down the casserole dish she'd removed from the oven.

Opal came in, and just as she did every evening, she dropped her briefcase and slumped into a chair. "I'm whacked!"

Brenda tangled her hands in the material of her apron. How on earth was she going to tell her about Bob? Tell her that there wasn't much chance for him. She'd rather do anything than do this!

"What is it?" asked Opal alarmed, sensing tension in the air.

"I've got some bad news for you," Brenda said gently.

"My parents?"

"No, not your parents, Opal."

She let out a sigh of relief. "Who then?"

"Bob."

"Bob. What's that to me?"

"Come on, now's not the time. I know he's very much to do with you."

Opal's fingers tightened on the back of the chair. "So, what's happened?"

"I'm afraid he's very ill - accident - came off his bike."

"His bike?"

Explaining, she placed a consoling arm about Opal's shoulders.

She sat trance-like for some minutes, then trembling, got to her feet. "I must go."

Brenda nodded. "But his mother?"

"I'm still going."

"Of course you are, but have some dinner first. I'm just about to dish up."

"I'm going now!"

"I'll come with you."

"It's all right, you've got the kids, and I'll be OK." She hurried into the hall. Brenda heard her stifled moans.

The front door slammed.

As she dished up the children's dinners, she thought, so Opal isn't so very different to me after all.

CHAPTER 23

Opal's heels clicked along the depressing green-painted corridor of the Radcliffe Infirmary; the hospital smell, a mixture of disinfectant, paraldehyde and boiled cabbage invading her nostrils. She passed porters pushing trolleys; doctors in white coats with stethoscopes dangling from their pockets; a motley array of visitors like herself; or outpatients, lost on their way to the X-ray Department with the inevitable slings, crutches and plaster casts, well in evidence.

She entered the ward, moving past the sister's desk, and down the centre of the twin rows of beds occupied by grey-faced males, many elderly, clad in striped pyjamas and with their counterpanes smoothed so tightly over them that they could scarcely move. Beside them on lockers sat the identical bottles of squash and bowls of dusky grapes. Glasses crammed with dentures were often visible. At the far end of the ward was the private room in which Bob lay, his head swathed in bandages and his body attached to various tubes and complicated apparatus which she didn't really understand.

Opal peeked in at the door, chest pounding. She breathed again, his mother wasn't there!

She didn't really fancy confronting that woman again if she could help it. She had that first evening when she'd visited. They had sat stoney-faced on either side of the unresponsive Bob for over three quarters of an hour, each pretending that the other wasn't there, but in reality, each noting the other's slightest movement; neither of them intending to be the one who left first. In memory she saw Mrs Brown, her back unbending; smelling again the discreet perfume that the woman had been emitting – Opal hazarded a guess, it must at the very least be Chanel No 5.

She pulled up a chair next to Bob's bed and clasped his limp hand that lay inert on the counterpane. She began to tell him of her day, the doctor having said that this was the thing to do, that talking to him might possibly help. A small pulse moved in his throat. He just looks as if he's asleep she thought. Surely he must be getting better? It was ten days since his accident. A tear ran unchecked and splashed onto his hand. Wake up, Bob, please wake up, she willed. Nothing happened.

Outside, a nurse hurried past with a covered bedpan. In the Sluice Room, water flushed, but Opal never heard it, she was reliving the happy times that she and Bob had shared, strolling along the towpath ... at the Ashmolean... in the back row of the Scala Cinema. And those never to be forgotten moments at Shotover. It seemed impossible that everything could be over for them both. She thought regretfully of all those weeks, days and hours that had been wasted because of her pride. Somehow, in the light of Bob's accident, his mother's disapproval no longer had any significance.

She looked at her watch. To her astonishment it was already seven-thirty. She had been with Bob for over thirty minutes. What time did they have their dinner at the Randolph Hotel? she wondered. Could the meal be over? If so, Bob's mother might appear at any moment. She certainly didn't want their paths to cross for a second time if she could avoid it. In her head she heard the detested Southern drawl, "How's my honey-chile today, doctor?"

She got to her feet. She wasn't hanging around until imagination became reality. She stood looking down, trying to imprint those dearly loved features into her memory. She bent and lightly kissed his cheek. She shivered. Did his flesh already have a waxen feel to it?

At the entrance, she saw Bob's mother approaching. Mrs Brown, recognising her too, averted her face and hurried past.

Opal gritted her teeth. How had someone as obnoxious as that bigoted woman managed to give birth to such a wonderful son, one with completely differing views?

She waited at the bus stop. She'd felt bad enough before running into his mother, but after seeing her disdainful eyes, she'd felt ten times worse. As if to match her mood the sun went in and black clouds gathered overhead. She felt a spot of rain on her cheek, followed by a second, then a third. In the distance thunder rumbled. That's all she needed, she reflected wryly, to be caught in a storm – and without her brolly! Why on earth hadn't they erected a covered shelter outside the hospital? If she wasn't feeling so distraught, she'd have been tempted to write a stiff letter to the Council Offices. She looked at her watch; peered into the distance for the bus, but there was no sign. The lightning flashed, and the heavens opened up.

She was soaking wet and shivering by the time the bus eventually arrived. Hair plastered to her scalp, skirt flapping wetly against her legs, feet squelching as she walked, she thankfully climbed aboard; inwardly cursing Bob's mother.

* * *

"How is he?" asked Brenda.

"No better than yesterday. It's heartbreaking seeing him so unnaturally pale and still."

"It must be awful for you, sitting there and talking to him without any response?"

Opal sighed, "Awful's hardly the word."

"Did you see his mother?"

"No, not this time, thank goodness! I keep an eye on the clock. I've got it to a fine art, the business of avoiding her."

"Well, that's something I suppose. Tea?"

"Please, I'm so dry you'd have thought that I'd been to the Sahara and not the Radcliffe. Not like the other day; I couldn't have been wetter." She slumped into a chair.

"No sign of a cold?" asked Brenda.

"No."

"That'll be because you took my advice and put your feet in a mustard-bath." She busied herself with the kettle and cups.

"I don't know what I'm going to do if..."

"While there's life there's hope," said Brenda. She felt so helpless. Why couldn't she think of something more comforting to say than that awful old cliché? How on earth was she going to cope with Opal if the worst happened? Send for her parents? Surely, they'd drop everything and come.

"If Bob dies I'm going to want to die too," Opal said, her voice breaking.

Brenda hurried over and put an arm around her shoulders. "Let them come," she advised, "let the tears come."

"It's so unfair, he's too young." Opal fumbled for a handkerchief.

A freshly ironed one was plucked from the clotheshorse. "Here have this."

"Thanks." She blew her nose and wiped her eyes.

The tea was poured. Brenda handed her a cup. "Drink that," she ordered.

Opal sipped obediently.

"Look, why don't you do what I did when the girls went

missing?"

"What was that?"

"Go and see Father Arnold."

"What, at St Mary's and St Johns church?"

"He was a great comfort to me. We said a prayer together for the girls' safety, and it worked."

"Yes, I suppose it did, didn't it," Opal said.

"Are you going to see him then? I always think that doing something is better than doing nothing in stressful circumstances. It can't do any harm."

"You're right." Opal drained her cup and rose to her feet. "I wonder if he'd be in if I went down to the Vicarage now?"

* * *

Brenda adjusted the clothes prop and eyed with satisfaction her line full of whites blowing in the wind. She picked up her empty clothes basket and peg bag.

Mrs Briggs came briskly out. "Shoo! Shoo!" The birds, wheeling around her washing, scattered to the nearby trees to watch. "Yohoo, Brenda. Do you think it'll stay fine?"

She raised her head. Over the fence her neighbour's grey head of curls bobbed. "Oh, hello, Mrs Briggs. Well, the forecast on the radio predicted good drying-weather." She moved closer to enjoy a few minutes chat.

"You're a dark horse," said Mrs Briggs.

"Whatever do you mean?"

"I heard your talk on how you got started as a novelist on Radio Oxford yesterday, it was just luck that I had it on. Why didn't you mention it to me?"

Brenda reddened. "I didn't think it was worth bothering you about."

"Well, I wish you had. I felt real proud for you."

Brenda hesitated. "I've been asked to give a talk at the Womens' Institute, too, next Wednesday afternoon; you can come along with me if you like; give me moral support."

Mrs Brigg's smile widened. "I'd love to, if you really mean it?"

"Of course I do."

"You're getting to be quite a celebrity. Well, good for you."

"I was shaking the first time I faced an audience. It's one thing writing a book, another talking about it to a room full of strangers. I still feel nervous, but I'm beginning to get used to it. It's strangely exhilarating."

Her neighbour suddenly turned serious. "What's wrong with Opal? I saw her this morning going for her bus. She looked so drawn. All the pep's gone out of her. Is she ill?"

"No, it's her boyfriend."

"I didn't know she had one, not a regular one anyway. Not since that nice lad with the motorbike - what was his name? Bob?"

"Yes, that's him, Bob. He's had an accident and is seriously ill in the Radcliffe."

"Never! An accident?"

"Yes. A near fatal one, I'm afraid. He came off his bike. It's such a shame; when you think of all the rotten sorts walking the streets and him… " Brenda's voice shook.

"But I thought he was out of the picture?" puzzled Mrs Briggs.

"She'd just been fooling herself when she said she'd forgotten him. I knew different. And of course once she knew he was at death's door, she ups and dashes to his bedside."

"Poor girl, I feel for her. Is there no hope?"

"Well, I don't know. She's had a word with the specialist. He says that the longer Bob's unconscious, the less chance there is. I dread to think of that day. "

"When I lost my Bill, I felt that the world had ended," said Mrs Briggs sadly.

"I know exactly what you mean. When they told me about my John…" For days and weeks she'd felt she was in the middle of a nightmare – one she'd imagined at the time would never lift.

"You had the children."

"That's true."

"They must have been a great comfort."

"I don't know how I'd have gone on without them. If it hadn't been for my children, well," she shrugged.

"I'll say a prayer for her, for them both."

"I've been praying," she admitted, "I sent her off to see Father Arnold at the church."

Mrs Briggs nodded. "Good idea. I'm a great believer in the power of prayer. I don't know why God let us invent motorbikes, they're the Devil's transport if you ask me."

"You never said a truer word," said Brenda.

* * *

Holding Bob's hand, Opal talked to him. She'd done as Brenda had suggested, visited Father Arnold at St Mary and St Johns. Sympathetically, the Vicar had let her talk out her dread and despair. "Would you like us to pray together for him?" he'd asked gently. She'd nodded her agreement. She would have agreed to anything, even to scaling Mount Everest, without oxygen, if by doing so she could have helped Bob. They had knelt before the crucifix in his study, her halting tongue following his, in a plea for God's mercy.

"Come again, my child, "he had said, "whenever you feel the need."

She'd walked slowly back to Brenda's. Father Arnold's comforting words still in her ears. Her hands tightly clutching the small prayer tract that he'd given to her.

She looked down at Bob. Was he paler than before? Wake up! Wake up! she willed.

But nothing happened. Did she really imagine that it would? In the light of what the doctor had said was she not fooling herself that there was a future for him, for them?

Her thoughts swung back to that picnic at Boars Hill. They had climbed an ancient mound with steps cut into its side, their legs aching by the time they reached the top. Afterwards they'd spread a blanket on the grass, and she had set out the food that she'd made and the sausage rolls bought from Weekes' Bakery. Later, she'd fallen asleep, and had woken to find him bent over her with a loving expression in his eyes. She'd quickly lowered hers, pretending to be still asleep and he'd tickled her nose with a blade of grass.

A nurse checking the apparatus over the bed brought her back to the present. She averted her eyes from the tubes and paraphernalia that was helping to keep him alive. The nurse smiled sympathetically as she left.

"I love you, Bob," Opal whispered, "don't leave me."

An eyelash flickered.

She stared, willing it to be true.

The eyelash flickered again.

She leapt to her feet. It had happened, hadn't it? She wasn't just imagining it?

"Nurse! Nurse!" she yelled.

The nurse came running. "Shush!! What is it?"

"I'm sure his eyelash moved."

The nurse bent over him and took his pulse, eyeing him intently. "I'll fetch doctor." She hurried out.

Opal clenched her fists at her sides. Her chest was thudding as if it was about to burst. Was it true? Was Bob really coming round? Please God, please God.

The doctor appeared, a stocky middle-aged man with tired eyes.

She stepped back. The doctor examined Bob.

He turned to her. "These are hopeful signs." As he spoke the hand on the counterpane stirred.

"His fingers!" exclaimed Opal.

As they looked, the fingers moved again.

"Doctor!"

He turned to the nurse.

"His eyelids," she said, "they're fluttering."

They all looked.

"Bob!!"

The doctor bent over him.

"Opal," he whispered weakly.

She took his hand, "I'm here, oh, darling, I'm here."

She felt the answering pressure of his fingers.

There was a movement at the door. Opal turned to see Mrs Brown with tears in her eyes. "My honey-chile!" she cried, hurrying towards the bed.

The doctor ushered out the nurse, saying, as he left. "We have to do more tests on Mr Brown. I'm sorry, but in a few minutes I must ask you both to leave."

* * *

They sat on either side of Bob's bed each holding a hand, tears of happiness staining both their cheeks. Opal sensed a warmer feeling coming from the older woman towards her. Was it possible that Mrs Brown's animosity was lessening? Could something like this alter her? No, someone like Mrs Brown, brought up as she had been would never change. Opal bit her lip. It was no use fooling herself. Just because she wanted it so very much, didn't mean that it would happen.

She shrugged the idea away.

* * *

"He's going to be all right, Bob's come round," cried Opal, dashing into the kitchen. Brenda put down the sock she was darning and leapt to her feet. "Thank God!" she exclaimed, hugging Opal.

"I was there when it happened. He spoke. He said, 'Opal'."

"That's wonderful news."

"Yes, for me and for his mother."

Brenda frowned. "She was there?"

"Came in just as he spoke."

"And did she acknowledge you?"

"Not really, we just sat on either side, each holding a hand and weeping silently." Opal sniffed and dabbed her eyes with her fingertips.

"And do you think she'll see things differently now?" asked Brenda.

"I don't know. It would be better for Bob if she could accept me, but with someone like her, with her background, it's not very likely."

"No, it's like expecting a leopard to change its spots. Anyway, I've had a visitor."

Opal eyed the two empty cups on the table.

"David?"

"Yes, he dropped in to invite us over to Rose Cottage for the day on Sunday. It's mainly so that I can keep my promise to take the kids to visit George Farmer, or as those two call him, Farmer George. He's a widower, and a really nice man, according to David. He always gives a generous donation to the village school for the children's Christmas party. With his daughter and grandchildren being so far away, it's as if he's completely alone in the world."

"Poor man. It must be awful to have no family around when you're old."

"Yes, David says he feels quite sorry for him."

"Well, I'm sure the children will enjoy feeding the rabbits."

Brenda laughed. "There'll be no stopping them, once they know about the outing."

* * *

CHAPTER 24

Bob gulped his orange squash, his thoughts in turmoil, wishing that there was a shot of whisky in it. He eyed the door apprehensively. At any moment his mother would appear and he would have to say what he'd mentally rehearsed so many times. He had asked Opal not to visit this evening. She'd nodded, knowing the reason, and hoping that at last he would find the strength from somewhere. But he knew from experience, this would be far from easy. Once, in desperation, he had even thought of trying a hypnotist. He'd read that one was appearing at the New Theatre. On the evening in question, Bob had been in the audience. When the Great Marvo had asked for volunteers to go up on stage, he had frozen in his seat, unequal to the challenge.

Footsteps in the corridor alerted him. Was this her? They passed by and he breathed again.

He just couldn't risk losing Opal a second time. He had to tackle his mother, do his best, at least, for Opal. He recalled the Christmas that he'd spent with her family in Birmingham. They had sat around the family table, eating a better meal than any he'd ever previously tasted, even his mother's French chef couldn't come up to Beulah Walker's standard. They'd pulled the brightly coloured crackers, worn the festive hats, read out to each other the jokes and got merry on the very potent home-made elderberry wine. Afterwards they'd opened the presents that lay beneath the tree. Opal's gift had been a pair of dazzling red socks, which were embroidered with his initials and caused a lot of merriment all round. Kneeling beside the tree, surrounded by wrapping paper, her face flushed by wine and the heat of the fire, she'd looked so desirable, so very loveable.

Again footsteps in the corridor brought him back to the present and the ordeal that he would have to face when his mother arrived.

The door opened and in she came, smiling, laden with flowers, fruit and magazines. "How's my honey-chile, today?"

"Fine, Mum."

She looked at him sharply, as she settled herself on the chair by the bed and removed her fox fur. "It's a lovely evening," she said, “quite warm in fact. By the time you come home to Tunbridge Wells to recuperate it’ll be almost summer.”

Between thumb and finger he twisted a loose thread on his counterpane. Now or never, he thought, taking a deep breath.

“Look, Mum, I shan’t be coming home when I leave here.”

Mrs Brown’s brow darkened. “Not come home?”

“No, Mum.”

“But you must.”

“Why must I?”

She reached for his hand. “You need me to care for you. I’ll order you all your favourite dishes - build you up.”

He removed his hand. “I’ll be all right. I want to stay near to Opal. Look, Mum. I’ve got to tell you this. I know you won’t like it, but I love Opal, and I intend to marry her.”

There he had said it, and the ceiling hadn’t crashed onto him.

Mrs Brown’s face became rigid and she clasped her handbag to her as if it was a life-belt. “Now, dear, don’t make any rash decisions yet, you’re still ill. Let me take care of everything.”

“It’s no good trying to avoid it, Mother. I’m going to marry Opal, with, or without your approval; but I’d rather have your approval.”

“Honey-chile, I know now that she’s a nice enough girl, but she’s not for you. I can’t understand why you stopped seeing that pretty Denise Robins. She’s always asking after you. She comes from such fine family. She’s really got breeding.”

“She’s not got a brain in her head.”

“There are other girls. This Opal would be better off with one of her own sort.”

“Her own sort?”

“Yes.”

“Opal is my sort!”

“But she’s a...”

“She’s a what?”

“Your granddaddy would turn in his grave if he knew what his grandson was planning.”

“What’s so terrible? I only want to marry the woman I love. Opal’s not a leper.”

“No,” said Mrs Brown, in a strained voice, “but she’s a negra.”

“Don’t ever let me hear you call Opal that again,” said Bob quietly.

“I’m only stating a fact.”

"And what makes me so much better than her?"

"You're white, and naturally superior."

"Who says?"

"I say; your mother."

"That's rubbish!"

Mrs Brown got to her feet and gathered up her belongings. "I'm going. You know where I am when you come to your senses."

"I shan't."

"I shall never accept that girl."

"That's up to you, but can you take the consequences? You'll be cut off completely…"

"And I'll cut you out of my will!"

Bob groaned inwardly. How could his mother use money as ammunition against Opal? It was below the belt. He'd never really known what it was like to be short of money – not like some of his fellow students. All the same an inheritance could never compete with Opal. "I don't care about that! I'll make my own way."

"That's easy enough to say now. You'll think differently later."

"No, I won't!"

"Money can be very useful."

"It's no good, Mum. You're wasting your breath. My mind is made up. It's Opal for me. And if you can't see reason and accept her as my wife, you'll miss out on your grandchildren."

"Grandchildren!! She's not...?"

"Don't insult Opal. But we will have children."

"But they'll be black!!"

"So what!" said Bob.

His mother never replied. Turning on her heel, she swept from the room.

* * *

"It's very good of you to visit me," said Bob, taking the bag of grapes from Brenda.

"I'm pleased to see that you're almost recovered."

"He looks more human without bandages," teased Opal, "and that small scar on his forehead should soon fade."

"I suppose I got off more lightly than I deserved," reflected Bob.

"Yes, no more motorbikes for you, Bob Brown."

He smiled. "We'll see about that." He turned to Brenda, "We're not even married yet, and already she's trying to boss me!"

"Someone's got to!" Opal turned to Brenda. "He's coming out next Monday. I've just seen the doctor and he's confirmed it."

"It can't be soon enough for me. I'm fed up with their steamed-fish and lumpy mashed potatoes."

"Is that what they feed you?" asked Brenda.

"That, and some kind of stew."

"He's exaggerating. He loves the food here really. I'm going to take lessons from the hospital cooks."

"Don't you dare!!"

"So when's the wedding then?" laughed Brenda.

"Six weeks next Monday, in Birmingham said Opal. My mum's so excited, she's invited half the neighbourhood. The reception's going to be in the Community Centre. Now, it goes without saying you're coming Bren. David, too, of course, and as I've said I want the girls as bridesmaids. I've got that lovely pattern for their dresses."

Brenda's eyes lit up with pride. "They'll be over the moon at the idea. I'll have to get a film for my camera. I must have some snaps for the family album."

"My mum's hiring a photographer."

"Everything in style?"

"She's says that you only get married once."

Not always, thought Brenda. Sadly life didn't always work out the way you expected. She'd always love John, of course she would, but she undoubtedly loved David too. If things carried on the way they were going; well, she could have a second husband in the very near future.

"My mum's sending me down some money that she's been saving for just such an event," said Opal. "I'm going to get the material for the bridesmaids' dresses from the Cattle Market; my dress, too. I fancy cream brocade with a mandarin collar."

"You'll look lovely in it."

Opal pursed her lips. "There's only one problem."

"What's that?" asked Brenda.

"Do you think you could make them? I know you don't get much spare time, what with your writing and everything else."

Brenda laughed, "I'd be offended if you asked someone else."

Bob pretended to yawn. "I'm a captive audience, that's what I am."

"Are we boring you, darling?" asked Opal sweetly.

"Men always find talk of weddings a bit much."

Bob popped a grape into his mouth. "I suppose we're just not extroverts like you women. No, I don't really mind all the fuss, just as long as you don't expect me to wear a top hat and tails."

"But I've ordered them for you from Walters of the Turl," said Opal, endeavouring to keep a straight face.

He dropped the bag of grapes. "You'd better not have done!"

She exploded with laughter. "I was only teasing, darling."

"So what about the honeymoon, where do you plan to spend it?" asked Brenda.

Bob waggled a finger. "Where did you spend yours?"

"John hired a boat on the Norfolk Broads." She blushed, "We spent the whole week in bed."

"But what about food?" asked Opal.

"There was a cafe nearby. We surfaced once a day to stock-up with eatables."

"Re-charge your batteries! I get the picture," laughed Bob.

Brenda blushed again. "We were talking about your honeymoon, not mine."

"Sorry, well, we've been giving it some thought. But can't make up our minds." He turned to Opal, "Can we, darling?"

"We'd love to go to Paris, but don't think we could afford it. I've thought of London, but I haven't suggested it yet. I'd love to see the Tower and Madam Tussauds."

Bob saluted smartly. "Your wish is my command," he said.

* * *

The two women caught the bus home. Brenda eyed her watch, "We should just make it back before the girls and Mark's ambulance. If I go anywhere in the afternoon I always worry about being late for them."

Opal nodded.

Brenda glanced out of the smeary window, catching glimpses of colleges and pavements thronged with tourists. "So everything's set for the wedding, then?"

"More or less."

"I never really thought that Bob would stand up to his mother. He must love you very much."

Opal smiled. "I rather think he does."

"But what about his mother, will she be coming to the wedding?"

"I shouldn't think so."

"How does Bob feel about that?"

Opal bit her lip. "Pretty bad, but what can he do? What can anyone do?"

Brenda nodded. "It's a pity she's got to be like she is."

"Yes, but I don't suppose she can really help it, being brought up as she was."

"That's magnanimous of you."

"I'd like her to come for Bob's sake. Of course I would. But I suppose she'd be too proud to ever climb down."

"So pride'll make her miss the most important day in her son's life."

"That, and dyed-in-the-wool prejudice."

"I can't understand the woman. If it were one of my girls getting married, I'd be there if I had to fly to the other side of the world."

"Maybe, but not everyone is like Brenda Bellinger," said Opal, "more's the pity."

* * *

Brenda's front room resembled a great lady's boudoir; everywhere one looked being draped with lengths of materials that glistened as they caught the evening sunshine that streamed through the window.

There was a length of cream brocade for Opal, a length of peach satin for Melanie and a length of blue satin for Miranda, whilst the cushions of the settee and armchairs were strewn with paper patterns, reels of thread, cards of lace, pearl buttons and press-studs. At one end of a table, the Singer Sewing machine stood waiting.

Opal popped her head around the door. "Do you need any help?"

Brenda opened the packet that contained the bridal gown pattern. "You can help me pin this to the cream brocade if you like."

"All right, I'll just wash my hands."

When she returned Brenda had carefully laid the brocade over an old sheet on the floor with the pattern on top. Together they pinned it to the material.

Light footsteps neared and two small faces peeked around the door. "Can I help?" asked Melanie.

"Me too," said Miranda.

Their mother, expertly wielding the cutting-out scissors, pulled a face, "Not on your life!" she said.

The girls looked crestfallen.

"If there are any snippets of material left," said Opal, "you can have them to make some clothes for your dollies."

Melanie's face lit up, "We can! Oh, goody, goody."

"Will you help us?" asked Miranda.

"Of course."

"I shall need Opal's help myself if I'm going to get all these dresses finished in time," stated Brenda.

* * *

The garments were pinned and tacked together. Opal and the girls stood on stools in the half-made dresses while Brenda did the final adjustments.

"How do I look, Mummy?" asked Melanie.

"Stop wriggling, do. I don't want to stick a pin into you."

Opal, from her perch, winced ruefully. "One's just stuck into me. It's fair giving me gyp!"

"Oh, no!" Brenda hurried over to readjust the pins that held Opal's gown together, "How's that?"

She sighed with relief. "Better, thank goodness."

"Aren't you going to see to my dress, Mummy?" asked Miranda, "I'm getting stiff stood up here."

"Sorry darling. I'm just coming." Nimble fingers made some darts in the waist of Miranda's dress. She stood back. "Yes that's just right." She studied the girls and Opal with satisfaction, "You all look as pretty as a picture."

The little girls preened themselves at her words.

"I feel more like a statue stuck up here," remarked Opal wryly, "can't we get down yet?"

* * *

Later that evening, and for several evenings to come, the whirr of the sewing machine could be heard all round the house, whilst the front room lino was littered with snippets of cream, peach and blue cotton and resembled a multicoloured snowstorm.

Brenda sighed and stretched, her right hand falling limply to her side. She rubbed her wrist. "It's as stiff as a board. Thank God, that's the final stitch!" She eyed with pride the finished dresses that were draped across the back of the settee. "They look like Paris models, if I do say so myself."

"They certainly do," agreed an admiring Opal. "I can't thank you enough for all your hard work, not to mention flare."

Brenda blushed, "Well, you helped."

"Yes, but you masterminded it all, as well as doing most of the machining."

"It was nothing. Come on, let's get the dresses upstairs."

Holding them at arm's length, careful not to step on the hems, they carried them up. With the utmost care they slipped them onto coat hangers and hung them in the wardrobes; to await Opal's wedding day, that was now exactly a fortnight off.

* * *

As Opal lay in her bed that night, she visualised the beautiful gown behind her wardrobe doors. She saw herself getting into the dress and then floating down the aisle on her father's arm. She had a full dress rehearsal, without leaving the confines of her bed.

She had never really thought that a marriage with Bob would ever come off. First there had been the difficulties with his mother, then the terrible Cynthia. She didn't really think that there'd ever been that much between Cynthia and Bob. Her snide remarks about him being a fantastic lover, and her claim that he'd said that he could never get enough of her, had rankled. Cynthia, to no one's surprise had been 'sent down' when she'd got herself pregnant, by some chinless young lord or other.

Opal turned over, and settled herself to sleep. Her last conscious thought being of Bob, and his tender embrace.

CHAPTER 25

Brenda pulled-to the front door and turned the key in the lock. She hurried out to David's car. Already the girls were wriggling excitedly on the back seat; Mark held upright between them.

In the car boot, alongside Mark's chair and the luggage was a wicker basket that contained a picnic lunch. This they planned to eat in a lay-by along the way. On top of the basket were the bridesmaids' dresses, carefully folded and wrapped in an old sheet to keep them clean.

It was the twenty-eighth of June and lovely balmy weather. Brides' weather thought Brenda happily. The following day, the twenty-ninth of June was Opal and Bob's wedding day, they, having planned the date to coincide with the end of term break. Opal was doing a further year at college. Bob, meanwhile had acquired a position at the Bodleian Library. Both Opal and Bob had left Oxford the previous morning for Birmingham; Opal to spend the remaining time as a single woman with her parents; Bob to book into Shirley House, a two star hotel, situated in Westley Road.

Brenda climbed in beside David.

He grinned, "All set, darling?"

The two girls in the back exchanged knowing glances and giggled.

David started the engine and the car moved smoothly away. Next door, a bedroom window shot up to reveal a beaming Mrs Briggs, "Safe journey!" she called, waving.

The car picked up speed.

"Off we go," said Melanie.

"Off we go," repeated Miranda.

Mark, laughing and waving his arms wildly almost gave Melanie a black eye.

"Here, watch it, squirt!" she exclaimed good-naturedly.

They turned into the Cowley Road. Brenda pointed out the local Supermarket. "Well, Opal'll be Mrs Brown the next time I set foot in there."

"Will you be Mrs Certes, Mummy if you marry David?" piped up Melanie.

Brenda's cheeks flamed. "Shush!" she admonished.

But eyeing the girl in the driving mirror he replied coolly, "Yes, yes, she would, if ever she did me the honour."

"Will you, Mummy?" asked Melanie.

At that moment Miranda began singing a Beatles' number, which all joined in, saving Brenda the necessity of replying.

The car purred through Marston, the Northern By-pass, and finally on to the A 34, heading North. The children sucked at barley sugar to prevent car sickness. They parked on a grassy lay-by for their lunch. David lit a primus to make Brenda and himself a cup of tea; the children preferring the Coca-Cola that they'd brought with them.

He savoured the last crumb of his sandwich. "Those ham and chutney sandwiches were delicious, darling."

"Glad you enjoyed them." She tidied up the remains of the picnic.

"I wanna wee!" insisted Miranda, hopping on one leg.

"So do I," said Melanie.

Brenda frowned. "I should have known this would happen with you drinking so much." She pointed, "You'll have to squeeze through that gap in the hedge."

"What, go in that field?" said Melanie aghast.

"There's nothing else for it. There's no toilets out here. I'll just check it first, make sure there's no stinging nettles for you to fall into."

"I can't wait for that, Mummy!" Miranda squirmed through the hedge and disappeared.

Minutes later she returned. "It's all yours," she grinned.

So, taking turns to relieve themselves, they followed her example. David going last.

But the field had an occupant.

At the far end was a massive black bull. David unfortunately was wearing red. The bull, inflamed by his sweater, glared with bloodshot eyes and tossed its head, a ray of sunlight winking on its wicked-looking horns.

He blenched. With one eye on the bull, he hurried towards the hedge.

With an almighty bellow it began to charge.

He started to run, his chest competing with the thudding hooves that pounded nearer and nearer.

Alerted, Brenda and the girls were horrified to see David being chased by a murderous bull.

"Quick! Quick!" Brenda screeched, clutching at the girls.

They screamed too, their eyes wide with terror.

With a superhuman effort, skimming the hedge, David dived to safety, rolling over as he landed on the grass.

There was a splintering of wood, but the hedge itself held, and the bellowing bull backed off.

Brenda held him close, "Oh, darling, are you all right?" she cried.

He patted himself gingerly. "I think so."

Both girls hugged him, shivering at the thought of the bull who was snorting angrily on the opposite side of the hedge.

Everyone turned, hearing laughter. It was Mark. Seated in his wheelchair beside the car, with a wide smile on his face, he seemed to find David's predicament a huge joke.

"It's not funny, Mark," scolded Brenda gently.

"He took no notice. "T… t… t… t," he spluttered.

"I'm sure he is trying to say something," said Melanie.

Brenda's eyes shone. "Do you think so? The Speech Therapist did say that Mark might say his first recognisable word at any time."

It was Miranda who was the first to realise what Mark was laughing about. "You've got a rip in the seat of your trousers, David," she giggled.

"So you have," agreed Brenda and Melanie, struggling to keep straight faces.

He reddened. "Caught on the hedge, most likely. I'll have to change." He rummaged in the car boot for his overnight bag. "You'll all have to turn your backs," he insisted, "I'm definitely not going behind that hedge again."

* * *

It was just after one-p.m. when they saw the Birmingham skyline, dominated by the new high-rise flats. They drove through the crowded town centre, clamorous with hooting cars, taxis, lorries and buses. A vast grey-stoned and lichen-covered church came into view. A large placard read, 'St Martins'.

"Isn't that the church where Opal is going to be married?" asked Melanie.

"Yes, unless Birmingham has another St Martin's church,"

replied Brenda.

They parked in the Bull Ring Shopping Centre. "All right, all right, Melanie, you can stop worrying. We'll go and look for a little present for the three of you to take back to Farmer George." Brenda laughed and turned to David. "They've only got me calling George Farmer, Farmer George."

David laughed too. "Well, it does suit him – he even sucks a piece of straw when he's not sucking the stem of his pipe."

Since that first visit, he and Brenda had taken the children to the old man's cottage several times. Not only did Farmer George keep rabbits, but also chickens. Melanie and Miranda, with Mark looking on from his wheelchair, had scattered corn for the squawking fowls. The children especially enjoyed the feeding of the rabbits with lettuce leaves. She smiled as she recalled how one baby rabbit had suddenly leapt onto Mark's lap, causing him to squeal. They couldn't help but laugh at the expression of astonishment on Mark's face.

They all got out, and with David pushing Mark's chair, went around the arcades.

The idea of handkerchiefs was discarded, as was buying a pair of red woolly socks.

"I know!" exclaimed Melanie, "how about some spills for his pipe?"

"Good idea!" said David.

"Yes, Farmer George has a pot of spills on his mantelpiece. He sticks a spill in the fire and then lights his pipe with it," said Miranda.

And so it was agreed, and a pack of coloured spills was bought.

They returned to the car, and set off again. "Do we turn ahead?" asked David.

Brenda studied the map. "I think so. Yes, this is New Street."

They turned into it.

"There's the hotel," pointed Melanie, "isn't it huge."

"It's as big as a palace," said Miranda.

"It's bigger even than the Randolph," exclaimed Brenda, apprehensively.

They drew up at the four star, Midland Hotel, where David had reserved a family room and a single room, both en suite.

A uniformed commissionaire stepped from the foyer and opened the car door. He saluted smartly, "Good afternoon, sir. Good afternoon, madam, welcome to the Midland."

"He looks like a walrus," remarked Melanie to Miranda, "do you think he won all those medals in the war?"

David got out and opened the boot and the commissionaire carried in the luggage.

Meanwhile the girls were scrambling from the car, looking around and pointing, their eyes round with excitement.

"Don't be so boisterous," admonished Brenda, feeling rather embarrassed by their exuberance, "people will think we're not used to stopping in places like this."

David smiled, "Does it matter? You're every bit as good as anyone else here."

She looked for confirmation at her smart cream coloured two-piece. "Yes, you're right," she said, "and this hotel is no smarter than the one I stopped at in London when I went to see my publisher."

"That's the ticket." He removed the wheelchair from the boot, unfolded it, lifted Mark from the car and into it. With David pushing the chair, they entered the hotel and went up to the reception desk.

"I've a family and a single room booked," he said, "name's Certes."

The receptionist consulted a list. "Yes," he said, "Mr Certes and party." He pressed a buzzer. A porter appeared.

"Rooms ten and twelve," said the receptionist.

"Come this way, sir, madam," invited the porter.

They followed him into the lift; the children trailing. He pressed the third-floor button and the doors slid together.

Seconds later they stepped out onto a corridor, David pushing Mark's wheelchair.

"This way," said the porter. He opened the door marked 'ten'. "This is the family room, sir," he said, "room twelve is the single; it's one door along."

They entered. They found their luggage awaiting them. The porter hovered.... David handed him a twenty pence. "Thank you, sir," he replied, leaving.

Brenda looked around. The room contained a king-size and two single beds. She admired the white wood furniture. At one end of the dressing table there was a dish of fruit – soon to be raided by the girls - and at the other a display of pink and white carnations. At the tall windows were red velvet curtains that were looped up with matching cords. "Such luxury," she exclaimed. She pressed her toe.

"The carpet's inches thick."

She pulled back the lace bedspreads and fingered the sheets. "Linen," she said, "the same as the Russell in London. I'll have to tell Opal."

David looked puzzled.

She explained as how she and Opal had once wondered whether a four star hotel, such as the Randolph in Oxford would have had satin sheets on their beds; never expecting that either of them would ever stay in such a place.

Melanie and Miranda were preening themselves in a full length ornate mirror.

Brenda laughed. "If they stay here too long they'll become as vain as peacocks."

But the girls were off to examine the bathroom. It had pale pink fixtures and fittings, and hanging on a heated towel rail were four pink fluffy bath towels and four hand towels.

Melanie pointed. "There's two toilets Mummy."

Brenda looked puzzled. "They're not quite the same."

"One's a bidet," explained David, "they're popular in France."

"In France, you say. But what's its use?"

He smiled. "I'll leave that for you to work out for yourself."

By the tone of his voice she thought it best not to enquire further, with the children present.

He left them to get unpacked and to tidy themselves up. "I'll just check on my quarters," he said, "don't forget we're due at Opal's home at seven o'clock."

"As if I could," replied Brenda.

Mr and Mrs Walker had invited them all to have a meal with them that evening. Brenda was looking forward very much to meeting Opal's parents whom she'd heard so much about. She wondered if Beulah Walker would match up to the picture she had of her from her daughter's description. She saw her as a jolly, older, plumper version of Opal. Joseph Walker, according to his daughter was very tall. Brenda guessed that Opal must take after him as regards height.

She did some unpacking, laid down for a while on the king-size bed, had a bath in the elegant bathroom, supervised the girls' toilet and attended to Mark.

At twenty-past-six, they were all waiting for David's knock. The girls dressed in rose muslin dresses with pink sashes and matching hair-ribbons. Mark in new trousers, white shirt and blue bow tie. Brenda wearing a smart taffeta cocktail dress in cerise.

A sharp rat-a-tat came at the door. He popped his head around. "Are you all ready?"

"Ready and waiting."

He took the chair and wheeled Mark out. Brenda's heart fluttered. He looked handsomer than ever in his dark evening clothes. A lock of black hair fell over his brow and he flicked it back carelessly.

They descended in the lift. Then out to David's car.

Their destination was a private housing estate on the outskirts of the city.

The car came to a halt outside Opal's parents semi-detached. Brenda saw a well tended garden at the front and side. In it were six-foot high larkspur with a fine deep blue effect. Orange-flame, apricot and shrimp-pink gladioli. And tiny blue irises. A glimpse of the back garden revealed a row of bean-sticks with green leaves and red flowers.

The front door opened and out ran Opal, followed by her mother; she was as Brenda had imagined her, even down to the bead necklaces and the blue dress patterned by red roses. Opal's father, Joseph Walker, who was even taller than she had expected had a ruddy complexion, silvery hair and a thin white moustache. Behind him was a nervous-looking Bob.

The kissing of cheeks and the shaking of hands followed.

Inside the house they were made very welcome, with a glass of beer for David, sherry for Brenda and lemonade for the children. She took out the straw from her handbag and popped it into Mark's glass. "It's easier for him to cope with his drink," she explained, holding the glass beneath his chin. He sucked up the lemonade thirstily.

She took in the comfortable room; its furnishings all rather jazzy in hue. There were colourful prints on the wall that she imagined were of Cape Town and Table Mountain. And on the sideboard and mantelpiece photographs of people that she guessed were family members. A black man in a silver frame stood out from the others. There was a gladioli in a glass stationed beside it.

"Nelson Mandela," whispered David.

Beulah Walker, her accent still retaining Afrikaans overtones, jumped up from the settee where she had been talking to Brenda. "Excuse me, but I must see to the food," she said apologetically, "it wouldn't do to let it spoil. I hope you like chicken cooked in red wine?"

"Sounds lovely," said Brenda.

Beulah Walker smiled widely. "That's good." She indicated the table that was set out with a floral centrepiece and gleaming cutlery, "Please take your places."

Brenda sat next to David, with Mark in his chair on her other side.

As well as the delicious chicken and sauté potatoes there were several dishes of vegetables, each served with their own special sauce, also baskets of bread rolls that Beulah had baked herself.

There was a never ending supply of home-made elderberry wine. Joseph constantly refilled their glasses.

The dessert was a cake flavoured with coffee and cognac and smothered in whipped cream.

"That was wonderful," said Brenda, thinking if she ate like this regularly, she would have to let out the seams of her clothing.

It was almost eleven when they left Opal's house, promising to be back at eight-thirty the following morning; the wedding service being at ten.

David wheeled the sleeping Mark into the hotel. The girls, half asleep themselves, being hauled along by Brenda.

"Which bed?" he asked.

She pointed to the single one upon which she had placed a small rubber sheet beneath the hotel bed linen to be on the safe side.

He lifted him from the chair and laid him down gently, and Brenda pulled off his socks and trousers and covered him with a sheet. "I changed him at Opal's, and with his plastic pants, he should be OK"

David nodded. "He's exhausted. It'd be cruel to disturb him." He looked towards the girls who had flopped down onto the double bed fully clothed. "I think we could all do with a good night's sleep."

Brenda followed him out. In the passage, he took her into his arms and kissed her. "See you tomorrow darling," he said.

She returned to the slumbering children, with a slight feeling of disappointment.

* * *

It was bedlam at Opal's house. Downstairs, David had taken Joseph Walker in hand, pouring him a stiff whisky, he, being overcome at the thought of giving his daughter away to another man.

Upstairs, it was far worse. Brenda was vainly trying to calm down Beulah Walker, who at the last moment had remembered that her daughter should be wearing 'something old, something new, something borrowed and something blue' and was frantically turning out every drawer in the house. Brenda needed to hunt for a pair of the girls' white socks, which had inexplicably gone missing. Pin the floral headdresses onto her bobbing daughters' heads. Zip-up Opal. Do a million-and-one other jobs, including mending a shoulder strap that had come adrift.

* * *

They sat on the bride's side of the church, with Mark in his chair beside them. In the pew in front of them was Beulah Walker, dressed in a scarlet two-piece and matching hat with a veil and with a handkerchief held in readiness in her hand. The pews behind them contained scores of the Walker's friends and neighbours – a mix of black and white. In the front pew, on the bridegroom's side sat a hardly recognisable Bob. Smartly-suited, his fair hair shone as if polished. His best man she recognised immediately, it was redheaded Geoff Hallett, his friend from Oxford. He and several others from Bob's former college had arrived earlier that morning. With white carnations in their lapels, they were seated in the pews immediately behind the bridegroom and best man. But there was no sign at all of the bridegroom's mother, Brenda thought sadly, feeling for Bob. She wondered if Opal and her father had left the house as yet? She'd spotted a flash of peach and blue at the back of the church, moments before, so she knew that the bridesmaids had arrived.

A whisper ran around the church. The organ that had been playing well-known hymns changed into the Wedding March. Every eye turned to watch as on her father's arm, Opal, veiled and wearing the brocade and lace dress that Brenda had made, and carrying a red rose bouquet, approached the altar steps and the waiting Bob. Behind them, with posies of white rosebuds, followed Melanie and Miranda.

The age old words were said and repeated and the ceremony ended to a background of happy weeping.

The vicar pronounced them man and wife. Opal lifted her veil, revealing an ecstatic face. Brenda felt her eyes smart as Bob bent and lingeringly kissed Opal's trembling mouth.

Outside the church, the photographer arranged everyone for the portraits. The bride and groom smiled self-consciously, but the bridesmaids were obviously loving every minute of it, as they preened and postured for the camera. At last, having taken all his pictures, the photographer was satisfied and packed up his equipment, ready to transport it to the Community Centre where the reception was to be held.

Brenda then went into action with her own small camera. She had taken it to the chemist on the Cowley Road and they'd put the film in for her.

She finished clicking.

Opal, with a knowing smile in Brenda's direction, turned her back and threw her bouquet - to find out who the next bride would be. Hoping it might be herself, Brenda thrust her camera into David's hand and she, along with all the other young women, stretched upwards with open palms in an attempt to catch the flowers, as with much laughter, the bouquet came whizzing over. Her hands closed over them. They were hers.

Blushing, but delighted, she breathed in the perfume of the red roses.

"Everyone's leaving," said David, taking the wheelchair and ushering her down the drive; just in time to see Opal and Bob being serenaded by a steel band as they climbed into the back of a beribboned car. The steel band, atop a lorry, consisted of four negroes who were stripped to the waist. Their muscles rippled as they energetically struck out the Wedding March on oil drums and dustbin lids.

Cheering loudly, Brenda joined in, throwing confetti. As the vehicle drew away, a wolf whistle rang out, for it could be seen through the back window that the bridal pair were kissing.

As they left, the giggling bridesmaids, followed by Mr and Mrs Walker, were the next to be sprinkled with confetti.

A car drew up and David helped Brenda in; he lifted Mark from his chair and seated him beside her; finally getting in on the opposite side. The driver having folded and placed the chair in the boot, drove off.

They arrived at the Community Centre. Recently built, it was of glass and chrome.

Entering, a waitress greeted them with a tray of sherry. Brenda took a glass and looked around for the bride and groom. They were surrounded by guests and looking the worse for wear, having been hugged, kissed and shaken hands with for far too long for comfort.

Running the length of the room and forming the letter T was the white-clothed table. In the centre of the top table was a three tiered wedding cake. This cake had been made and iced by Beulah Walker.

They took their places. The sit-down meal was served. Brenda fed Mark all the tasty pieces – and there were very many of them. Each course was accompanied by elderberry wine; their glasses being continually topped up.

Afterwards came the congratulatory cards and telegrams, read out by Geoff Hallett. He then made a speech.

Bob, red-faced, followed.

The bride, holding the handle of the knife with her bridegroom's hand over hers, pressed down and cut the wedding cake whilst the guests cheered. Thin slices wrapped in paper napkins were passed around, and everyone readily admitted that this cake was the best that they had ever tasted.

Brenda was watching the steel band setting up for the dancing when she suddenly realised that something was going on at the door. A waitress came over and spoke to Joseph Walker, who immediately left his seat. He returned shortly afterwards and whispered something to Bob, who jumped to his feet and white-faced went out. Brenda craned her neck in an effort to see who he was talking to. He moved slightly and revealed a smartly dressed middle-aged woman with greying hair.

CHAPTER 26

Bob gazed in disbelief at the well-dressed woman stood in the entrance hall of the Community Centre.

"Mother!"

She held out a hand. "Yes, Bob, it's me."

He took and held it joyously. "I'd hoped, but I never really expected to see you here."

Mrs Brown's lips trembled. "I had to come. I know that I said that I'd never accept your choice. But since then I haven't been able to eat or sleep. It's made me quite ill. Then it came to me just how lucky I was that you were still alive. That was when I 'woke up', when I realised that I couldn't let myself be cut off from you, no matter what the circumstances. I had to come and make my peace with you." She hesitated. "And with Opal too, if she'll forgive me."

"She will! She will!" said Bob.

"I hope you're right, but I couldn't really blame her if she didn't want to know me."

"Opal's not like that. You'll love her when you get to know her."

"I hope so. I know I said that marriage wasn't right between the two of you, because of colour, but I've been thinking seriously. I was wrong. This is seventies England and not twenties Alabama, and we all need to change with the times."

Bob touched her shoulder. "Thanks, Mum. I understand how difficult it's been for you."

"Yes, it hasn't been easy."

"So will you come and meet Opal?" he asked hesitatingly. He still couldn't really believe that his mother was actually here. He would have sworn that he had more chance of being struck by lightning than that his mother would have a change of heart. But he was glad, so very glad that she had found the strength to overcome all the ingrained prejudices that had been instilled into her, almost from the cradle. It was a miracle!

She straightened her shoulders. "That's what I'm here for."

"And meet her parents?"

She smiled thinly. "Why not."

He heaved a sigh of relief. "Oh, thanks Mum."

She slipped her arm through his and he led her into the reception. "I hope you've saved me a slice of wedding cake, I'd hoped to be here before the church service but got caught up in a traffic jam on the outskirts of Birmingham."

"So you've not eaten?"

"I came straight here."

He beckoned Opal.

Opal looked shaken when she recognised Bob's mother. "Mrs Brown, I never thought... I'd hoped, of course."

Trembling, Mrs Brown took her hand. "I've come to give both of you my blessing, and to apologise, my dear, for the way that I've treated you."

Opal looked disbelievingly, then pulled herself together. "There's no need Mrs Brown, I'm just happy you could come."

"Mum hasn't eaten," put in Bob, glad to find something definite to smooth the awkwardness of the situation.

"I'm sure there's some food left in the kitchen. I'll ask the waitress. I'll only be a moment," said Opal.

Mrs Brown nodded. "Before you do that, my dear, could you ask your parents if they'd come over and make my acquaintance?"

Opal nodded and hurried off to where her parents were ostensibly talking to a neighbour. Bob could see the anxiety on his in-laws' faces, and although he couldn't hear what they were saying, he could well imagine the conversation.

Minutes later, Opal said, "Mrs Brown, this is my mother."

"How do you do," both women said, shaking hands warily.

"Mrs Brown, this is my father."

Joseph Walker shot out his hand to grasp the smaller feminine one. "Pleased to meet you," he said.

"Likewise," replied Bob's mother more warmly. Although sixty, Opal's father was still an attractive man.

With this difficult part over, Opal began to move away. "I'll just see if I can find the waitress."

Mrs Brown caught hold of her hand. "No, let Bob go, you stay and talk to me, dear." She turned, "You don't mind going, do you?"

"Of course not." He disappeared in the direction of the kitchen.

"Mrs Brown," said Opal hesitatingly, "I should very much like to introduce you to a dear friend of mine. Since I've been at college in Oxford, she has made her home mine." She brought Brenda forward.

Mrs Brown put out her hand. "Pleased to meet you, Mrs Bellinger. Bob has told me all about you. You've been a good friend to him too."

"It was nothing," said Brenda modestly.

"And are these beautiful bridesmaids your daughters?"

Brenda beamed at her praise. "Yes."

Mrs Brown eyed the handsome man accompanying Brenda. "And you are?"

"David Certes. I'm Mrs Bellinger's friend and also her literary agent."

She turned back to Brenda. "You write. How wonderful, I've always fancied writing a book. How did you get started?"

"It was Opal. She was the one instrumental in getting me interested in the first place," she explained.

Joseph Walker filled a wine glass with elderberry wine and offered it to Mrs Brown. "Try this," he said, "it'll go down well with your meal."

"Thank you." She picked up the glass and sipped cautiously, "It's good," she exclaimed. She took another sip, "In fact, it's very good!"

"Everyone says that," he chuckled, "here let me top you up."

"I shouldn't really, Mr Walker."

"Call me Joseph."

"Joseph, you'd better call me Belinda Lou."

"Belinda Lou. What a pretty name."

She held out her glass for him to refill it.

Bob returned with a piled plate. He set it before his mother. Solicitously he watched her eat. She daintily wiping her mouth with her paper napkin after each mouthful, and to his astonishment, sipping with relish, the elderberry wine.

Four glasses later, and she was in almost a mellow mood and chatting in quite a friendly fashion to her new in-laws, especially, as he noticed, Opal's father.

Their conversation was interrupted by the steel band who swung into a very skilful rendering of the popular, 'Let's twist again like we did last summer.'

Several girls and youths immediately took to the floor and began gyrating wildly.

"Looks like a dance straight out of the jungle," commented Mrs Brown. Her glance fell on Beulah Walker. Flushing, she shot a hand to her mouth, "I'm sorry, I never meant anything..."

Bob frowned at his mother's faux pas.

Joseph Walker chose to ignore it. He chuckled. "I believe it's called the 'Twist'. It's all the rage amongst the younger generation. It's a wonder they don't dislocate all their bones."

Mrs Brown nodded.

Bob, noticing Brenda and David 'twisting', turned to Opal. "Would you like to do it?"

"What with my floor-length wedding gown. I don't really think I'm suitably dressed."

"Just look at that!" he said.

"Look at what?" Opal followed his direction. Seated opposite the band, Mark was smiling and waving his good arm in time to the music. Suddenly one of the musicians grinned and said something to the others. They nodded in agreement. He got up and went over and spoke to Brenda. She smiled and turned to Mark. "This kind gentleman," she said, "wondered if you'd like a bit of fun. They want you to go up on the stage and play a tune with them. You'd like that, wouldn't you Mark?" He gurgled, "Of course, you would." She unfastened him from his chair.

The musician picked up the handicapped boy as if he weighed no more than a basket, and carrying him over to the oil-drum, seated him on his knee. He grinned. "Mark is now going to play a tune for you," he announced.

The room went quiet.

The musician fastened the small fingers around the stick used to beat out the rhythm on the oil-drum. Then he carefully guided Mark's hand so that he picked out a recognisable tune.

Everyone cheered and clapped, none more so than Brenda.

The applause died down.

Mark eyed the stick that was still in his hand, "B... b... b... b," he spluttered, "B a n g!"

"Did you hear that?" cried Brenda in amazement, turning to David and hugging him, "he's spoken - he said Bang - it's happened at last."

He hugged her.

A woman laughed. "That little chap'll probably be chattering the hind leg off a donkey before long. You'll no doubt soon wish that he'd hush-up a bit."

"Never," cried Brenda, wiping her eyes. She dashed over, hugging and kissing Mark. "You've done it at last, my little miracle, Bang!" she mouthed.

"B... b... b... b... B a n g!" came back from Mark.

Bob pulled Opal to him, "To think he should say his first word on this day of days."

"Brenda will never forget our wedding day, that's for certain," laughed Opal.

The band announced that they would now play something more suitable for the older generation, starting with a waltz.

Joseph Walker turned to Mrs Brown. "We're not going to let the young ones have all the fun, are we, Belinda Lou? Will you give me the pleasure of this dance with you?"

She went quite pink. But got to her feet and was soon being spun around the room.

"I'd almost forgotten," she said breathlessly when the music had stopped and he'd escorted her back to her chair, "I've got their wedding present outside."

"You mean in the car?"

"Yes; in a way. It's something that they could really do with. Something, that I hope will really transport them."

She turned to Bob and Opal, "Come outside and see what I've got for you."

"You've got me curious," said Joseph Walker, "can I come too?"

"And me," said Beulah Walker.

They went outside.

A red Morris Minor gleamed in the sunlight. "It's yours and Opal's, Bob." Mrs Brown took a key from her handbag and handed it to Opal. "A car's far safer, my dear. I don't really want him riding a motorbike again."

A woman, even rounder and browner than the bride's mother remarked, "You'll not be able to add that to the wedding present display in your front room, Beulah, it'll take up more space than a toast rack."

"A guest with grey scraggy hair, giggled. "It's a far cry from my pink nylon bedspread."

Beulah nodded and turned to her husband. "It's a pity they've already got the train tickets to London. They could have used the car to go on honeymoon."

Joseph Walker shook his head. "Too much hassle. The London traffic's terrible. No one with any sense would take a car there." He turned to Bob. "You can park your Morris in my drive until you get back."

"Thanks, Mr Walker."

Opal nudged Bob," Your mother agrees with me about that motorbike. I don't want you to ride it again either."

"We've only been married five minutes and already you're both nagging," he chided playfully.

"I'm not." She turned to Mrs Brown, "He's only been on about getting that bike mended and riding it again."

"You mustn't do that!"

"I've tried and tried to talk him out of it."

Mrs Brown took Opal's arm and together they strolled back into the Community Centre. The older woman smiled warmly. "If we join forces, my dear, I'm sure we'll be able to persuade him."

* * *

Bob and Opal leant out of the carriage window and waved at the wedding guests on the platform. They were off to London for their three day honeymoon.

Bob's mother put a handkerchief to her eyes and Beulah Walker laid a consoling arm about her shoulders. "We've got to let them fly the nest, Mrs Brown. We can't keep them with us forever."

"Beulah's right, Belinda Lou," agreed Joseph Walker sympathetically.

"I know we have. It's just a smut from the engine."

Brenda, with Mark in his chair and David beside her, waved and called out good wishes, whilst Melanie and Miranda jumped up and down and attempted to throw more confetti into the carriage.

"Please no more confetti," begged Opal, "it was lucky I thought to undo my umbrella. Fancy filling it up like that!"

Brenda laughed. "That was Miranda's idea."

Opal eyed the elder girl. "I hope you haven't put confetti into anything else, Melanie?"

"You'll have to wait and see," she replied smugly.

"I think I saw her doing something with a needle and cotton," teased Brenda.

Opal looked alarmed. "She better not have done!" She shot a look at Brenda's face,

"You're having me on, aren't you? You are awful! I'll be on tenterhooks now until I get to London and can unpack my suitcase."

Bob kissed Opal swiftly upon the cheek. "Take no notice. She's just pulling your leg, love. You can get your own back when she weds Certes."

Opal waggled her finger playfully at Brenda. "I certainly will. You can bet your sweet life on it."

Bob admired the profile of his bride. Dressed in a smart yellow going-away costume, a feathered close-fitting hat curved over her head; exactly complimenting the black corkscrew curls; while sparkling in her ears were the diamond hoops that he'd bought her as a wedding gift. He had won himself a beauty - a beautiful dusky rose. How he'd longed for this day. From the very first moment that he'd set eyes on Opal in Blackwells Book Shop, he had loved her. He thought of the scoffers who said that there was no such thing as 'love at first sight'. How wrong they were. He turned his attention to the wedding guests, all well-meaning people, he knew, but at this moment he wanted nothing more than for them to disappear. For the train to get under way and he and Opal be alone together in the compartment that he had reserved so that they could have complete privacy. He certainly didn't feel like making small talk with strangers, and he didn't think that Opal would either. His attention was drawn to his mother who was wiping her eyes with one hand and waving with the other. She and Opal, to his astonishment, seemed to be warming to each other. Just before they left the reception she had asked Opal if she would help her to write her life story. Evidently, she had always wanted to. He knew that his mother was very fond of reading, that she had always acquired the best-sellers when they first came out. But writing. This was a new one on him, and certainly a surprise; the second that his mother had given him that day.

The guard waved his flag.

A whistle blew. The wheels began turning.

"We're off," said Bob.

"Goodbye! Goodbye!" shouted the guests, one or two endeavouring to keep up with the train, but soon falling behind.

Bob shut the window, "Alone at last," he said; taking Opal into his arms. His lips met hers in a long passionate kiss.

CHAPTER 27

They returned to the Midland Hotel. Brenda ordered a light supper for the children to be served in their room. But they just picked at it; too tired even to eat. Afterwards she got them all to bed. Minutes later they were fast asleep.

She took a leisurely bath, pouring in the sweet-smelling salts that were in a porcelain jar. They sparkled, red, blue, gold and lilac as they touched the steaming water and turned into rainbow bubbles. She patted herself dry with a fluffy pink bath towel, admiring her sleek curves in the full-length mirror, smoothing her hands over herself, shivering deliciously, imagining his strong hands doing just that. She eyed the new underclothes draped on the chair nearby, white, silk panties edged with lace, matching bra and slip; undergarments chosen especially with David in mind. Would he ask her to marry him tonight? Would tonight, after the romantic dinner, be the night that they would, at last, come together. She powdered herself with Lily of the Valley talc; slipped on the undies, turning this way and that, feeling the heat running through her as her own erotic image flashed into view. She imagined his fingers removing her dress and then.... If they didn't please him, nothing would.

She chose a blue cocktail dress. He'd said he liked her in blue. She anointed her neck, wrists and temples with perfume. Finally she piled her fair hair onto the top of her head as Opal had taught her, securing it with two blue and silver-edged combs. Before she left the room she turned on the intercom. The hotel staff would listen out for the children whilst she was downstairs at dinner.

David was waiting at the entrance to the dining room, elegant in his dark evening clothes and smelling freshly of aftershave. Her heart missed a beat. A trickle of perspiration ran down her back. Would he always have this effect on her? Her bones felt as if they might melt at any moment.

He turned at her step, his eyes lighting up with love and admiration. "You look beautiful," he said.

She smiled her thank you, feeling the luckiest woman in the world as she slipped her arm through his. He pushed open the door and led her inside.

The Head Waiter appeared as if by magic. "Table for two," he said, ushering them to a candlelit table within a secluded arbour, screened by palms. He clicked his fingers and another waiter materialised with the menus, which, to her astonishment, were even larger than those at the Randolph in Oxford.

Brenda sighed. "I suppose it's all in French?"

"I'm afraid it is, darling," he replied, "but how about melon to start with followed by chicken in white-wine sauce? That's what I thought of ordering."

"That'll be fine."

He rattled off their choices in French. It was scribbled down and he then disappeared.

The Wine Waiter took his place.

David ordered champagne. As before, he lifted his glass, partly as a toast, partly, she realised, in homage to her. His eyes, soft in the candlelight and promising, she felt, a night of loving passion. She shivered with hopeful anticipation.

They ate, finishing with strawberry sorbet. The waiter removed the dishes, replacing them with minute coffee cups.

David reached across the table, his fingers curled about hers, gently caressing them.

She looked into his eyes, feeling she could drown within their depths. "Brenda," he said softly, "Darling, Brenda. I love you, so very, very much. Would you, would you make me a very happy man and marry me?"

Her eyes shone, "Yes, oh, yes," she breathed, "as soon as you like."

"You will! I feel so happy that I could... I could get up on this table and proclaim to the whole world, 'Brenda's going to marry me!!'"

She giggled. "Go on then, I dare you to."

He leant across the table, his lips meeting hers in a kiss.

The Head Waiter appeared with the coffee pot, he poured the fragrant coffee, then discreetly withdrew.

"I'll see about a Special Licence immediately. We won't have to bother about banns being called then. I don't want to wait any longer than necessary to make you Mrs Certes."

Brenda paused. "I'll tell the girls and Mark of our plans, first thing tomorrow."

"You do think they'll be pleased?"

"Pleased! Melanie will probably say, 'What took you both so long, Mum?'"

He chuckled. "So you think that they'll accept me as a step-dad?"

"I'm sure they will. They all think the world of you."

"I feel the same way about them." He became serious, "And John?" he asked, "what do you think he'd think of all this, of me?"

"I'm sure he'd want me to be happy. And Angela?" she asked.

"She would too, I'm sure of that."

"That's settled then. I'll go and see Father Arnold at St Mary and St Johns as soon as we get home. Find out how soon a wedding can be arranged."

"I'll visit the Travel Agents."

"Travel Agents?"

He grinned. "I was thinking of a honeymoon in Australia, in Adelaide in fact; that's where your mother lives, isn't it?"

"Australia!! Oh, David, David, yes, yes - I never thought, I never expected." She shifted excitedly on her seat. "I just can't believe it - to actually see her again - it's been twelve years you know, a lifetime. It'll be a dream come true; the most marvellous thing that's ever happened to me."

David smiled. "I thought Mark's first word had that place in your heart?"

"Well, yes."

"And what about getting your novel published? I can remember you saying that was your top priority."

"Oh, go on, you're teasing me."

He laughed. "I'm sorry, but I just couldn't resist it."

Her face clouded over. "But the children?"

"Well, couldn't you arrange for Mark to go into that home attached to his Training Centre?"

"I suppose so. He was very well-cared-for there while I was in London seeing my publisher, but that was only for a night. Australia's so far away."

"Not if we go by plane."

"Fly?"

"Yes."

"Good Grief! I never expected to ever set foot on a plane. But even then, we'd be away ages."

"Three weeks."

"I don't know if I could bear to leave Mark, or the girls for so long."

"Not even to see your mother?"

"If you put it like that. I'll find out if that home can take Mark. I'm sure Mrs Briggs would be only too happy to look after Melanie and Miranda for us. Mind you, I don't know that those two will be all that pleased about missing out on a trip abroad - even if it is our honeymoon."

He laughed. "I'll bribe them; promise them a holiday on my parents' croft later on; tell them all about the rabbits and baby goats."

"That might do it." She sighed ecstatically, "What a lot I've got to divulge tomorrow. I know the girls'll be thrilled to be bridesmaids again. Thankfully, they haven't had time to grow out of the dresses that they had for Opal's wedding, so can wear them again; get a bit more use out of them."

He smiled. "That's my careful Brenda. You'll just suit my mum."

"Will your mother be well enough to travel down from Harris, David?"

"Hopefully. I'll ring them tomorrow. They'll be over the moon. Now let's get down to basics. Where are we going to live? We've got to decide that. How about my cottage in Clifton Hampden. It's much larger and…"

Brenda cut in. "But the girls' schooling, not to mention Mark's Training Centre? They've only just said that they're going to teach him the Bliss Symbols."

"The what?"

She explained. "It's a board with symbols on that mean different things. When he's learnt it, he'll be able to point out whatever he wants to convey so that people will understand him."

"That's good. But, Brenda, there's an excellent Training Centre in Abingdon, and before you say it, a well-thought-of Grammar School, too."

"Oh."

"My cottage will be far more suitable. Miss Tribble will enjoy giving you a hand with the children, and later on, when Mark gets too heavy to carry upstairs, I can have a bedroom and shower room built on. We'll be able to wheel him from his bedroom straight into the shower."

Brenda laughed. "You seem to have thought of everything. We'll have to put it to a family vote. Oh, but what about Opal and

Bob? I've told them that they can lodge with me until Opal finishes at college; I couldn't see them out in the street."

"You don't need to. Surely they could rent your house?"

"Yes. Of course." She drained her cup.

"More coffee?" he asked.

She shook her head.

"Let's go then."

Holding hands they went up in the lift to the third floor.

As if by mutual agreement, they moved towards his room. Suddenly she paused. "I'd best check on the children first."

He nodded.

She eased open the door, tiptoeing into the room. Minutes later she exited. "Sleeping like lambs," she whispered.

He smiled invitingly. Wordlessly she followed him into his room.

He flicked a switch. Wall sconces flushed palely, casting a romantic glow. In the centre of the room were two armchairs, covered in red moquette. She sank down into one. Between the chairs stood a polished occasional-table. On it was an ice-bucket and two tall crystal wine glasses; within the bucket, a bottle of wine.

David busied himself with the corkscrew. The cork shot out with a loud pop. Brenda giggled. "I hope the walls between the rooms are thick. I wouldn't want the noise to wake the children. If Mark started crying I should have to go."

He poured wine into both glasses. "That goes without saying. But I shouldn't think there is any need to worry. This place is quite solid. Eighteen-fifties, I believe. No jerry building in those days." He handed Brenda a glass.

"I don't know if I should drink anymore. I've already had champagne. You'll get me tiddley."

"It'll relax you. Go on."

She took a sip. "Lovely, nice and sweet."

He perched on the arm of her chair and they clinked glasses. "Here's to us, darling."

"Here's to us, darling." she repeated.

"You like the wine?"

"Mmmm." She drank some more, "Aren't you going to drink any of yours?"

"Later." He leant over and pulled her to him; his lips met hers in a lingering kiss. She felt his fingers searching for the zip at the back of her dress. With a deft movement she undid it, and his fingertips began exploring the silken flesh of her back. At his touch love's warmth surged strongly within her, casting out any feelings of embarrassment. She moaned as he unfastened her bra, releasing her breasts from their prison. His hand moved sideways and covered one of them and he began to tease the nipple.

Brenda squirmed with desire.

Suddenly his fingers halted. "I'm sorry darling, but it's so darned uncomfortable on this chair." He rose to his feet and she with him. "I want our first lovemaking to be something special, something that we'll always remember." He lifted her easily and carried her over to the bed.

He slowly removed her clothing, his mouth nuzzling her neck, his fingers tangling the long fair hair that was now in glorious disarray, her blue and silver combs lying neglected on the carpet. He explored her full breasts with their pink tip-tilted nipples. He caressed her neat waist and the soft curves of her bottom. "You're beautiful," he murmured, as he pressed his lips over every inch of her body, his tongue gently investigating the blonde triangle between her thighs; she, crying out with extreme delight, and clawing at the hair of his vigorous dark head.

She slid off his clothes. Her fingers stroked his flat belly, smooth buttocks and muscular legs. She ran the tip of her tongue over his chest-hair and nipples, until, he too, was ready to explode.

Eagerly she spread her legs. He entered her. She gasped as he thrust and thrust again. She matched his rhythm stroke for stroke. Higher and higher their excitement mounted. On a peak of pleasure, a thought ran corkscrew through her head, how on earth had she managed to do without this for so long? Her mind went blank, given up to delight, until, finally, with long drawn-out exquisite groans their act of love peeked in an excruciating mutual crescendo.

They lay satiated, lip clinging to lip, arms around each other. "I must go," she finally said, gently disengaging herself and slipping from between the sheets. "If the children should wake, they'd wonder where I was."

David drew her back. "Just one more minute, darling," he pleaded, pulling her again into his embrace.

"Just one more then," she replied, snuggling close.

* * *

Brenda opened her eyes. The pale light of dawn was peeking

through the crack in the curtains. She sat up hastily, and looked at David's alarm clock. It was six-a.m. "Good Grief! The children!" She should have gone back to her own room ages ago. What if they'd missed her?... and Mark! Not only that, what if someone should see her wandering along the corridor? She knew people were more broad-minded than when she was a girl. But she didn't want to get talked about, even if it was just by the hotel-staff whom she would possibly never see again.

She kissed David's bare shoulder and he stirred but didn't wake. She slipped out of the bed, reddening when she found her garments strewn about the place. What on earth would her mother say if she could have seen what she'd been up to? She probably wouldn't think it much of an excuse that she and David were to be married in the very near future.

She stepped into her dress and twisting and turning, struggled to zip it up. Then picking up her shoes she tiptoed from the room. She looked apprehensively up and down the corridor. At what time, she wondered, did the chambermaids start delivering early morning tea? She certainly hoped it wasn't yet awhile. She wouldn't know where to put herself if she should come face to face with one of them.

She carefully opened her bedroom door. The children were fast asleep. Mark, rapt as an angel. What a relief. She wouldn't have known how to have answered their questions. She smiled. Miranda had kicked off her bedclothes and had a thumb in her mouth. She picked up the bedspread from where it lay in a heap on the floor and covered her with it. Miranda stirred. Was she waking up? If she started chattering, the others would be awake in a trice. But no, she just turned over.

Brenda flung her dress on a nearby chair. Suppressing a yawn, she climbed into bed. She lay back on the soft mattress and closed her eyes. Smiling, she relived their magical moments. Soon she was asleep.